Praise for *The Glowing Life of Leeann Wu*

"Absolutely shines! Featuring shimmering magic, strong female characters, a captivating romance, and a touch of haunting suspense, Mindy Hung has crafted a memorable novel about the power that comes from recognizing you're good enough—extraordinary, even—just the way you are."

—Heather Webber, *USA Today* bestselling author of *Midnight at the Blackbird Café*

"Mindy Hung remains one of my all-time favorite storytellers. The beating heart of the story rests in Hung's deft, aching portrayal of multiple generations of Wu women, whose love for one another is fierce but fraught with tension and contradiction."

—Olivia Dade, *USA Today* bestselling author of *Zomromcom* and *Spoiler Alert*

"*The Glowing Life of Leeann Wu* is wise, hopeful, powerful, and—yes—incandescent. I couldn't put it down. I'll be thinking about this book for a long time."

—Hazel Beck, author of *Small Town, Big Magic*

"Clever and deep and slyly funny, *The Glowing Life of Leeann Wu* is . . . a story about truly looking at and loving ourselves at even the most fraught and confusing stages of our lives. I loved it."

—Kate Clayborn, author of *Georgie, All Along* and *The Paris Match*

"*The Glowing Life of Leeann Wu* by Mindy Hung was like reading a wish that came to life. This romantic contemporary fantasy gives a refreshing look at what happens when a woman carves her own path, despite ghosts of the past. I loved every bit of it."

—Nichole Perkins, author of *Sometimes I Trip on How Happy We Could Be*

"This novel literally glows with tension, and readers will be breathless . . . *The Glowing Life of Leeann Wu* offers a magical, sexy, midlife midwife for readers to fall in love with."

—Annie Mare, author of *Cosmic Love at the Multiverse Hair Salon*

"Every page was beautifully written and perfectly observed. With this book, Mindy Hung instantly positions herself as a major voice in women's fiction."

—Emma Barry, author of *Bad Reputation*

The Glowing Life of Leeann Wu

Writing as Ruby Lang

Uptown Series

House Rules
Open House
Plating House

Practice Perfect Series

Clean Breaks
Hard Knocks
Acute Reactions

Writing as Opal Wei

Wild Life

The Glowing Life of Leeann Wu

♦ *A NOVEL* ♦

MINDY HUNG

alcove press

Published in the United States by Alcove Press, an imprint of The Quick Brown Fox & Company LLC.

Alcove Press and its logo are trademarks of The Quick Brown Fox & Company LLC.

Library of Congress Catalog-in-Publication data available upon request.

ISBN (hardcover): 979-8-89242-273-4
ISBN (paperback): 979-8-89242-169-0
ISBN (ebook): 979-8-89242-170-6

Cover design by Natalie Olsen

Printed in the United States.

www.alcovepress.com

Alcove Press
34 West 27th St., 10th Floor
New York, NY 10001

First Edition: November 2025

The authorized representative in the EU for product safety and compliance is eucomply OÜPärnu mnt 139b-14, 11317 Tallinn, Estonia, hello@eucompliancepartner.com, +33757690241

10 9 8 7 6 5 4 3 2 1

For everyone who's going through it.

You may house their bodies but not their souls, For their souls dwell in the house of tomorrow, which you cannot visit, not even in your dreams.

—"On Children," Kahlil Gibran

♦ 1 ♦

THE FIRST ACCIDENT HAPPENED on a Friday.

I'd planned to meet my clinic partner, Parisa, outside the life sciences building. She was teaching a couple of classes over summer term, and I'd swung by to get an early lunch with her on campus. The last few weeks had been busy—it seemed everyone had decided to have a baby over this long, oppressively hot summer, so I'd tried to build extra time into my schedule today in case something unexpected came up.

We met for lunch regularly—the intention was to go over paperwork for our midwifery practice, but usually three files in we'd end up talking about our clients, or our kids. Or sometimes we'd sit under the shade of a tree and simply watch the world go by. Parisa always had a story about the people passing, and the grounds of MacDougall University at Reineville made almost a fairy-tale setting. My mother, the esteemed Dr. Shu-ling Wu, eminent obstetrician/gynecologist, taught and terrorized residents at the nearby hospital, and I'd almost finished premed on this campus. When I was a kid, I thought it looked like the castles in books, the facades blunt and imposing, old without being beautiful. It seemed a perfect place to fight imaginary battles or roll around on the grass. In a way, this place had been my playground, my babysitter.

But this year, it was too hot and sticky to sit outside. It was early June. It hadn't rained for weeks—always threatening, never falling. The air was pregnant with water. Air conditioners fought useless battles against the humidity, and my clients complained they couldn't sleep; I didn't have a baby weighing down my insides, and even *I* could barely sleep. When I did, restless dreams had me waking up in a sweat, and the echoes of my nightmares pursued me throughout the day. Already it seemed that summer had come and draped itself over Reineville like a lazy, malevolent beast.

I was making my way past the rugby field when I heard the shouts. I looked up, and the first thing I saw was the clock tower, its stark white limestone scarred with the burn of a strange lightning strike that had hit yesterday in the wee hours of the morning. Against the pale length of the tower, the damage looked like a set of jagged teeth.

Like the mark from the storm I'd been dreaming of.

A team of construction workers was erecting scaffolding around the damaged tower. Classes were already out. Campus never completely emptied over the summer, but at least most of the undergrads had left. I, and probably many of the townies, breathed a sigh of relief when convocation was over each year and there wasn't a constant stream of young, *new* people, with their raucous, unformed voices and drunken, flailing limbs. Of course, there were tourists, but they usually stuck to the lake and avoided the sprawling old campus near the south side of town.

After the shouts, I heard creaking, and this time someone screamed as the hot wind gusted through campus. Then I saw him. A man in a hard hat, clinging to the wall as the scaffolding he and others had been trying to erect started swinging in the wind. The collapsing structure groaned, alive and terrifying. At first, the workers under it put their arms out as if they thought they could catch it, but almost immediately abandoned that plan and turned to run away. Another punch of wind shrieked through the wide green pathways of the school, almost knocking me off my feet, and an awful crack rent the air. Shielding my face, I pulled out my phone to call 911 as the structure collapsed.

Choking dust swirled around. I started forward, yelling into my phone.

The wind was still strong, but workers and onlookers ran toward the heap, pulling at the biggest pile of planks and metal in the middle.

After hanging up with the 911 operator, I ran toward the wreckage, too. "Does anyone need first aid?"

Reineville General Hospital occupied the bottom quarter of the university's sprawling campus. Ambulances wouldn't be that far away. But I had a pair of hands, and my training.

And more.

The thought curled through my mind like smoke, and through the dust I could see the faint glow in my hands that had first begun appearing about a month ago. They weren't hot or cold, just bright. As far as I knew they only emitted light—not that I'd used a Geiger counter to test them. It had happened only a couple of times so far, and it never lasted long, but it was enough to spook me—and fascinate me. I didn't know what it was or whether it was a good thing or a terrible one, but now was not the time to dwell on it. All I knew was that there was something in the dreams, the restlessness I felt crackling inside me, in the glow.

No time to think. I shook my head and tried to keep my hands out of full view. I inspected the first person to stumble my way, a construction worker with a gash in his hand.

Emergency workers were pouring onto the site now, their vehicles barreling across the lawns, but I focused on my corner of the chaos, where EMTs had already begun setting up. I examined people with less serious injuries—people with debris in their eyes or cuts from going at the wreckage with their bare hands to help pull workers out—triaging those who seemed more severely hurt.

It could have been worse. Everyone said so afterward. Miraculously, no one died. If students had been on campus, if more people had been on the scaffolding . . . *If.*

By midafternoon, a police officer took my name and told me firmly to see an EMT. Luckily, it was Daywin, one of my favorites, who checked me over briefly—at least the glow was gone—and told me to go home.

But I couldn't. I didn't think I would have been able to drive.

I trudged to the car, promising myself I could at least sit down in it, maybe take a nap in the back seat. But once I got inside, of course I rolled down the windows, pulled out my phone, and saw the messages from Parisa.

"Oh my God," I said when she picked up. "Did you see what happened at the clock tower?"

"Yeah, don't worry. I spotted you in the cordoned-off zone. Are you okay?"

I laughed suddenly, maybe a little hysterically, because I wanted to apologize for no good reason. *Sorry I dreamed of the storm that hit the clock tower. Sorry I've been keeping secrets about lightning and fire. Sorry I can't sleep. Sorry I long for rain.* But whose subconscious—or consciousness, really—wasn't longing for rain these days?

Instead, I told Parisa I was emotionally shaken, but physically all right. "I have postnatal visits late this afternoon."

"Do you want me to cover?"

Parisa wasn't just the director of our practice. She was my mentor and best friend. She'd delivered Lulu and been the one to suggest that I should train as a midwife. After I'd gotten pregnant with Lulu, I'd dropped out of premed, to my mother's dismay, and I'd broken up with Paul, Lulu's father. When Parisa met me, I was very pregnant, very alone, and very stubborn. Somehow, she looked at the charming bundle of hostility I was at that point and thought I'd make a good colleague.

"I'm good. I probably just need to go home and change."

"Eat something, too," Parisa said, ever practical. "Get some sugar."

I laughed lightly, but I wanted to cry. "I'm telling your kids you told me I should have candy."

"They wouldn't believe you."

But after she hung up, I stayed in the parking lot. I felt guilty. There was no explanation for it. The accident hadn't been because of me; I couldn't have warned anyone about a strange storm approaching, one that seemed alluring and powerful. Even if I had told someone that I knew the restless dreams I'd had the other night would come true, what could anyone do about the weather?

The wind had done this. Workers had been trying to put together scaffolding on a rickety old building. There was no reason for me to feel responsible for the lightning from the morning before, or for the heat and the weird lethargy that seemed to surround Reineville this summer. Even if the weather seemed to reflect my unease.

And even if, along with having prophetic dreams, I had started to glow.

Aside from being alarming, there wasn't anything connecting these phenomena.

Except me.

My eyes were gritty, my mouth was full of dust, and I had all these contradictory feelings swirling around me. I didn't want to go home to my daughter with the sounds of yelling and fear and the wind—that terrifying wind—echoing in my ears. The dirt seemed to permeate my clothing. There was a smear of blood on one sleeve. I felt as if I'd infect my house with all that bad energy. There was already enough malevolence in the humid air.

I had only a few months left with my daughter as it was. Lulu would be off to university in Toronto by the end of summer. Three hours away. I joked that I had so little time left to be a proper, loving, fun parent who was cooler than all the other moms but didn't try too hard. But even though I was excited and happy for her, I was already anticipating how lonely I'd feel with her gone.

I really didn't want her memories of these last months together to include me falling apart. So, I did the only thing that felt safe. I cowered in the bubble of my SUV, lay my head gently on the steering wheel, and closed my eyes.

I don't know how long I sat there, but too soon, someone tapped on my window. I started, registering the fact that Kenji Hartell, the brother of one of my recent clients, was outside my car gazing at me with soft-eyed concern. "Hey there. I thought it was your car. I don't know if you remember me from Andrea's the other night—"

"I do."

"Oh, good. Good. Well, it's kind of hot out here. Are you all right?"

Even in my exhausted state, I wished that I didn't look like I'd spent part of the morning in a collapsed construction zone triaging people's wounds.

Get some sugar, Parisa had said. I almost laughed at the memory, because young—too young—Kenji Hartell was definitely a snack.

It had been hard the other day not to notice his big dark eyes, the wide shoulders on a lean frame. Today, the bike shorts he was wearing emphasized the long deep groove of thigh muscles, and despite all that happened earlier, I was tempted to trace them with my thumb.

Whoa, where did that come from?

I turned back to face my steering wheel.

I'd only met Kenji two days before, when I was attending the home birth of his niece. His half-sister, Andrea Hartell, was the vice provost of MacDougall, and when he answered the door in the wee hours of Wednesday morning, I had a briefly unprofessional wish that I didn't appear so practical, clad in a plain t-shirt and leggings, with my hair in a ponytail. Midwifery was messy work, and my clothing couldn't get in the way.

But today I looked even worse. In addition to the dirt, I probably had the imprint of the steering wheel on my forehead. Not that I should care.

"I'm fine. I really am okay," I finally said.

Undaunted, he continued, "Did you hear about all the excitement on campus?"

When I didn't answer, he gave me a closer look. "Wait, were you there? Is that why you've been sitting in your car for the last while?"

I breathed in and out once before nodding.

"Leeann," he said, and the way he said my name sounded soft on his lips, smoother than petals. "You're sure you're all right? Physically, I mean. You weren't hurt in the collapse, were you?"

"I wasn't injured." I sounded like a robot.

"You look a little gray."

Oh, it was just what any middle-aged woman wanted to hear from a beautiful young man, even if it was true.

But Kenji continued. "Do you need me to drive you home? I only have my bike, but we could throw that in the trunk."

I shook my head gently, a little afraid that if I moved it too much, things would start to fall out of it. Like tears.

"Then can I get you some water? Or something to eat?"

I swallowed. I didn't want food. What I wanted was to peel out of this parking lot and drive screaming until we passed the limits of town, beyond the trees and the gas stations and barns, the sparse fields and plain expanses of land, out of this province, this country. But I couldn't make my limbs move.

So, I handed him the keys and slithered my way across the front seat, knocking receipts and coins to the floor. Kenji stowed his bike in the back and climbed in. He pulled out of the parking lot, avoided the center of town, and went down the highway until just past the *Welcome to Reineville* billboard, and took us to the old Caravan Lodge and Diner, its heavy neon sign still burning bright in the heat of the afternoon.

Later, when Lulu asked me about my day, I realized what it looked like to let someone I barely knew take me out of town in my car. But you can learn a lot about a person by the way they behave during a birth. Kenji had stayed in the house during the hours I spent there, keeping a respectful distance when Andrea needed privacy, but when she needed him, he'd let her squeeze his hand, quiet but encouraging. He'd fetched things when I needed them and didn't complain. He hadn't—as one birthing partner had—tried to switch the TV on in the living room to watch the game and shush his partner during an important play. He'd been in tears when he held his niece for the first time. In my professional opinion, a cis man's tears, although a beauty to behold, weren't a measure of how good a parent—or uncle—he'd be, but I'd grudgingly allowed myself to like him.

Well, there was also the fact that the way the lines of exhaustion had pulled at his face only made his cheekbones more stark and sharp, and that his unruly hair practically called to me to smooth it down.

And that I thought at the time he might ask me out.

But no. I wasn't about to go on a date with a new person right before my daughter was set to leave the nest. I hadn't dated much at all since Lulu was born, and I didn't miss it. Men were more exhausting than babies, so I really wasn't planning to take up with a younger one. This summer was for Lulu and me. I couldn't afford to get distracted. It might be tempting to forget my sorrows in someone's arms, especially when the arms looked like Kenji's, but I was trying to be mature and wise.

It didn't help that last week when I tentatively asked my longtime doctor about the sleeplessness and the strange glow, she'd told me I was likely entering perimenopause and that everyone reported weird symptoms. She'd referred me to an ophthalmologist to check my eyes and muttered something about hot flashes. "Given your profession, I'm sure you know all about this."

In my professional opinion, she could suck it. I was pretty sure hormonal temperature dysregulation wasn't responsible for incandescent digits.

But I swallowed my outrage. I made the eye appointment, upped my dose of vitamin D, kept staying away from men, especially the young, attractive ones, and tried very hard not to glow.

Not that Kenji had asked me out, in the end. This diner outing was just him being concerned about a fragile older woman he found crying in a parking lot.

I didn't really want to go out with him anyway. Getting dressed up for an actual date, making stilted conversation in order to know the other person's career goals, remembering my table manners, talking about movies and shows I didn't have time to watch. Being disappointed.

That all seemed tiring and required too much long-term planning. All I actually wanted from Kenji was to pull his body down onto me and feel his weight on mine, like a big, sexy weighted blanket.

I must have been more exhausted than I thought if I was ready to wear the man. Especially in this heat.

I cleaned myself up in the diner's washroom as best I could, glad I kept a change of clothes in the car, and went back to the booth where Kenji sat waiting.

The waitress had brought over some water. I gulped mine down, and when Kenji slid me his glass, I drank that, too.

"I'm usually better in a crisis," I said abruptly.

He went with it. "From what I've seen you were great. You convinced my sister to go through with labor even though at several points, what did she say? She wasn't sure about this having-a-baby thing anymore?"

He probably wanted me to laugh.

"Childbirth isn't a disaster."

"It's no picnic either. You were probably fine out there at the accident. What happens afterward doesn't count."

A pause. "I don't think I can talk about it."

"We don't have to talk about it."

I took another breath. "You're very calm. I've noticed that about you."

He looked me in the eye. "I didn't have to help people during a scaffolding collapse."

The water had cooled me down, and I was starting to feel normal again thanks to his unruffled responses. I squinted at him over the rim of the glass. "I never did find out what you do. Or how old you are. Are you a shrink?"

He laughed. "No, I'm a middle school teacher."

Oh. Well, that explained the ability to deal with people's intense emotional states.

"And I'm thirty," he added.

Eleven years younger than me. I definitely shouldn't be thinking about him like this. I changed the subject and tried to sound like a normal human being who wasn't a mixture of worn, numb, traumatized, and strangely horny and who definitely hadn't had to see her doctor last week because she was lighting up like a firefly. "How is your niece doing?"

His face softened. "She's perfect. You said she'd sleep a lot, and she does. Andrea and I have spent hours just staring at her and listening to her little noises. Being able to hold Andrea's hand when my niece was born . . . it was the most incredible, messy, terrifying emotional experience I've ever had. Andrea was amazing. *You* were amazing."

I basked in it, until he added, "It was like you radiated some sort of competent energy."

His choice of words startled me. Had my hands lit up during the birth? No, he'd kept his back turned to the proceedings, facing Andrea, holding her hand and talking calmly, not watching me. He couldn't have seen anything—if there had been anything to see.

Best to change the subject. "How's Andrea doing?"

"She's tired. But happy." He looked down and rubbed his face. "Do you . . . do you know who the father, or I guess I should say sperm donor, is?"

I shook my head. "I don't."

Having similar questions about my own background, and also having been the subject of the town gossip mill when I was pregnant with Lulu, I grew quiet again. Every conversational path seemed to hold traps.

But Kenji didn't really expect more of an answer. He kept his head bowed. "She told me it was a longtime acquaintance but wouldn't say more. I get the sense she's unhappy he hasn't come to see her but . . . Well, as long as she and the baby are healthy, that's what matters. I know Andrea really wanted a child. More than she wants a partner. I don't understand why she won't give me a name. Maybe she didn't want me to go all medieval on someone, challenge them to a duel for my sister's honor. And child support."

"I think lawyers work better than duels for that kind of thing," I said a little tartly.

He looked woebegone and young at my words. *Too young for you*, I thought even as I reached to pat his hand. At the last moment he turned his palm over and captured mine.

The waitress came by at that moment, thank goodness. "What do you want?"

I pulled my fingers back. "Oh. Uh. A really hot coffee."

"It's always hot."

I'd been to Caravan many times before. That's how I knew now was not the time to argue. "And can I have a slice of the cherry pie? With ice cream?"

Without looking away from me, Kenji said, "I'll have the same."

The waitress rolled her eyes and left.

I gave a shaky laugh. "I guess it's not the healthiest lunch. But we probably won't run into any clients."

"Do you mind what your clients think of what you're eating? Or what you're doing?"

I thought about that for a moment. I supposed I did consider what people expected of me. Maybe too much. But I said lightly, "Some of my clients have been told to limit their sugar intake. I'd feel bad chowing down on dessert in front of them. Don't you feel like you have to set a good example for your students?"

"I'm new to the school district, so I haven't met any from here yet. If any future students are here, I doubt anyone will remember me sitting in this booth very innocently drinking coffee and eating pie with you."

His look was too bright and mischievous for me to be comfortable. I shifted in my seat. "But they'll know me. They might speculate about what this might be."

"Hmm. So what does it look like?"

"Sort of a date." I drew in a breath after admitting it. I'd just spent the morning staring at a pile of steel and wood, bandaging hands, and talking to paramedics and police. Now here I was, another world away, sitting with a handsome man in the hangout of my high school and university years. "Sorry," I said. "I don't—"

"It could be a date if you wanted."

His voice was carefully neutral, but he watched me closely. "I wanted to ask you out after Rose was born, but I figured it wasn't the best time. But I'll back off now if you'd like and let you make up your mind. I can go slow. Or fast."

I didn't feel like he wanted slow. Or maybe that was my own pulse ticking at a breakneck pace in my wrists and throat.

"I don't know," I said truthfully. "Today has been a lot."

"Yes, it's true. I'm sorry. But why don't you think about it?"

Oh, I will.

The waitress set two cups of coffee down and two enormous slabs of cherry pie, glistening with fruit and juices, each topped with a round mound of vanilla ice cream.

The sugar and coffee were going to course through my veins like a drug. I felt a little lightheaded just looking at them. Or maybe it was because Kenji put his hand over mine again, briefly, before taking it back.

We started to eat.

I thought I wasn't going to be able to swallow anything. But a steady shovel and chew kept me from doing something stupid, like jumping across the table right into Kenji's lap. Or bursting into tears.

"So Andrea named the baby Rose?"

"Yes. After her mother." He rubbed his eyes. "I'm sorry. I didn't get any sleep. I wanted Andrea to rest, so I ended up holding Rosie, and I think I spent half the night just staring at her little toes and fingers. I'm around kids for my job, but I haven't seen many babies, especially newborns. Her skin is so fine, it's almost translucent."

I had to laugh a little bit because even while talking about how exhausted he was, he gestured energetically. Maybe he was up with Rosie, maybe there were shadows under his eyes, but his face was still unlined.

He said he was tired, I was tired, and no one I knew was getting any sleep. Looking back, I should have seen the patterns, connected the dots: Exhaustion. Bad dreams. Oppressive heat that seemed to weigh down on the soul.

My glow.

But I was too preoccupied with my own worries. The only thing I remember thinking about in the moment was the way he talked about the baby. That he'd want children someday. That he was too young, that I couldn't date, and that I was getting ahead of myself, which meant I should definitely put a stop to this. Now.

"It sounds like she's healthy," I said. "I'll be checking up on her and Andrea soon."

Kenji nodded. "What about you? Any kids? Or nieces and nephews? Niblings?"

Right on cue, there it was. The beginning of the evaporation of his interest. I should have welcomed it, the way he gave me the opportunity. "I have a daughter. Lulu. She's eighteen. She's off to university in eight weeks."

Kenji sat back. Ah, there it was, the beginning of the end. "You must've been pretty young when you had her."

"Not that young. I was twenty-three. But I did have to drop out of university for a while. Lulu's dad and I didn't work out." I paused. "My mom was horrified when I decided to be a single mother, especially because she's an obstetrician and a professor at MacDougall and ought to have taught me better about birth control, according to her."

I finished with a shrug then pushed at my pie, waiting for him to do the math, waiting for the eventual backing up when he realized that despite the fact my black hair didn't have any gray in it yet and my small face with its pointed chin was still smooth, I was more crone than girl.

Time for him to say regretfully, with a sad smile, that he was making a mistake. That this had been fun, but a little harmless flirting was all he was in for this summer.

He touched my hand again. "What will you do with your daughter gone?"

I looked up and saw mischief in his eyes and no retreat. If anything, he seemed to press forward, and that made me want to run and hide and think about everything he was saying and how he was looking and examine it under the microscope of my memory. What the hell was he up to if he'd heard everything I'd had to say for myself, and didn't mind? Did he really . . . like me?

Or maybe he simply saw me as an opportunity.

I don't know what I might have answered because in that moment a mighty crash sounded across the diner.

I jumped, my knee knocking the table so hard that the cups rattled and tears sprang to my eyes.

"Are you all right?" Kenji leaned forward in concern.

"I'm fine," I choked out for the millionth time today, swiping under my eyes. "What was that?"

As had become my habit, I glanced at my hands to make sure they weren't glowing inappropriately. I turned them palm up before lowering them, trembling.

Nothing.

But now Kenji was staring at my hands, too.

They were fine. Normal. I resisted the urge to hide them under the table.

He'd seen nothing. After a moment, he blinked rapidly and glanced away. I swallowed and turned to look at the scene in front of us. Our waitress had upset an entire tray of dishes and was scrambling to gather the shattered pieces.

A plate was still spinning on the floor. Martin, the crotchety manager of the diner portion of the Caravan, was staring aghast at the pile.

I let out a slow breath and the pain in my knee subsided. But my heart was still beating fast.

Too much had happened today. How could I even sit here flirting with Kenji when too much of my life was still up in the air? I had to focus on my daughter, on what my life would look like after she left, and on researching whether glowing hands was a lesser-known symptom of perimenopause.

I'd allowed myself to be distracted.

"I should go. Thanks for bringing me here. I have clients." I stood up and put some money on the table.

Kenji did the same. It was probably too much, but the waitress was probably going to need all the tips she could get.

"I'll drive you back into town," I said, avoiding Kenji's eyes.

"It's okay. I'll get my bike out and ride."

As we walked out, I saw the waitress rubbing her eyes. "I'm sorry, Martin," she said. "I'm just so tired. I can't sleep. I'm so sorry."

◆ 2 ◆

"MOM, MAYBE I SHOULD drive."

I turned to find Lulu bristling with impatience. Evidently, I'd been standing with my keys in hand, staring at the car door a little too long. Although my mother's was at most a ten-minute ride away, we weren't going to be on time for Friday dinner.

My daughter hated being late. She probably got that from her father, the eminent cardiologist.

Lulu grabbed my keys and nudged me aside, stepping into the driver's seat. She made a great show of adjusting it so that it would accommodate her longer legs, then she flicked a glance up at me. "You coming?"

Truth was, I didn't want to hang out with my mother. Even under the best of circumstances, dinner with Shuling was . . . trying. But it was going to be worse tonight, because with the memories of the scaffolding collapse and more bad dreams, I hadn't managed to sleep much for the past few nights. A combination of restlessness mixed with a good dose of unease over my nightmares and so-far secret glowing, and, I hated to admit it, horniness kept my mind active even when it should have been resting.

Something about having a lean, dark-eyed young man staring at me from under hooded eyes, brushing his hand against mine, making my skin prickle. All of that attention and care and intensity focused on me—it made me think of him in the late hours of the night, as the sheet tangled around my sweaty legs. It made me ache.

Of course, while I shared a lot with my daughter and tried to be as open with her as possible, this wasn't something that I particularly wanted to divulge. I hunkered down in the passenger seat. With Lulu's perfectly straight back and pressed linen shorts, she looked more like the mother and I the slouching teen.

I focused on her, as I should have all along.

Lulu was a wonder. Clear-eyed, dewy-skinned, and with a sitting posture that could serve as a right-angle ruler, she was the determined and strong and competent young woman I'd wanted to be. She'd been accepted into all the schools she'd applied for and had chosen the University of Toronto; she would be leaving at the end of August. People always said I'd done a marvelous job, *especially as a single mother.* But I always told them I was the lucky one, because it had been all Lulu. Lulu at age five sitting in a corner of the public library reading a book meant for a much older kid. Lulu at nine telling me she didn't want to go out for Halloween anymore because she didn't really like walking around at night just for a little candy. Lulu raising money to save the whales. Lulu making friendship bracelets and selling them in the park. Lulu making me go to dinners with my mother. Lulu writing out a chore chart for us to follow so the house would be in decent shape.

She would have been welcome to stay here with me and go to the excellent university in our town where her own grandmother taught. But Lulu wanted to expand her horizons. I couldn't blame her. After all, remaining in the town I grew up in hadn't exactly been the greatest choice for me. Because of my mother and her reputation, I'd felt the need to go against every warning she'd given me.

Then again, I'd gotten Lulu out of it.

But Lulu's father was in Toronto, a few hours' drive away. So, even though in the years leading up to high school graduation she'd been close-mouthed about her plans for university, I'd already taught myself to let her go.

I hadn't given it much thought beyond that.

I watched Lulu through half-closed eyes as she navigated around a line of police cruisers and emergency vehicles on Division Street. "I wonder what that's about," she muttered.

I let my head fall back. "I feel like I keep hearing about accidents around town lately. Or maybe they're more frequent in summer."

"You know, they're saying it was human error that caused the scaffolding collapse you saw."

I squinted at my daughter. "That's bull. The wind was like some sort of tornado. I don't think anything could've withstood it."

"A tornado in this part of the country, though?"

I shrugged. "We've had strange weather."

Lulu nodded. She was clearly working the complex meteorological problem out in her head, maybe linking the whole thing to climate change or trying to figure out how to solve it all. I settled back again and watched her, thinking that it was so much easier to be proud of her than to try to find joy in my own accomplishments: her first step, the first word she read, the first joke she ever made, the As on her essays, the way she could speak seriously or teasingly with the kids and adults in her life. It was all so easy to love the things she did and would go on to do.

"What?" she asked me, never taking her eyes from the road. "You're staring."

"I'm just thinking about what a good driver you are."

Lulu snorted. "Next thing you know, you'll be telling me to do this more often. Then I'll have to drive you places. Soon you'll be sitting in the back seat and calling me with your phone to tell me to slow down. And by the way, please pick up some brandy on the way home."

"Brandy? I don't drink brandy."

"You will when you start believing you have a chauffeur."

"You've got some nerve complaining, considering how many swimming and violin lessons I used to take you to."

"*Stranded me at* is more like it. I was always the kid shivering in the cold waiting for my mom to get back from delivering a baby."

"That happened twice. And eventually we worked out a system with Madison's mom."

Lulu made a face, which told me what she thought of our neighbor, Madison, who was Lulu's age.

"What are you going to do when I leave at the end of August?"

But we'd pulled into my mother's driveway, and there wasn't much more time to talk. "I'm quite self-sufficient. No need to come around, Jeeves." I opened the door, "See? I can let myself out."

Joke was on me, though. Lulu didn't even laugh at my sad little attempt to sidestep the question of her leaving but hopped out and headed for the door. "Jeeves was a valet, not a chauffeur," she said over her shoulder.

Like I knew anything about domestic servants.

My tired forty-one-year-old body creaked once or twice before hauling itself up. Lulu was already through the open door before I got up the steps, and when I finally reached the door, my mother stood there glaring at me. "You're letting in the heat," she said in Mandarin.

"No, you are," I muttered.

It was true. She could have shut the door before I came in, and despite her belief in my incompetence, you'd think she could at least trust me to be able to figure out how to turn the knob and step over her threshold. Then again, it wasn't as if I really wanted to enter my mother's lair, so maybe it was understandable that I made her stand there waiting. She didn't believe in turning on the AC when I was growing up, so I don't know why she had a sudden zeal for cold air now.

I ignored the slippers she'd set out for Lulu and me and walked barefoot into the kitchen. My mother didn't like living in old houses, like the Victorian manors nearer the hospital; but she'd been settled in this faux-Tudor suburban spread for the past ten years, and somehow it felt like it had been here forever. The air was heavy with the medicinal aromas of her cooking. For as long as I remember, Shu-ling had been trying to prolong her life and ours, with exercise and vegetables, vitamins and herbs. She believed in science, of course—she was a practicing ob/gyn and an instructor at the university. But science didn't preclude experimenting on oneself, within reason.

"Can I help with anything, Ma? Run some carrots through the juicer? Massage some kale? Give some chia seeds a foot rub?"

"Stop talking nonsense," Ma said irritably.

She was wearing a pair of elegant lounging pajamas, as she often did when she was at home, her short silver hair neat and shiny. It had been that color even when she was a young woman. Most often, she told me I'd turned it gray, and once, only once, she said my father had done it. But she and I had the same brows, although she kept hers plucked to dark, emphatic lines. We had the same pointed chin. But I had bigger features—larger eyes, a sharper nose. Even when I wasn't dressed in jeans and a t-shirt, I always felt messy next to her.

"Chop up this garlic," she said, while she sliced kohlrabi and dressed it with sesame oil.

Lulu was already in the living room, pulling out the old photographs. "Not until after dinner," I called.

The photographs were the latest thing that kept us both coming to visit my mother. They'd arrived in a couple of small boxes years ago from my āyi, my mother's older sister Shu-chuan, in Taiwan, but it wasn't until last year that Lulu had started to wonder about our heritage. Ma had told me stories from her girlhood here and there, but she was close-mouthed about her teen and university years. But when Lulu asked, it was different. So we came to sift through old pictures, and because Ma had extracted a promise from me when I felt her out about helping with a portion of Lulu's upcoming tuition. Although to be fair, Ma had not grumbled about that either. She'd given Lulu good advice about premed courses and what to expect. Shu-ling was more useful than me, the not-so-dutiful daughter who hadn't finished her degree in the first round.

"I'm only taking the pictures out so they'll be ready," Lulu yelled.

She was still a child sometimes. My heart wept.

Lulu was fascinated with the pictures from her grandmother's girlhood. I'd never even known they existed until recently. When I was young and had to bring in a photo for some sort of family history assignment, Shu-ling had told me that we didn't have any. "The old house is gone," she'd said. "Your aunt told me it's been taken over by snakes."

I never knew how to respond to statements like that, so I didn't push. But the snakes apparently had little use for pictures, because two years ago, the packages arrived from Shu-ling's sister. We'd been going over them, a few every week. There was a story behind every one, and Lulu wanted to hear it all. My mother had something to say about all of them, even the ones she didn't remember.

Or maybe she was making things up. She did that sometimes.

"Andrea Hartell gave birth a couple of nights ago," I told Ma. "Girl, seven pounds, five ounces. Apgar 9."

She grunted. "Did she say who the father is?"

"Ma!"

A glint appeared in her eye as she cleared the chopping board with her Chinese chef's knife. "I'd keep it confidential."

"You're not her doctor."

Ma had some nerve to ask, considering how close-mouthed she'd been about my other parent my entire life.

Another grunt. "I suppose she's got nannies and nurses all lined up if she's going to go back to work in August, like she told the *Chronicle* she would."

"Yes. And her younger brother—her half-brother—is staying with her."

That made my mother look up.

I probably shouldn't have mentioned it. But my mother had a sixth sense about these things. If I'd left out that detail, and she heard it on the university grapevine, it would have been more suspicious.

She turned away, calling "Lulu, put the pictures down and help me carry this to the dining room." I thought I'd won a reprieve, until she turned to me and said, "He's not right for you."

How did she do that? It had to be some kind of magic.

Still, even though I had already told myself the same thing a truly embarrassing number of times, I couldn't help pushing back. "He doesn't have to be right for me. He just has to be right for right now."

"Who's right now?" Lulu asked as we headed into the dining room.

"A young man that your mother met at a birth."

"All right, Mom! Birthing babies, stealing hearts."

"*Assisting* with birthing babies," I said with a pompous glare. "Still, yours sounds better as a clinic motto. Let's get the t-shirts printed up."

"You make jokes," my mother said, "but you always end up crying."

"Are you writing country songs now, Ma?"

She gave Lulu a helping first, then told me, "Now you serve me. Because I'm the oldest." Trust Shu-ling Wu to slam the doors with her last words. There wasn't much else we could do except crunch our way through the rest of dinner.

It wasn't as if I wanted to get involved with anyone anyway, but my mother telling me I shouldn't do something was usually what made me want to do it. Acting on it, however, was a different story.

Surely it was okay for me to daydream a little. After all, it wasn't as if I was enjoying my nightmares. I allowed myself two minutes to think of Kenji's lips: one for the upper, the other for the lower. But anything beyond that I probably should save for when I was away from Shu-ling Wu's table. She could read minds. Probably.

I took a very big bite of kohlrabi and hoped the loud crunching would drown out any telepathic signals I might be transmitting.

"Did you know Mom got caught in the scaffolding collapse?" Lulu asked.

Ma swung around to look at me. "You are all right?"

"Of course, I'm fine."

Satisfied, my mother gave a sharp nod.

"You should have a boyfriend if you want," Lulu whispered when Ma got up to get the soup. In hot weather, we always finished with cold, sweet soup.

"It's been a while," I whispered back.

"I'm just worried you'll get lonely."

"What lonely?" Ma called. "Your mom can go back to school and finish her medical degree."

Ma had great hearing. She returned with three bowls on a tray.

I cut her off before she could start that old argument again. "Ma, I'm happy with midwifery, and I'm not going to medical school."

"Even if she finished another degree, she wouldn't have to give up on her social life," Lulu said.

Shu-ling snorted. A woman who changed into one of several sets of lounging pajamas the minute she got home from work had little use for a social life. I couldn't remember the last time she'd gone out to dinner. She didn't trust restaurants—was convinced she'd contract hepatitis A from contaminated flatware. A butterknife could be deadly. She hadn't dated even when I moved out.

I swirled my spoon in my bowl. Ma had made cold taro soup with tapioca. Back when I was a little kid, she'd only cooked it for special occasions. On her rare days off, we'd drive off to Toronto in the big station wagon she'd bought secondhand on a quest for ingredients. We didn't have car seats back then, and I sure didn't use a seatbelt. So on the way there, I'd start out shotgun, or climb to the back to nap, or if we'd left the rumble seat down, I'd sit facing the back and wave at other drivers until a big rig tooted at me and Shu-ling finally realized what I was doing.

I had to stay up front after that.

We'd always kept to ourselves when I was young. Ma was acquainted with a lot of people, of course, but she couldn't really be friends with her patients. There was a small, ever-evolving Mandarin-speaking community in Reineville—having a well-regarded public research university and a large teaching hospital could quickly make any town a little more diverse—and I'd sometimes befriended other Asian kids, whose scholarly parents inevitably left for other schools. But Shu-ling shunned her mainland Chinese and (even more mysteriously) her Taiwanese colleagues. She slammed the door, muttering under her breath when East Asian Christians of any country came knocking at our door with pamphlets. I was told not to answer their persistent rings, although she didn't explain why. When I was in junior high, I sometimes let them in anyway, because they were always accompanied by a white lady who'd start talking in whatever dialect she assumed was the Chinese all my people spoke, and I'd answer in English.

It was only fun the first few times.

Now I could admit a grudging sympathy with my mother about her situation. A single mother, one who was Asian, invited curiosity, questions. Or worse, propositions from people who thought she'd be easy, starved for any kind of attention. I knew the Ob department had been surprisingly unenlightened when my mother started out. I could feel for my mother now that I'd gone through some of it myself.

But empathy, as always, was short-lived when my mother began to *mother* again.

"Ever since you were little you said you wanted to be a doctor," Ma said now. Thank the gods I'd outgrown that desire. But I didn't say that out loud. That had only been fun the first few times, too.

I gritted my teeth. "I said I wanted to be like you and deliver babies. Goals achieved."

She shook her head. "You're not like me."

"Let me remind you that I also wanted to be a police officer, a dolphin, and Sabrina the Teenage Witch. But this is the only aspiration you conveniently remind me about. I'm 41, Ma. I do important work that I love. I like my life."

"So don't mess it up by getting a boyfriend." She pointed at Lulu. "That goes for you, too."

"What about girlfriends?" Lulu asked.

Ma narrowed her eyes and didn't answer.

After dinner, we settled in the living room, Lulu and Ma on the couch by the window. Lulu had taken out the albums and the box of photographs, and a couple of frames, even though the truth was, Ma never wanted to put any of them up. Shu-ling wasn't scared of much, but I got the sense that she found the idea of having those pictures of long-dead people, the family she hadn't seen or spoken to for decades, unnerving rather than comforting. Or maybe she was afraid of being confronted by her younger self, the one who had felt the need to leave them all behind.

"And who's this, A-mà?" Lulu asked, holding up one photo.

"A cousin on my mother's side—I don't know how you say it—third cousin twice removed or something. Everyone is a cousin in English. How does anyone know who's important in the family this way?"

"You could always just use their names," I said, even though I knew why we didn't.

"That is not respectful."

No, we never used names. Just titles: older sister, second uncle, little cousin. The one time when I was young and I'd called my mother by her name she'd scolded me until my ears rang. I never said it to her again—except in my head.

Shu-ling was examining another photograph, "This cousin was a dressmaker. Your grandmother must have been getting a gown made for a wedding or something like that. That's why she's holding the tape measure over her arm. I didn't like her. She used to tell me my eyebrows were too thin, and I shouldn't pluck them." Ma frowned. "Old women should mind their own business."

I snorted.

"But *you're* my business," Shu-ling said in response to the words I didn't say.

"The board voted you out years ago."

Lulu ignored us. "Your clothes and hair are just perfect here, A-mà."

"Your great-grandmother, and me, too, we used to go to the salon once a week to get our hair set. I never washed my own hair until I came to North America."

I rolled my eyes. Oh yes, my mother had been such a pretty, pretty princess. "Even when you were a kid? A teen?"

Ma regarded me, gimlet-eyed.

But Lulu was used to our sniping. She had picked up another photo. "Who is this?"

Ma looked at the photo for a long time. Long enough that I became curious enough to get up and go around the couch. Then I saw.

In the black-and-white photo a woman stood by herself, a road open behind her. She was dressed in plain, dark clothing. I was sure I'd seen her in the background of a few of the other photos. Her appearance niggled at me, but every time I'd been about to ask my mother about her something had happened. A box tipped over. The doorbell rang and no one was there. A bird smacked into the window.

But in this photo, she was by herself. She was looking right at the camera. Right at me.

"That was your great-aunt, you'd call her your Yi-beh," Ma said to me. "My mother's oldest sister. This is the village they grew up in. She never married but she was a midwife."

"Wow, it really does run in our family."

"Yes." Ma gave a slow nod. "Many things do."

I shivered.

Lulu asked, "Like what else?"

Shu-ling waved her hand as if brushing the question away. "Thin eyebrows, longer second toes, age spots when you get older, other things."

"Other things like high blood pressure?" I asked.

Shu-ling ignored me. Then she said quietly, "Some people said she knew magic."

I felt the words whoosh into me. My mother wasn't fanciful. She didn't say this lightly.

I had been staring at the picture before, but now I felt myself having to pace and cross my arms over my chest to suppress the sudden tingle in my fingers. I resisted the urge to untuck them and stare at them.

"She knew a lot, your great-aunt."

"Magic?" Lulu repeated, excited. "I want to know more about these powers."

Ma didn't meet our eyes. "Not powers. People just said things about her."

"That's helpful, Ma." I was trying to sound casual and cynical, but I don't think I fooled anyone. Lulu and my mother glanced at me.

I flexed my fingers again; they wanted to do something.

Lulu turned and waved her arm. "How come you never talked about her before if she was magic? If I'm a witch or something, you should let me know in case I turn someone into a toad accidentally by looking at them cross-eyed."

Ma shook her head. "Because it's not real and you aren't a witch. We've been midwives. That's the real magic. In every generation, there's at least one Wu woman who attends births and heals people. That's why we keep our last names. In Taiwan you can have your mother's surname, but many don't take it. We do."

"So you and Mom are part of the whole Wu woo." Lulu grinned, pleased with herself.

"You, too," Ma said. "Good thing you'll be going to premed."

I glared at my mother, then to Lulu I said, "You can choose your own path based on your interests and what you love. It's a big legacy to live up to."

Ma thinned her lips. "Some of us haven't."

"You just said that your aunt was a midwife. Which means I'm the one actually following in her footsteps. I feel like I'm upholding just fine."

"Your aunt could have been a doctor, if she'd been given the opportunity. But she was the first of six children. She took care of her brothers and sisters while training to be a midwife. Later, she even raised you when you were young, Leeann, while I was here during my fellowship."

I frowned. I'd always known vaguely that my mother had left before me, that she'd had to come back for me. But I always assumed I'd stayed with my grandmother and aunt in Taichung. Not this unfamiliar person, staring out from the photograph.

Lulu looked up from the picture. "What?"

Ma nodded.

"She came here?"

"No, I left your mother there. Then when Leeann was three, her Yi-beh disappeared in a typhoon." Under her breath she added, "And there was nothing I could do about it." She said more loudly, "So I brought your mother back here to live with me."

Lulu swung her gaze at me, puzzled. "I didn't know this until now. Why didn't you tell me? Why haven't we heard more stories of her?"

"I don't really remember her, Lulu. I must have been too young."

Besides, the question of what I'd done in the first years of my life had never been as urgent as questions about where my father was, who my father was, and what happened to him. All my mother had ever said was that he died in Taiwan before she left for Canada and that his family hadn't known much about her—or me. But now, I stirred uneasily, wishing I could remember something, knowing that even if I did, it wouldn't ever be enough. As for Ma, she only answered questions when she felt like it.

My mother shrugged. "She lived in the country." She turned the picture face down on the coffee table, and announced she was going to make some tea and would return with it shortly.

We never drank tea in the living room.

Lulu picked the photo up again. "Just think, all this time we had a witchy midwife in the family. How many generations of Wus have been delivering babies? She probably mixed herbs and knew about pressure points and things like that. You really didn't know?"

"I didn't." I stirred, feeling restless and uncomfortable. There was a lot, it seemed, I had no idea about. "Maybe there was some folk medicine mixed in with her midwife training? Healing stuff. Like A-mà says, there's a lot of that in the family."

"But this is different." Lulu held up the photo. "Look at her eyes—the way she stares into the camera, like she can see us. She knows things."

Maybe she could have told me about my glowing hands. I shivered. "People always say that about old photographs. It's probably just bad light." I shook my head to clear it. "I'm kind of surprised at how fascinated you are with this. You're usually all about facts and science."

"Doesn't mean I don't enjoy a good family story." She gave me a lopsided smile. "And A-mà is clearly leaving things out—and you're acting weird. Sounds to me like there's more to it than 'family tradition.'"

Maybe there was, maybe there wasn't. I was never sure myself. My mother, constantly pointing out how I'd disappointed her, had made me sure whatever had been passed down in the Wu blood had probably managed to skip me. After all, who the heck suddenly became a great power after 40?

But the hands said otherwise.

Luckily, Ma came back with the tea before I could start psychoanalyzing myself to my own daughter, and she started telling us a story about her sister and a motorcycle, and before we knew it, the evening was over.

As I went to help put away some of the albums we'd managed to put together, I thought of nabbing the photograph of my great-aunt. Although she'd apparently taken care of me for the first years of my life, I didn't remember one thing about her. I didn't know why I suddenly wanted this picture of her. It was a little unnerving. Still, the thought of having her image, and the memory of those eyes gazing straight out at me, made my fingers tingle as if electrified.

It called me. I just wasn't sure I should heed it.

When I quietly tried to sift through the pictures we'd set aside, it was gone.

• 3 •

THIS MORNING HAD STARTED off unsettled. It wasn't often that I had to shake my daughter awake. "Come on, Lulu, your phone alarm has been going off for the last fifteen minutes."

A faint whine came from the tangle of black hair.

"I'm turning it off," I threatened.

"Fine. I don't care. Leave me alone."

I picked her phone up off her night table and switched it off. Then I sat back on Lulu's bed and lay down on her covers. In less than a minute, she began to complain. "Hey stop that. I'm pinned under this thing."

"I'm tired," I complained. "I want to sleep, too."

"Mom, I have to get up."

I snuggled closer to her. "But it's so nice and comfy here."

"*Mu-um*. I'm going to be late."

"Fine."

I rolled back and when she struggled out from under her sheets, I wrapped them around me.

"I want to make the bed."

Lulu sounded impatient now, and of course, because my brain was totally normal, that made me sad because I was going to miss her being snippy and competent at me.

"I thought you said you were going to be late." I grumbled trying to cover up my stupid mom feelings and stood up. "Who taught you to be so neat and responsible anyway?"

"When did you get in last night?"

"Four, four thirty. The baby was a little over nine pounds."

We'd all been exhausted after that one.

"Yikes."

"Grab a shower. I'll make you a smoothie."

"I thought you were going to go back to sleep."

"I can't sleep now. I'm so close to having a breakthrough." I swooped the blanket over my head and bent over, so I looked like a crone.

"What do you mean?"

"What if . . ." I swallowed. "I'm starting to have visions. My hands are radiating power." I stuck one finger out. "Maybe I'm like our spooky great-aunt after all."

But Lulu had ger back to me, and my expression was hidden by the blanket anyway. "Whatever, Mom."

"What do you mean 'whatever'?"

"Stop playing around," Lulu said, irritated. She sounded like my mother. "And your Yi-beh wasn't spooky. Okay, she was a little intense looking. But she was powerful, not scary."

She grabbed clothing from her drawers in short, jerky movements, clearly wanting me gone.

I don't know why I said anything. I wanted to test the waters, I guess. But as usual, I could never tell people important things in a serious way, so I shouldn't be surprised when no one listened too closely.

Of course, I couldn't let it go. "Well, be careful. I might chant over your smoothie, do something unsettling to you. *Lulu, you will have the sudden urge to clean my room. And bake me pastries.*"

She turned around finally, and I could see she was suppressing a grudging grin.

She threw a pair of underwear at me. I was used to ducking.

⋆ ⋆ ⋆

I was still tired when I arrived at the clinic that morning. I should be used to the lack of sleep by now, but there was an extra heaviness to my exhaustion lately. Maybe because I knew that soon scenes like this morning with Lulu would be rare.

What will you do with your daughter gone? Kenji's question echoed through my head.

No one had actually asked me that before. They'd told me: *This is your time*, a few people said, *You can remodel your house. Travel the world.* I resented the conversations. It wasn't like my whole life revolved around Lulu, but the way people talked, it sounded like it did. But the sad thing was that I was beginning to worry I would have no useful function after she left.

At least I still had my work.

Cato and their partner Sol were expecting their first child in November. I was filling them in on what to anticipate while taking their history. At first, they were both a little reluctant to talk. They scanned their surroundings warily and watched me with equal trepidation. Cato was

37 and Sol was 29. As I took down that information, I swore my hand tingled. It was probably my imagination.

"We'll have you into the clinic about once a month around the beginning," I was saying. "Then when you get to 28 weeks, we'll start seeing you more frequently, once every two weeks. And starting at 36 weeks, I'll see you once a week until the baby is born.

They listened to me carefully. Sol was also taking notes on his phone, so I scooted my rolling stool closer and spoke a little slower. "We'll also talk about any tests and test results coming up."

Cato shifted on the exam table, their movement making the paper rustle. "We're both a little anxious."

A look passed between the pair, even though they weren't touching. I liked them despite the reserve—or maybe because of it—which was good, because we'd be spending a lot of time together.

"It's natural to have worries. I mean, it's your first. If you do feel yourself preoccupied with these thoughts, I hope you'll talk to me or anyone else at the clinic. We're here to answer any and all the questions you have, and we're not going to rush you. At the end of the visit today, I'll also give you my contact information."

"Can I ask about home birth?" Sol asked. "Is it true we can just do this in our living room?"

"As long as we think it's safe and best for the baby and you, yes. You're only at 8 weeks, Cato, so as long as everything proceeds well, we can revisit this at 36 weeks."

They nodded. "We'd just like privacy. I feel like I'd be more comfortable that way."

"I'd like to be surrounded by things we love," Cato added.

I thought of our long, squat clinic building with its plastic siding, and looked around at the drab colors of the exam room, the chipping paint, the blocky worn furniture. I couldn't help laughing. "I can see why. The birthing rooms at the hospital are much cozier than this, and we even have some new pools for water-assisted birth. But a lot of people understandably prefer being somewhere familiar and less institutional. And for the days after the birth, one of us will come and do home visits to make sure the baby is thriving and gaining weight and check if lactation is going well, if you want to breastfeed. But also to make sure you're holding up alright, emotionally."

At my laugh, they both relaxed. Sometimes it was the little gestures.

"So next, I'm going to test your blood pressure and measure you so we can have a baseline to see how much the baby grows over the next few weeks. We may also be able to listen to the heartbeat."

Cato stiffened again when I brought my equipment out. They hadn't been kidding about being nervous, and I sensed that it wouldn't help if I tried to tell them there was nothing to worry about. So I took care to warm my stethoscope so that they wouldn't have a cold metal disk placed on their body when they were feeling jumpy and vulnerable.

My hands were strangely heated, even under the chill of the air conditioner, but I couldn't dwell on that now. I concentrated on inflating the cuff.

It wasn't until later, when I was chasing the fetal heartbeat, that I saw the glow.

I almost dropped the Doppler.

Under the fluorescent lamps of the clinic, my palms and fingers appeared golden, the tips of my nails almost pearlescent. They *radiated.* I blinked at them, thinking it was some sort of hallucination again. Maybe I was tired, and my pupils were smearing the lights. Maybe I was developing an astigmatism or having a stroke. Maybe it was perimenopause, as the doctor said.

I glanced up to see if the couple had noticed anything. Sol was gazing at Cato, his arm around them. Cato had their eyes closed.

Cato murmured, "Thank you for being gentle."

So it wasn't my eyesight. I looked down again at my hands hovering above Cato's still flat belly. Everything was as it should be, except my glow.

I took a deep breath and applied the Doppler wand. The rapid pulse of the fetal heartbeat filled the room.

"Oh." Cato opened their eyes and looked around. They were crying. So was Sol.

I forgot about my hands and held the instrument as still as I could and let the sound march on, each beat a lifegiving thunderclap.

"Thank you," Sol said fervently.

I smiled. "I just did my job. We're all in this together."

As I put the Doppler equipment away, my fingers looked almost normal.

A trick of the light. That must have been the problem.

But Cato had felt the warmth . . .

A voice whispered to me, *What if it really is something magical?*

* * *

I parked behind Andrea's house, pausing for a moment to look at the birds roosting in the big oak tree in the back. It felt like they were watching me expectantly, although, admittedly that was how birds often looked.

Be like the bird, I told myself.

I hadn't seen Kenji since that day at the diner, but I couldn't pretend he wasn't in my thoughts. This, of course, was why I couldn't allow myself to go out with him. Because even though there was no rule saying I shouldn't see the brother of my client, it was awkward to be driving to his sister Andrea's house for a postnatal visit and wondering if I would run into him. By awkward, I mean that when I, a middle-aged midwife, began to nonchalantly inquire about where the brother of the house might be, I turned bright red. It wasn't just my hands that glowed, apparently.

Hearing my knock at the back door, Andrea called out to tell me to let myself in. It took my eyes a moment to adjust to the gloom of the house. I entered through the small kitchen, observing that the sink was empty of dirty dishes and the counters clear. It was always clean, as if someone, too conscious of how old houses so often seemed aged and marked with the fingerprints of years, had scrubbed until the past was gone.

For some reason, that made me shiver.

Andrea was feeding the baby in a big chair in the darkened living room. She'd drawn the curtains to keep the light out, and even though a fan circled slowly and shiny ivy grew in a pot on the windowsill, the air seemed stale. Still, it was quiet, except for the ticking of the old clock. Someone had been keeping everything up. I hoped it wasn't Andrea. I wondered if it was Kenji.

I perched on the edge of the couch to observe. "This looks like it's going well," I said nodding at the baby.

"Yes, I don't think eating is a problem. She's a frequent feeder."

"How often is she getting up at night?" My voice sounded oddly hushed in the dark room.

"Every hour and a half."

"Oof."

"Yeah, it's a lot to do, but she seems to really need it. Kenji, my brother, he's taking some of those feedings, though. But it does mean that I have to pump a lot during the day."

At the casual mention of Kenji, my stomach flipped. But I kept my eyes on Andrea. "She isn't confused by the switch to the bottle?"

"No, she'll drink down whatever we put in front of her."

The baby did indeed seem to have a lot of energy for eating.

"I see her cheeks are filling out a lot. That's some good growing, baby. Now how about you? Are your nipples getting sore?"

Andrea winced. "They're starting to. Mostly with the pump, though."

"Okay, so I think it might be a good idea try a different size pump flange, maybe one that's bigger. I can leave you information or email it to you so that you don't have to remember all of this."

She looked up at me for the first time since the visit. She and Kenji had the same kind eyes, I thought. Brown and large, although Andrea's seemed far more shadowed, fatigued. "Okay, yeah, I think leave it here," she said. "I keep forgetting to check my messages, which is funny because I used to be attached to my phone." She laughed. "Used to be. It's only been a couple days and I'm acting like it's two lifetimes ago." Andrea shook her head. "I'm too tired to take any of this in right now. I'm sorry she's still nursing. I wanted to be done before you came over so that you could examine us right away and you wouldn't waste your time."

I waved a hand. "Don't apologize or rush. You also don't have to tidy before my visits. I'm used to this. This is about you and the baby and making sure you're adapting to each other well. My schedule is flexible."

Unless Mariam Ahmad needed to give birth in the next hour or so. But I trusted my instincts, which told me it wouldn't be today.

Besides, Andrea needed me right now. Despite the fact that the baby seemed to be thriving and the house was well kept, I knew that didn't necessarily tell the whole story.

"Why don't you talk to me a little bit about how you're doing?" I said.

Her eyes filled with tears. I was ready with a tissue. "I'm doing really great," she choked out. "You know, the baby's eating, and she's an absolute perfect angel. And Kenji is really good about cleaning and running the dishwasher and making sure I eat."

"But how about you?"

She shrugged. "I'm feeling fine."

I glanced at my hands—they were pale but at least they didn't appear to be glowing—and I waited.

"Well, I'm tired. I'm really exhausted. I mean, even with Kenji here helping me, I'm having so much trouble sleeping. I'm a little afraid to close my eyes. When I do . . . The other day when I was lying in my bed trying to get myself calm enough to nap, I looked over at the dresser, at the little pulls, you know? And it was like suddenly I saw my grandma's face in the cabinet overlaid on it, as if it became her? I don't know how to explain it. Was I hallucinating?"

Andrea sobbed a little again as the baby unlatched, asleep.

But in a moment, she said determinedly, "It's not post-partum depression, is it? I've read all about it. I'm just tired, that's all. It's not serious."

"It's normal, but it can develop into postpartum insomnia—" I held up my hand at her incredulous laugh. "I know, it sounds like insult upon injury. First you can't rest because you're trying to keep the baby fed, then you can't doze off because your brain is a jerk. But you can cycle from being tired, to being so tired that you can't even sleep. So maybe what we should track it."

"Another tracker. I had one for pregnancy and I've already got one for how much the baby feeds."

"It could be as simple as a tally on a piece of paper, or an app that you don't have to enter much info into. I can show you a few my clients have liked. If it persists, we can talk to your physician about medication that's safe to take while you're nursing. But in the meantime, be careful about the caffeine and alcohol."

She gave another bitter laugh, but as she tucked her breast away, she looked relieved to hear the insomnia was at least normal, as normal as anything was in these days after the baby was born.

Still, despite the fact that I'd kept my voice light, I was vigilant. It was a difficult period made worse by that stew of hormones, fatigue, love, and milk. A lot of my clients were reporting postpartum insomnia lately. It was already a vulnerable time for many of them, and not being able to sleep made it worse. I made a note to myself to talk to Parisa about it and finished the exam.

"Another thing that might be a good idea," I said as I began to put my things away. "I don't know if you're getting outside at all."

"I haven't set foot outdoors once," Andrea admitted faintly.

I nodded, understanding. "I know it feels like you have to cocoon with the baby, but maybe you should try to take a walk in the mornings or afternoons, get some sunshine on your skin, so that when you come back inside, your body can be ready for sleep. You can take the baby with you, as long as her face and eyes are shaded from the light. Even just sitting on the back porch in a chair would help."

"It might be nice to go out. Kenji's been trying to get me to, but I feel strange, like I've almost forgotten how. She was only born last week, and I feel like we've just been here together my whole life, and we can't ever leave."

"Well then, you definitely should get out, just a short distance. You can even leave her with someone else for a little bit."

"Kenji says to let him sit with her sometimes. He loves her, and I know he'll feed her and change her."

"So you feel like she's safe with him," I said encouragingly.

"Yes. Yes, I do. I just . . ." She trailed off.

"I know it's hard to let go even with people you trust. But it's a suggestion. Where is Kenji now, by the way?" I tried to sound bland but, as predicted, blushed hotly.

Andrea didn't seem to notice. She stroked the baby in her bassinet and leaned down to smell Rose's downy hair. "He went out. He checked to find out your appointment time, saying he wanted to give us privacy. I told him he could stay in the house, but . . ." She shrugged.

Kenji was avoiding me.

It was fine that he wasn't there. I wasn't supposed to be thinking about him anyway.

With a cheerfulness I didn't feel, I said, "It's nice to have such a helpful sibling. I'll stop in again. But you call me if you need anything."

I left by the back door again, shivering despite the heat of the day. Andrea's yard was dark and gloomy, hemmed in with huge trees on each side. The air smelled faintly of decay, and no birds sang.

Maybe it wouldn't be a good idea to bring the baby out to this ominous place.

No, I was being dramatic. The back offered good shade from the sun. It was shielded from noise. But maybe that was also unsettling. I shouldn't let myself get keyed up because I was preoccupied with thoughts of Kenji and strange magic. I scolded myself for letting my imagination run wild.

Still, I wished that I didn't have the feeling that there was something out here waiting for me. Listening to my long shaky breaths. Oh, how I wished it were cooler and that the hot choking air I drew into my lungs sustained me better. I raised my hands slowly, as if they'd be able to do something.

Maybe they would.

Out of the corner of my eye, I caught a flash of movement from the patch of garden near the yard. Dark clothing, the swoop of a heavy hem. I don't know why my mind went to the photograph of my great-aunt. But when I whirled around with a gasp, no one was there. The stolid wood of the fence stared back at me.

"Who's there?" I called.

My head swiveled back and forth.

Nothing.

I took in another breath and my voice came out stronger than I expected. "Who's there?"

"It's just me," a male voice replied.

From the opposite corner, the gate unlatched. Kenji.

His smile flared up bright and then faded as he stepped toward me. "Are you all right?" he asked carefully.

He glanced at my hands, which were still held up as if I were trying to push someone back. *It would have done little against a ghost.*

I wasn't sure why that thought flashed through my mind.

At least there was no sign of the glow. "Jumping at shadows," I said. "Maybe it was the wind."

There was no wind.

"It's secluded here. I can understand why it would make someone nervous. I ought to cut back the branches a little when I get some time."

Now that my fear had faded, I felt like a fool. Not because of the way he talked, so sensibly, but his eyes had run over me to make sure I wasn't hurt. His presence made me feel safe again. Although it shouldn't have.

Kenji had his helmet tucked under one arm and the other slung casually over the handlebars of his bicycle. Sweat had darkened his t-shirt and made his strong fore-arms shine.

It was too hot and bright to be exercising. He'd ridden out at this hour to avoid seeing me.

Kenji came just a little closer and let me look at him, which I did slowly and carefully before glancing away self-consciously.

Whoever I'd just seen couldn't have been him. I'd had the barest impression of someone smaller, clad in black, a dress. But there had been a presence. My senses had screamed it.

A crow settled on the fence.

I took a breath. "Let's start again. Hi. How've you been? And before you ask, I'm fine."

He laughed, and now we were both self-conscious—yet unwilling to leave each other's presence. I stood for a moment watching the bird as it preened, then my eyes slid to meet Kenji's again.

Kenji gestured at the bird. "They say crows are pretty smart," he said. "They can use tools, mourn their dead, and take revenge."

I tried to keep my tone light. "It's so human to think that taking revenge is a sign of intelligence."

He smiled fondly at my prickly words. "It requires planning."

"So does finding food and feeding your young. Revenge takes intelligence, yes, but it also takes having your pride injured."

"Are you saying being proud is a human failing?"

"I guess I'm saying that sometimes we see the things we want to see in others."

A pause.

Then he said, lightly, "Is that what I did the other day?"

I had the feeling we weren't talking about crows anymore. I exhaled. "No."

He took a step closer, holding my gaze.

My heart was in my throat again. Although for another reason. "I'm not in a playful mood," I said to myself as much as to him. "I need sleep, and I've had a rough morning. Plus, I've just been startled by a bird. Or you. Or maybe a ghost."

He took a step closer, and it was stupid, but I felt like closing the gap when I should have been running.

"I'm not making fun. I take you very seriously," he murmured.

I didn't look away.

He hadn't planned to see me. He was fine leaving well enough alone. I reminded myself I should do that too. I was probably just a distraction for him. He was new in town. He didn't know that many people here. His sister was—or at least she felt—homebound. What was a man to do except flirt with any older lady who came along?

Yet, when I was with him, I didn't doubt he was drawn to me. I could feel the air change when he looked at me. It was only when I was alone that I wondered if it was as much of an illusion as my glowing hands.

My heart was pounding again. Who would it hurt if I did something stupid? If I got just a *little* involved with him? Just a finger. The merest touch of a toe.

Although, I'd want a lot more than a finger from him.

I swallowed. "Next you're going to say that I'm overthinking things."

"Is that what you've been doing? Thinking? Because I can't get you out of my mind."

"Is that so?" It came out softer than I wanted. A whisper, when it should have been a firm statement, full-throated in its cynicism.

"Why are you so surprised?"

I fiddled with the hem of my shirt. "I'm guessing this whole thing between us is because you're here in a small town with your exhausted sister and a baby, who though fascinating, is probably not a sparkling conversationalist. It's natural you'd latch onto someone who speaks in complete sentences and doesn't fall asleep in the middle of a visit."

He was smiling now, which I loved, but which I also wished he'd not do.

I said desperately, "I need to be responsible and think of consequences. I have to hold my head up high in this town."

Why was every word out of my mouth some kind of a cliché?

He'd put down his bike helmet now. "Is that the reason you're scared?"

I crossed my arms. "Who said I was scared? I have to be careful. I have a kid."

"She's going off to university soon you said. What's her name?"

"Luisa. Lulu."

"Your voice changes when you talk about her."

It probably did. I took a moment to get ahold of myself. "Yeah, well. She's my pride, and I'm a vengeful crow mother. I remember every wrong against her, every kid who ever pushed her in a sandbox. Everyone who ever told me I wouldn't be able to take care of her. I did it. She's amazing and responsible. She finishes her essays and applications weeks before they're due. She composts. She starts clubs at her school. She has plans."

He smiled and started moving toward me. "Makes us old people sound like losers."

"Oh, I am. But you've still got one or two good years left in you to make up for it." He was close now. I nudged him with my elbow. If he could tease me, I could do the same to him.

But touching him with that bony part of my arm seemed unsatisfying somehow. Instead, I brushed against him once, gently, with the side of my body. He turned his face enough so that I could feel his breath in my hair.

"Is that what it is?" he whispered. "Do you think I'm too young for you?"

I didn't answer. But I didn't move away from him.

He sighed and my hair stirred again. "We could see where it goes," he said.

But that was the problem. I wasn't worried about my wrinkles, the softening of my flesh. It was that I couldn't just meander down a path and try to find out where it led because I didn't have the luxury of time. Should I invest my precious days and months in a person who could afford so much more?

Yet, people kept telling me I'd have so much time now that Lulu was leaving me.

"I tried to stay away," Kenji said. "Went on a long bike ride. Got turned around and biked up one street too many times. The older residents probably thought I was casing the joint."

I needed to step away. But my feet didn't budge. "People don't case houses in Reineville. They get drunk on beer and break into their neighbor's to get back the weed whacker someone borrowed and never returned."

He laughed softly and I felt the breath fan lightly over my nose. He was so close now. I could smell his sweat.

"You make it sound like a tiny town instead of a city."

"It's barely a city. You couldn't even call us midsize—we're a large town," I said, my voice hoarse. "But I guess the population swells when the students are here."

His nose was close to my hair. I shut my eyes and swallowed.

"There's a lot about large-town life I could get used to," he said.

His hand was on my back now, his palm warm through my thin shirt. One little push and I'd sway right into him.

"I've hardly been anywhere," I said. "This is all I know."

"Leeann, why do you do that?"

"Do what?"

"Tell yourself you're uninteresting. Say you don't know anything. You've been trying to convince me you're nothing special when I know you are."

"How do you know?"

"Because you glow."

I felt a hitch in my breath. *He knows. How?*

But he wasn't staring at my hands. He was looking into my eyes.

I took a deep breath and stepped in, getting used to the closeness of him. Even that was electric. He swallowed, but his eyes never left me. He kept his arms at his side. He was letting me do what I wanted in my own time. I put my hands slowly up to his face. Maybe they *were* glowing faintly now, or maybe it was a trick of the light, but at this moment, with these feelings, it was almost like power coursing through me. I didn't care if he saw me—I wanted him to see me. And he never looked away. Even as my thumbs stroked over his cheekbones, even as I drew his face down to mine, he never stopped seeing me.

I ghosted my lips over his and I felt him shiver. Or was it me. A warm, golden haze enveloped me as I brought him closer, and I could feel his breaths, quick, a heartbeat. I could feel his whole young life in my hands and I kissed him.

Oh, it was soft and good and I could feel my whole body ripple with the energy of it, the yearning for more. He was holding my arms, keeping me more firmly in place as if urging me to drink from him, and I couldn't stop. I kissed him and kissed him, my tongue greedily taking every stroke and sensation he could give me. I drew everything in him to me.

Then I let go.

He looked at me dazedly for a minute in the brightness of the garden, in the more-than-sunlight, and I knew then it was me. I was radiating, I was glowing.

I dropped my hands and he almost staggered, as if I'd been holding him up.

"What is this?" he murmured.

I only smiled. Because I knew at that moment, it was me.

4

WHEN CAN I SEE you again?

The text came in not an hour after I left Kenji in his sister's yard.

I was scared and excited and terrified by all the strange possibilities stretching in front of me. So of course, I avoided thinking about it all, avoided replying to Kenji's text. I caught up on my paperwork, and then when it finally dulled my brain enough, I thumbed out a reply. Tomorrow maybe? My schedule is . . . difficult.

Good thing mine is easy.

I could almost hear the way he said it. I closed my eyes, and my head thunked down on my desk. I had no response to that.

A little later, he sent me a picture of Rose in her crib.

Another ping and he'd sent me a meme about crows.

He was . . . charmingly persistent, and I wondered why. Had he seen the glow? Had *I* even seen it? Because in the moment when we kissed the whole world could have been on fire. Besides, if he had witnessed something, he wasn't treating me like a freak. No, I was being wooed, which was so funny because I was just me. Except, I was also perhaps a little magical now, and I didn't know how to think of who I was anymore.

Maybe I *should* be wooed. Maybe I was *supposed* to glow.

As if in response, I felt it through my whole body, like a release of some valve, opening up something I'd kept in check for years. There was no visible glow—but something had changed.

I let myself breathe slowly for a few seconds. "OK, woo me," I said to my phone. Tomorrow afternoon at the Caravan Diner?

No one would see us there. Dots appeared on my screen.

Are you sure you don't want to go somewhere fancier?

I couldn't read his tone. Of course, I could always call him, but I didn't trust myself. This was why I didn't date; it was too hard to figure other people out. So I just wrote back, It's on my way, and let it go.

I didn't let myself call it a date.

We made nervous conversation—or rather, I babbled and he seemed fine. We shared some fries, but I didn't relax until he decided halfway through to slide into my side of the booth. Now that I didn't have to face his beauty and youth head on, when I was just feeling his warmth against me, listening to his quiet laugh, when I could just the barest catch glimpses of how he looked at me, it was easier to talk. When he draped his arm over my shoulders, it seemed natural to turn and kiss him, and kiss him again and again. I almost suggested we walk to the motel side of the diner, but something about the way he pulled back finally and looked at me, as if dazed, made me stay quiet.

It was wonderful to have that effect on someone. To stun them, to make them think you were special and wonderful and magical. It almost made me believe it could be true.

Later, at home, I texted, The waitress thought you were cute.

I thought she was going to offer me crayons and a coloring sheet.

A pause.

He texted, Did you think I was cute?

A little. But not in the same way.

Oh. What way was that?

It was harmless. This whole flirtation was just that—a flirtation.

Still, I didn't answer that last text.

* * *

"You look . . . good," my mother said.

"I—" I swallowed. "What?"

"You look rested," she said. "*Happy.*" She spat that word out like a curse.

As a matter of fact, I was exhausted, having rounded the bend of tiredness and stumbled into that overly bright-eyed, hectic, and horny state that often preceded a total collapse. But that wasn't exactly the kind of thing I could divulge to my mother and daughter while I was sitting through another Friday dinner, so I pretended I was absolutely fine and not a keyed-up wreck.

No, I'd been buoyant for other reasons: A glass of champagne or five after Lulu's graduation ceremony. All those pictures with my beautiful girl in her cap and gown, clutching an armful of awards. Her smile. Her relief that it was all over. Part of me felt sad that she was so eager to cast off her high school years and leave, but I reminded myself it wasn't about me, but about having some amount of freedom to explore who she was and what she wanted. And of course, there was Kenji.

I could have invited him to the graduation party, but that felt too official. Plus, I didn't want him to meet Lulu and my mother or even Parisa yet, and I sure didn't want him to run into Paul, Lulu's dad. But when I found myself getting depressed, I'd look at our texts and that kept me running high, sleepless, and permanently aroused for the rest of the week.

Too bad my mother couldn't be put off today.

When we'd arrived, she was in the middle of attempting to clear out her basement. You had to get dirty to get clean, I guess. It wasn't that Ma didn't spray and vacuum and sweep when she could—sure, given the chance, she would have come to my home to disinfect it, and scrub me down, too—but Shu-ling also accumulated things. She couldn't bring herself to throw out an old shirt with holes in the elbows because she said she could wear it while gardening. (She didn't garden.) She kept every gift that anyone gave her—jam from a patient, even though Shu-ling didn't eat sweets, a set of crocheted toilet roll covers, Christmas wreaths from neighbors who never saw them grace her door. The basement was a city of shelves and bins, and now some of those boxes had migrated to the hallway.

I could never tell if Ma cleaned when she was stressed, or if she stressed when she was cleaning. While she appeared unsurprised to see us, she was wearing one of those old shirts with the holes, and she did glance at the clock when we appeared at the door.

"We can make dinner," Lulu had said, sniffing the air.

It smelled like a forest of artificial pines.

"I can make it. I've already—" Her shoulders slumped for one second. "Or we can call for take-out."

I cheered, and Lulu shot me a warning look, even though she probably hadn't been looking forward to cobbling together a meal with the kabocha and greens that were doubtless the only things in my mother's kitchen.

So that's why we were seated at a table loaded with containers of Golden Garden egg drop soup, beef and broccoli, dumplings, fried noodles, egg rolls, and the plain steamed vegetables and tofu that my mother insisted on ordering. She also always vetoed sweet and sour chicken for some reason—growing up, I didn't know what it was when classmates asked me about it—and fried rice. The rice was too filling, she reasoned. I never understood that, because didn't you want a meal to be filling? No, Shu-ling Wu did not.

Now I was too tired to enjoy any of it.

Luckily, dinner was unusually quiet—probably because there was a lot less crunching of fibrous and probably very healthy vegetables than usual. Ma had gone for the good stuff—she probably worked up an appetite hauling all those boxes up. Later, maybe, she would ask us to help her. I hoped not, because now I was more curious about the photographs. I wanted to see if there were any more of my great-aunt, the midwife.

"Mom does almost have a glow about her these days," Lulu said.

I almost choked on my tofu at Lulu's words, but she continued, oblivious to my reaction.

"It's amazing she looks that good, because it's been hard to sleep lately. Even I'm tired all the time."

I only then noticed that she was paler than usual and that there were dark smudges under her eyes. What kind of mother was I to not see she hadn't been as energetic as usual?

Both Ma and I reached for her forehead, as if to check her temperature. She batted us away irritably. "My point is," she said, "this summer has been hard on all of us."

"And it's only June. The hot weather is just getting started."

"They say that truck driver yesterday, the one who crashed into the bank, fell asleep at the wheel. I read that the accident on campus was due to the construction company's negligence making people work overtime, and everyone was too tired," Lulu said through a mouthful of broccoli.

I hadn't heard about that truck accident. Again, the sense I was missing something stirred in me, and my fingers twitched. I hid them under the table. But Ma clicked her tongue. "Overtime, undertime. In Taiwan, people work until it's done. If they don't, there are plenty more people who will take their place."

This was rich coming from a woman who, as far as I knew, needed only about 4 hours of sleep.

"Fatigue and sleep are public health issues. I might like to study that—or occupational health," Lulu said, reaching for more rice.

I helped Lulu snag a carton as Ma opened her mouth as if to object. But I headed my mother off before she dictated to Lulu. "You've hardly ever been back to Taiwan," I said to Ma. "It's not like that anymore." Even though in some cases it probably still was. The same could be said about here, though, considering what had happened at the clock tower.

Lulu asked a question about Taiwan, a place that was preserved in my mother's memory like an insect in amber, or maybe Han Solo encased in carbonite in *The Empire Strikes Back.* Despite infrequent visits, Shu-ling liked for me to think of the country as she'd left it in the 1970s. Young girls from Taiwan were always obedient, she told me. Of course, later I realized she never made any mention of my father and what had happened to him, no mention of the gap in years after I'd been born and when she'd left me with my great-aunt, so I wonder if this story about obedience was just a fairy tale she liked to tell about herself. It was too bad my Mandarin and Taiwanese were so terrible.

Maybe that's what I'd do when after Lulu left. Learn the languages, then get myself on a plane to get the scoop from Ma's sister.

After dinner, we went to the box of photographs again. I was eager to find the one of my great-aunt, or another of her, and maybe the village. I would have been too young to recall everything, but I wondered if I could jog my memory somehow. Maybe I'd learn something about why I was . . . this way.

Because ever since that day I'd first kissed Kenji, I'd started to think of my glow as magic. Maybe I was being silly. After all, the glow hadn't reappeared since then. There was no hard evidence that I was special, except maybe to my kid and this new guy who wanted to sleep with me, and even then, I was pretty sure there was another word for it. But *magic*—it was seductive to think about it when I was tired and it was late at night and the person giving birth was dozing next to me before the next wave of pain washed over her.

"A-mà, what happened to the photos we were looking at?"

"I put them away."

As if the house disapproved, there was a faraway thump, the sound of something tipping over in the basement. We all jumped. I had to admit, I was spooked. I followed Lulu and my mom downstairs to investigate.

A few old boxes had indeed fallen. No wonder, with the way things were stacked so haphazardly. Lulu glanced at the disarray around her and pursed her lips. "We said we'd sort through all of them together."

She grabbed the boxes as she said this and gazed deep into my mother's eyes. I had to laugh. Lulu did not like the flouting of rules. She'd wielded this authority ever since she was a child putting her blocks away in Roy G Biv order. While my mother's gimlet eye worked on quaking first-years, it never had worked on her granddaughter.

Shu-ling huffed then stalked up the stairs. We followed more slowly. When we'd settled again, Lulu grabbed a small box from atop her rescued pile. "Why were these downstairs? Were you hiding them from us?"

"They don't matter to me," Ma said simply.

Lulu said nothing, but her eyes were like fire. Shu-ling sighed loudly and set the photos down with an ungracious thump. Maybe we Wus had gifts, maybe we didn't, but our ability to be sore losers was probably our single strongest legacy.

Having won her point, Lulu was opening the box carefully, using only the tips of her fingers. If I'd handed her gloves, I'm sure she would have donned them. "These are mostly of you, A-mà," Lulu breathed.

She handed me a picture. It was my mother as a teen, but instead of the city scenes I was used to, this was another view of my mother, her hair messy, wearing a loose, button-down shirt and holding a wide-brimmed hat.

With an odd jolt, I realized she looked a lot like me. And Lulu.

Lulu was taller than both of us—she took after her father, Paul, that way—but all three of us had eyes wide with curiosity, the same slightly cynical mouths, and of course, that pointed Wu chin.

"Where are you in this picture? Are you on vacation?"

"We didn't go on vacation. I was with my aunt."

"The witch?" Lulu asked excitedly.

"She's not a witch." Ma scoffed. "You young people all want to be witches now. You think it's all living in the woods and being more powerful than men."

"Honestly, that sounds great," I said.

Ma waved her hand and continued as if I hadn't spoken. "I was sent to stay with your great-aunt for a while when I was sixteen."

"What did you do to get sent to the boonies?" I interjected. As if I weren't from the boonies myself.

She kept ignoring me. "I was a very spoiled girl. I was the youngest, and pretty. I did not want to go."

Despite myself, I leaned in. It sounded suspiciously like someone may have been a little wild at that age. Shu-ling might have resisted telling me about it, but she was not going to be able to deter her granddaughter.

I wondered if there was any popcorn in her pantry.

"My aunt took me everywhere. When she had to go to the market, I went to the market. When she had to pick vegetables from the garden, she made me crouch down beside her and put my hands in the leaves and pick them, too."

Ma's nose wrinkled, and I had to smother a laugh. She still didn't like gardening. The backyard of this house consisted of rocks and bushes. She hired a kid to trim everything—shrubs, trees, the small patch of lawn in front—once a month.

"She also took me on rounds. Visits. She had gone to Taipei for training, but being a midwife in the countryside she could do things her way. She taught me to ride a motor scooter and borrowed one for me so I could ride with her. The rural areas there aren't like the ones here, so plain and full of fields and trees and nothing else. There, there are fields with workers, and little houses, shacks, in bright colors, patched with tin, and green. All the trains run on time."

"And the roads are paved with gold," I muttered.

Lulu elbowed me. She wanted to hear more. Because I was a generous and loving mother, I tried to remember to keep my mouth shut.

"We rode far out one day to check on a woman and found her already in labor. She didn't have a telephone. She was young and her husband and all the workers were out in the fields somewhere, so she was completely alone when my aunt came in. Maybe your Yi-beh knew; she had a sense about her when these things would happen."

I rubbed my chest and looked down at my hands. Was that a faint glow from them? No, it was nothing. I was imagining things.

Besides, what my great-aunt had done wasn't necessarily some great magic power—that was experience. I'd gotten that feeling at the back of my neck myself, waking up a minute before my phone alarm went off. I'd turned down roads to check on clients even though it was not on my schedule, because I'd read the signs at our last visit.

Then why did it feel like magic?

I didn't know why in my forties I was suddenly hoping to learn that something special bubbled through my veins. I stared at my fingers again. Just a few weeks ago, I'd dreaded what would happen if my glow returned. But right now, it felt as though I needed it back in order to prove something.

But my mother was still talking. "The patient was in the kitchen when we found her. Her clothes were soaked, and there was water all around her. She'd dropped a pot she was trying to fill. She'd been trying to cook while going through her contractions. Back then, I thought she was a mature woman. I was sixteen, but she was having a baby. But now that I think about it, she was only a couple of years older than me. Maybe your age, Lulu."

Ma shook her head and pressed her hands to her eyes. For the first time, I realized that it may have been difficult for her to think about that time in her life. What had happened to make her this way? I would never truly understand.

It seemed impossibly lonely.

"My aunt took the patient into her room, and I was left to mop up. For the first time in what felt like weeks, I was left alone. I could have walked out of the house, gone down the road, taken a train, and gone back home to Taichung. But instead of taking advantage, I felt useless. I didn't know how to cook a meal or light the kind of stove they had in this kitchen to boil water. My aunt, even though she kept me around, she was impatient with me and usually just did things herself when she needed to be faster—"

That last part sounded familiar.

"I'd watched my aunt do it so many times, though. So I looked through every bucket and every bin in the kitchen to find kindling and ingredients. I managed to boil water and make a thin rice porridge."

I'd never heard this story before.

"I heard some cries, but my aunt was always able to keep the patients calm. I don't know how she did that. Then my aunt called me. She told me to wash my hands, thoroughly. Really, really thoroughly. So I did. And she handed me the baby. She told me to clean up the baby, gently.

"It felt like the heaviest thing, because I was afraid to hold on too tight as it squirmed and cried. It already had all this life. It had muscle. And I was afraid to scrub the baby with something too rough and make its red skin redder. But I cleaned it, and while I did that, my aunt took care of the mother. There was a lot of blood. On me, on my aunt, on everything.

"We gave the mother food before we left. Her husband and some workers had finally come home, and there were people to at least watch her and the baby. When we got back to my aunt's house, so tired, she told me I'd done well. That was the first birth I attended."

"A-mà, you were just a kid!"

"We had to grow up fast in those days. It was very different from how it is now. Even different from how you perform in someone's home, Leeann. You could have a spoiled teenage girl assisting you." She tried to smile at me.

I recognized that my mother was almost telling a joke.

"A-mà, did you decide you wanted to deliver babies then? Because you witnessed the magic of birth?"

My mother snorted. "No. I did not want to be a doctor after that. So messy."

One thing I actually enjoyed about Ma was that she never tried to appeal to our nobler instincts, probably because she didn't really believe people had them.

"You didn't even want to bring new, young lives into the world?" my daughter persisted.

Ma waved her hand. "Later I decided I wanted to be a doctor because I was smart. And I wanted to be free to travel and have my own money. I took what I learned from my aunt that summer, and I used it. I learned to live with the blood and the death and the birth and not be frightened so that I could finally leave."

Now this was more along the lines of the stories she told about herself: A young woman fighting for her freedom, coming to Canada with nothing except her brains and courage. The fact that I'd already been born, that she'd left me behind, complicated that narrative. Maybe I was one of the things she wanted to be free from.

"Did you ever witness anything magical?" Lulu asked.

"Isn't birth magical in itself?" I asked. "Basic equipment and facilities, few drugs, no help except a teenage girl. Isn't the fact that our great-aunt was a total badass enough?"

Lulu nodded, then shook her head. "Sure, but don't you want to hear about our *powers*?"

Did I? I glowed, sure. But it didn't help anyone. Did I really want to hear that we were supposed to read minds and throw thunderbolts? Did I want to let down the Wus by confessing I wasn't more than an unreliable lamp?

But before I could say anything, Ma growled. "There are no powers. We're not so special. Your mother is right. Safe childbirth is the miracle."

"She said I was right! Maybe I do have magic."

Lulu threw a cushion at me. "Is it that, A-mà, or that you don't know?"

"Of course, I would tell you if I knew," Ma said in an aggrieved tone.

But my anger blazed sudden and strong. "No, actually, you wouldn't," I said. "Since when have you ever told me everything you know? Hell, it's been forty-one years, and I still don't know anything about my father."

There was a shocked silence.

Ma finally said, "Sometimes I don't tell you things to protect you."

"Well, none of us is safe if we don't know what to expect. If we suddenly start shooting electricity from our eyes, if we vomit fire, if we can change water into acid."

I threw my hands up to find Ma and Lulu watching me uneasily. "What?"

"Are you okay, Mom?"

I closed my eyes. "No," I finally said. "Sometimes, I think I'm really not."

• 5 •

"THIS IS WHAT A hot date with me is like," I told Kenji as he led me out of the ophthalmologist's office and to the car.

I'd gotten my eyes checked and my pupils had been dilated. There were probably any number of people I could have called to pick me up. But Lulu and Parisa were working. And for some odd reason, I didn't want to tell either of them why I thought I needed my vision examined. That left Kenji. But now that he was here, I felt silly for even asking him.

As usual, I tried to crack jokes, because although we texted and we'd gone out—and made out again—I hadn't invited him to the graduation party, or to my house, or to meet anyone else important in my life.

Kenji laughed at my comment, but I felt him pause for a moment. Whether that was to open the car door, or because we'd run into a moose, or maybe it was because I'd called attention to my age again, I couldn't say. Evidently messing up my vision when the eye doctor had dilated my pupils had not heightened my other senses.

So much for powers.

But after a second Kenji had safely stowed me in the passenger seat of my car and I felt some remorse for constantly trying to put some a barrier between us, emotionally at least.

"Thanks again for doing this," I said. "Sorry about the mess in the back."

And for everything else.

"You've already said that," Kenji said gently. "My bike fit fine. Besides, I did offer."

"It's just that Lulu was working and Parisa was called to an emergency."

I stopped myself from talking more.

But I thought I heard Kenji laugh softly. "You really have no idea," he said.

Or something like that. I was determined not to make things any more uncomfortable than I already had.

A few days ago, I'd met up with him for only a few minutes in a little pavilion in a park near campus. When I saw him leaning on the gazebo, those firm shoulders relaxed, his eyes hooded, I felt that that pang of longing ripple through me. I don't know why I ached constantly for someone who was already here and—who would have me if I asked.

Of course, sitting in the car with him now, listening to him change gears and hum quietly, I couldn't help remembering how we let our breaths mingle, our mouths and tongues first hesitant then firm. I'd tried to flatten my body against him, wanting to be absorbed into him, yet afraid to let myself go.

I swallowed and shifted in the seat, trying to angle myself into the cooler air.

"You doing all right over there?" Kenji asked.

"I'm fine."

My voice was a little strangled.

I felt too much every time I was with him. I was scared and hungry and hot, too hot, and tired and alert and above all, I wanted—and every feeling made my skin ripple with energy, and if I let myself have it, I knew I'd begin to glow.

"Leeann, what are you thinking of?" Kenji asked.

I was probably blushing. "Bodies," I said. "You'd think after years of seeing people's bodies, of all shapes and sizes, that I would be used to how weird my own is."

"I like your body," he said simply.

I felt his hand take mine, felt him gently stretch and open my fingers so that he could lace his with mine.

He'd pulled in somewhere gravelly, probably my driveway, and we sat there holding hands.

I wondered if he'd kiss me, if I'd try to convince him to come inside with me.

"Are you tired from your checkup?"

I shook my head and grimaced under my sunglasses. "Everything is fine. No glaucoma."

"Glaucoma?" A laugh. A squeeze of my palm. "Aren't you a little young for that?"

"I was old enough to ask about reading glasses."

"And?"

"I don't need them. Yet."

He was quiet again. I felt safe and lulled. Until he said, "The age thing bothers you. That's why you hold back."

"That's not the only—it's a strange time for me. People have told me I should get some hobbies after Lulu's moved out. Redecorate. Learn to fix a car. Take up life drawing."

If the subjects looked like Kenji, I'd be willing to try that.

"It doesn't matter to me—the fact that you're older," he said, focusing on the more annoying thing I'd admitted.

I sighed. It was easy enough for him to say it didn't matter to him, because right now it didn't.

Maybe I shouldn't weigh this down—whatever this was—with thoughts about a future. It was summer. I could enjoy myself. I was not going to get emotionally involved. Even if Kenji was the kind of person to stick around, he had to want children someday.

It wasn't as if this could ever last.

And besides, I had secrets.

"You're right," I said. "I'm only in my very early forties. A baby forty. I have my whole life in front of me. Years of watercolor landscapes and restoring vintage autos ahead of me."

He played with my fingers. "What do you want to do with your life?"

"I'm already doing it." It was true. I was comfortable and sure of myself in this town, and I didn't want to leave that. And yet . . . "You went New Zealand for two years and hiked and washed dishes," I mused, recalling some of the things he'd told me about.

"They say there are more sheep in New Zealand than people. I did see a lot of them. But what I loved is that there were hiking trails all over the place, winding through hills and meadows and through cities and towns. I remember in one place, the shower water made everyone itchy, so the hostel closed down. A group of my friends ended up sleeping in a park and being woken by birds picking through our backpacks looking for food." He laughed.

"I wonder if Lulu will end up doing that. Having those kinds of experiences."

"How about you? Do you want to go to New Zealand and sleep in a park?"

"Well, I don't want Lulu to sleep in a park. Ever. Or at least if she does, I don't want her to tell me about it."

"But how about *you*?"

"Wouldn't want to piss off the sheep majority by adding to the human population," I said lightly, withdrawing my hand.

Kenji told me to stay put while he got his bike out of the trunk and came to the other side to escort me to the door.

I leaned my head back. I'd been pregnant midway through university. I wasn't worldly. I hadn't traveled much—and I didn't regret it. I loved Lulu, I'd loved being a mother to her. Being able to help her shape her life, to let her figure out things on her own, to see her grow had given me joy. Maybe because so much of what my own mother had done for me had been because she wanted to keep me from harm. That was love, too, but I thought it a grim, smothering kind of shell.

Then again, my love for Lulu was a shield, too. But whether it protected her or me more, it was hard to say.

The car door swung open. "Are you going to be okay in there?" he asked when I refused his offer to walk me inside. "You probably can't see very clearly yet."

"I know this place like the back of my hand."

Meaning I already knew it was a mess. There were clothes piled on the hallway floor next to unopened packages I'd hadn't kicked out of the way. If I let him inside with me, at least I wouldn't be able to see his reaction to the squalor we lived in.

But that wasn't the real reason. I wasn't ready to let him see all of this. I wasn't supposed to ever be ready with someone like him.

"And one of my clients might be going into labor." Unlikely, but it was my standard excuse. "I should try to take a nap. The eyedrops ought to wear off by then."

"I can keep you company, help you get settled. Make sure you're all right." He caressed my back, a delicate motion from fingers I knew could be strong.

"I have to try to get actual sleep. And not the kind where I have nightmares, either."

His eyebrows raised. "Nightmares? What are they about?"

"Oh, a huge mouth eating the sky. Nowhere to run. Lightning but no thunder. Ghosts that feed on your spirit. That sort of thing."

"Right, so the usual apocalyptic nightmare landscape?"

"Pretty much."

His voice was still light, his hand still gentle, not pushing me toward something I already wanted even though I shouldn't. "Well, let me know if you want someone to soothe you."

He took the key from my hand, opened the door, and pulled me lightly to him. A kiss, the smallest sip, and he slid my sunglasses gently up my nose and let me step inside without him.

I shut the door and slid to the floor in a puddle of need. These were just those pesky perimenopausal hormones my ob/gyn had been telling me about, a veritable stew of them cooking up feelings that were almost like a second adolescence.

Well, I couldn't masturbate here in the front hall. What if I kicked the hat stand and it fell over and brained me, and Lulu found me unconscious with my hand down my pants? Hardly the memory I wanted to send her to university with.

I pulled off my shoes, discarding them where I'd probably trip over them later, got up, and felt my way up the stairs to my bedroom. I shucked off my clothing and drew the covers over my head.

I didn't quite fall asleep, but neither was I entirely awake. I drifted along a stifling, sticky landscape of familiar figures lurking in gardens, flashes of lightning coming from my fingers. And there were the dead, who wanted something from me, begging me in in a language that I both knew and didn't quite understand. Every time I tried to grasp it, it eluded me, and I was exhausted from chasing it. But I couldn't stop. I tossed and turned until the phone rang.

Flinging the covers off, I rubbed my eyes while answering.

"Ms. Wu," the voice said. "There's been an accident."

* * *

They said Lulu wasn't critically injured, but until I saw her for myself, I wouldn't be okay. First step was to get to the hospital, then I had to call her father and my mother.

Why was she driving at night? Why was she alone?

Where were you?

Asleep. Unable to see. But at least by now the eye drops had worn off.

Traffic delays meant it took me forever to get to the Reineville General. I later learned it was because Lulu's accident had rerouted everyone through town. At nine-thirty that night, a truck veered off the highway, causing a five-car pileup. Lulu's little Civic had been hit by a vehicle that failed to slow down in all of the snarled traffic. I'd missed her message this afternoon saying she'd be out on a babysitting job. I should have been spending the time I had left with my daughter, not with a man I had no business being with.

Ma, of course, spelled it all out for me by the time I finally got to the hospital. "You should have been here ten minutes ago," she whisper-shouted at me before starting to walk away to lead me to the room where Lulu was being kept.

"Not all of us live at their workplace like you apparently do. Besides, traffic was heavy."

"Traffic is never heavy in Reineville. And your t-shirt is on inside out," she said without even turning.

Lulu was in a hospital bed, her face red with abrasions. But she was on her phone, texting and frowning.

We fell on her.

"I'm fine. It's just airbag injuries. Does it look bad?" she added anxiously. Without waiting for an answer, she added, "The car isn't doing so well, though. Dad's freaking out."

As we all watched, line after line of texts from my ex appeared on the screen. Questions: Are you sure you're all right? Do you feel drowsy? Has your mother finally arrived? And orders: Stop reading this screen if you feel dizzy.

That was Paul for you. He hadn't been around much, but when he was, he acted like I was the neglectful one.

"*Do* you feel woozy, though?" I asked. I should have asked first, dammit.

Lulu groaned. "Don't you start too, Mom."

The ER doc emerged, and I was relieved it was a somewhat familiar face. I'd delivered Dr. Rivkin's daughter's first child last year. "Dr. Rivkin. How is she?"

"She's fine, if irritable," Lulu snapped.

"I agree with that," Dr. Rivkin said smoothly. "No concussion, no broken bones. Ice and rest."

"What about my face?" Lulu said.

"You were lucky. Just a few scratches."

Lulu picked up her phone and turned on the camera to look at herself. "I look like a Frankenstein tomato."

I choked back a laugh and everyone—well, everyone except Dr. Rivkin—turned to glare at me.

"Your daughter was just in a car accident," Ma said. "Why was she driving?"

"She has to get to places because she's an adult. A responsible one at that."

I said it because it was true. But I didn't feel it. She was a kid. She was my tiny toddler baby child who was taller than me. She shouldn't be behind a wheel; I should have kept her in a stroller and never let her out.

"Yeah, A-mà. Come on. I drive all the time."

"What were you doing on the highway?"

"I was coming home from the Ledesmas. They live in that new subdivision outside of town limits. What am I going to do about work tomorrow? I need a car."

"I can take you," I said quickly.

"What if you need to attend a birth? That won't work."

"Ladies. *Wus.*" Dr. Rivkin clapped her hands. "We're going to discharge you, Lulu. But I'd advise that you don't go to work tomorrow. It's late, and you're still shaken up."

She held up a hand before Lulu could say anything. "Yes, that's my official diagnosis. By the day after tomorrow, I'm sure you'll have your transportation problems all figured out."

"Thank you, doctor," my mother said with dignity, as if she too hadn't been screeching just a few minutes before.

My phone rang as soon as we got in the car. It was Paul, of course. "Is she really okay?" he asked.

I fastened my seat belt and checked to see if everyone else had, too. No use risking further injury.

Paul added, "She shouldn't be driving out there. Maybe she should come out to Toronto sooner."

Oh, like she'll be safer in a city, I almost retorted.

I heard him sigh and felt an arrow of sympathy for him. He hadn't wanted a child, and we hadn't been as in love with each other as I'd thought, but he'd accepted my decision and tried to be as involved as he could be given how busy he was being ambitious and wanting to be important. I should have seen the signs of it. He was never satisfied; when I was young, I'd been impressed by his lack of contentment. Maybe I'd been drawn to him because I sensed I was missing that drive myself.

But Lulu was hard for him to resist, and he'd developed a kind of relationship with her that worked for them. He also provided money, and I'd accepted it for Lulu's sake. Now he and his wife, also a cardiologist, had a little boy, a chatty six-year-old named Mason, and Paul's ambition had turned, as it often did when one got older, into anxiety. Or maybe that's what it had always been in the first place.

"The thing she needs most is rest," I said. "I'm just about to drive us home."

"All right then. I won't keep you. At least you'll all sleep better in the country air," he said gruffly, then clicked off.

I wanted to laugh. He'd lived here for four years doing premed; this wasn't exactly the country. And no one was sleeping well. I already knew I wasn't going to be able to rest tonight.

I texted Parisa to tell her what happened. Unexpectedly, I thought of Kenji. But no, somehow I didn't know if I should share that part of me. He would care, he would be good to talk to. But even as I yearned for that, even as I knew how comforting he could be, I didn't want to depend on him for comfort.

We got Lulu home without incident. My mother, following in her car, insisted on spending the night. She was a doctor, she reminded us, as if we, her family, had no idea of her career path. I gave her my bedroom and made up the couch for myself. Of course I couldn't fall sleep. No one did. By three, mom had crept down to the kitchen and was opening and closing cabinet doors, and I was trying desperately to ignore the fact that she was probably studying the contents and judging me.

When I finally padded into the kitchen, she looked over her shoulder at me. "Why do you have so many teas?"

"People give them to me. They think, *Midwife, ooh, must like folk music and dancing barefoot. Let's get her an herbal tea selection for the solstice.*"

She grabbed a box and frowned at it suspiciously. "Where is your kettle?"

"I don't have one. If I want a cup of tea I can heat water in the microwave."

No electric kettle, no carafe of boiled water. I even occasionally clomped around the house wearing my shoes. I was a disappointment in so many ways.

Ma thinned her lips, filled a pot with water, and got down two cups.

We sat at the kitchen table in silence as we waited for the water to boil.

"Dr. Rivkin tells me they've been seeing a lot more accidents lately," my mother said. "Car crashes, people hurting themselves mowing the lawn, or scalding themselves. Now this big mess on the highway."

"Sounds like there is traffic in Reineville after all."

Ma ignored my crack about her earlier remark.

Still, it was strange. People were tired, making mistakes. More of my clients were struggling with fatigue. Hell, I was having a hard time. Moreover, I couldn't shake the feeling that there was something that connected all of these things. But like my dreams earlier, I couldn't make the links. *Why would I?*

Of course, when I look back, I feel like I should have noticed all the little accidents adding up. Old Mr. Nguyen running through a traffic light and ending up in a ditch. He wasn't hurt and he didn't do any damage, but his wife told me he was mortified and handed her his keys after the incident. He never did drive again after that, and we all got used to seeing his dignified figure, always with a hat and neatly pressed pants, at bus stops all around town. I thought of the kids working at their jobs, chugging energy drinks, all of my clients with circles under their eyes. It could be hard to sleep when you were pregnant, and it was hot, and the air conditioner made funny noises all night. I hadn't paid enough attention. Of course, the fact that I myself was barely sleeping didn't figure into it, because I was a midwife and my sleep was always disturbed anyway.

"It's this heat," Ma said, half to herself, showing she'd been mulling over the same problems that preoccupied me.

Oddly enough, I took a measure of comfort in that. It had been a long time since we'd done this. Sat in a kitchen together, simply talking. Probably not since I was in high school. But my mother had not been much for sleep even then. Useful in an obstetrician.

The kitchen was cool, though. The central air that came with this little block of a house was sometimes overpoweringly strong.

"What kind of tea are you having?" I asked.

She frowned at the package. "Lemon Tea-lite."

"I'll have some too. Can we add cinnamon?"

She nodded and cast the teabag into the pot. I added a cinnamon stick. We both stared at the darkening liquid. It was comforting to watch the tendrils of it come up and swirl around, so much so that we didn't notice when Lulu came up behind us.

"What are we doing?" she asked.

I whipped around to face her. "What are you doing? You're supposed to be asleep."

"I can't."

"Do you have a headache? Fever?" Ma held her hand to Lulu's forehead.

Lulu ignored my mother. "Is that tea? Is there enough for me?"

"Yes, definitely."

She turned and got out the honey bear. "Would anyone else like any?"

"Just add it to the pot," my mother said.

We all watched Lulu squeeze some honey in. I got a wooden spoon and stirred it. We all stared for another moment, blinking.

My mother got another mug from the cabinet. And I poured tea carefully into the mugs, managing not to splash anyone. Maybe we'd be able to rest well after this, I thought, as the last drop went into my cup. We'd made exactly the right amount.

I put the cinnamon stick and the teabag into the compost and washed my hands. We all sat at the little round kitchen table. And because it felt right, I took Lulu's hand. She took my mother's, and, after some hesitation, my mother held mine.

We were together. We were all right.

We were strong.

For a moment we glanced around at each other, surprised at what was in front of our eyes, because I wasn't the only one glowing.

We all were.

If I hadn't been startled and frightened—and yes, oddly guilty—it would have been beautiful to see our faces illuminated this way, by the power of something within us. Together.

But when Lulu let go of our hands to stare at her own, the glow that had enveloped all three of us vanished.

I let out a small breath that was almost a sob.

"What was that?" Lulu asked shakily.

Ma blinked. "I must be tired."

But I'd seen it, too. The glow had illuminated our joined hands. More important, I'd felt it—and they had, too.

It wasn't just me. *I wasn't alone.*

But Lulu, who'd been so eager to learn about my great-aunt's magic, wasn't having it. "Maybe it's a concussion. Maybe I do have one. Should one of you check me?"

I almost got up then to order her to bed. I was a bad parent. Of course it was a concussion aura. But as I started to get up, Ma stopped me. She and Ma had strange expressions on her face. Almost like . . . fear.

"Then why did we all see it?" Ma asked.

I cleared my throat. "I think it's the thing. The Wu thing. Is this it, Ma? Could this be it?"

Ma sighed. "I don't know."

"What do you mean?"

"I mean, I don't know! I never had any magic. I'm too old for this."

Tell me about it.

"Maybe we should try to do it again," I said.

"*No.*" This was Lulu. Firm. "We're tired. We're all tired and we're seeing things."

"But Lulu, weren't you excited before?"

"I don't like it," she cried.

My girl was scared. I moved to hold her, but she shook me off.

I dropped my hands and twisted them in my lap.

"They never told me exactly what it was," Ma said half to herself. "So, I told myself it was placebo effect. A healing touch when someone had a headache. Also, there were a lot of older women your great-aunt helped, and sometimes they just wanted attention."

"You're getting to be an older person. Is this a hint?" I couldn't help myself asking if only to break up the tension. My insides felt jumpy, and I flexed my fingers. Lulu had been afraid of the glow, but I wanted to try again.

"I have never liked that," Ma said. "And any time I am in the spotlight, it is because I deserve it because I worked hard, not because I look for it."

I wanted to snort, but I had to admit, it was true. Instead, I asked, "Are there any stories of miracles she pulled off? Reattaching limbs or reviving people from the dead?"

Making her hands glow?

My mother frowned. "She didn't always succeed. Working with the body can be a frustrating job. And in the end . . . there was an illness in one of the villages she worked in, she said. It was hot that summer, too—and hot in Taiwan is something extra strong. You sweat just from sitting and existing. Your clothes never feel clean—*you* never do. This was before air conditioning was commonplace. It was already hard to work, hard to think."

"Like it is here now," I said.

My mother nodded. "It feels like Taiwan this year."

She put her arms around herself and looked around her, suddenly seeming small. Unlike herself.

"What was the wrong with the people in the village?" I asked my mother.

That snapped her out of it. "I remember my aunt's first letter. I was already in Canada by then. She said the illness came in slowly, so slowly that people hardly noticed it.

Everyone was infected. I didn't have a chance to reply, and by the time she telephoned me, well, it was too late."

"What do you mean, too late?" Lulu asked. "What about Mom? Was she there, too?"

Ma gazed down into her tea. The story seemed to drag out of her, like we were dredging a lake for bodies. "My aunt tried to notify the local health authorities, but it was a different time in Taiwan, and by then she was older and they thought she was . . . not dependable. She was taking care of you, Leeann, but she'd gotten—" Ma frowned. "What's the word people use to describe old relatives? Eccentric. Started collecting all sorts of newspapers and piling them up. She used to feed birds and let them in her house, that sort of thing. Her hair never settled into a pretty snowy white. It was always so wild and coarse. So people thought she was stranger than she was."

Ma touched her own perfect hair. "The health authorities didn't have time for her. I didn't. She called me to make sure I took you back, Leeann. She tried to tell me that danger was coming, but I didn't understand her. I thought she was just a worried old woman."

Lulu looked aghast.

My mother added, "She said the patterns of the illness were too hard to see."

Lulu had started to relax again, her body uncurling. Her questions came rapid-fire now. "Was it an epidemic? What exactly was the illness? What was happening to people?"

"That was the problem. She said the symptoms were so scattered but she didn't describe them. I have to admit, I was beginning to believe she was not as sharp as she used to be.

I thought . . . well, all she knew was that there was something wrong and she thought I'd be able to help. It took me almost a week to get leave, but I flew back to Taiwan as soon as I could because I was worried about her and the baby."

About me.

She paused here. "I didn't always like my aunt. It seems wrong to say that, because she was my elder and I owed her so much. So after taking a plane to Taipei and then one train and then another, I thought I'd go and stay overnight, make sure everything was all right, and then come back to Canada."

"But when I got to Taichung, my sister had you. My aunt had returned to the village only for a typhoon to hit. We never found her body. But you, you wanted to go back to her there. You were three years old and you didn't know me, Leeann. Well, how could I expect different?" Her voice was harsh. "You were a baby when I left and I'd been away too long. My sister didn't want you, so I carried you screaming all the way back to Reineville. When we arrived, you didn't speak for a long time. Not a word for two years. But at least you were safe. You weren't sick. You hadn't disappeared with your great aunt."

Ma was quiet. The clock ticked. "Another storm hit that part of the country hard the next week. Luckily, we were already back here, and I was too busy trying to find someone to watch you and working in the hospitals. But my sister told me later that almost the whole village had been washed out. She was glad you and I had left right away, but whether it was because she was relieved or she thought we were bad luck, I don't know. I hadn't even stayed for the funeral."

Ma's voice stayed even, but I detected a small tremble at her mouth.

"A-mà. I'm sorry," Lulu said quietly.

"That was Taiwan," my mother said, as she often did. When I was younger, she told me it was an isolated island with a history made up only of tragedy and disaster, of strict teachers and even stricter relatives. But that's what we tell stories about, isn't it? We leave out the parts that are just life. Now I think that her stories were more her way of making a space between what was in her past and her present. But maybe she didn't know that.

She stood up. We all did. "You should be in bed," she told Lulu.

We put our cups in the sink, and Lulu went back upstairs, accompanied by my mother.

I settled back on the couch, and oddly enough, for the first time in a long time, I managed to sleep—not only drift off, but fall deep into slumber.

I should have felt great the next day. Rested. Ready to take on the world.

Except.

The next morning, as I washed the mugs from our late night, I looked down at my fingers under the running water, and I remembered.

When we all sat down around the table to drink our tea, we all saw it. We'd talked about it openly: Our hands had been glowing. All our hands.

It appeared that the Wu magic was real.

♦ 6 ♦

I SAT IN THE STUFFY car in the clinic parking lot and started to text Kenji. But I stopped myself before saying anything about Lulu's accident. It was too early to message him. Too early in the morning, too early in whatever this thing between us was. Besides, he'd probably been up at all hours feeding the baby. He'd told me he liked to walk around the house with Rose over his shoulder or cradled in his arms, singing songs he didn't know the lyrics to, patting her back, looking out the windows—and damn, the image made me smile. I was a sucker.

We weren't supposed to be close. I should treat him as a civic-minded young man who had merely driven me home from the eye doctor once and who made out with me a couple of times. A real public servant, that Kenji.

A corner of my mind reminded me that I had thought of him rather earlier in the morning than I thought of any of my other friends, none of whom I'd ever wanted to get naked with, except Parisa that time we drove out to Frontenac to try out a spa and dry sauna. Even then, there had been towels.

As I was holding my phone, a message from Kenji popped up.

That did it. Without reading the text, I shoved the temptingly easy, intimacy-enabling communication device in my bag and got on with the day. My mother had cleared part of her schedule to stay with Lulu so I wouldn't have to worry about my daughter trying to go to her internship, reorganize the closets, or save the world while she was supposed to be resting. By afternoon, I still hadn't read Kenji's message (although I thought about taking a quick peek at it, which probably defeated any claims that I was ignoring it). Instead, I checked in with a grumpy Lulu and got out on the road again for home visits.

Luckily, it was easy for me to avoid the stretch of highway that Lulu had her accident on. The clinic's territory covered our three bigger towns and a few of the smaller ones, and usually I enjoyed driving along the endless roads under the wide skies. But I kept remembering this same sky split by the terrifying weather of my dreams. I thought of the typhoon that had wrecked my great-aunt's village so long ago and wondered if I'd ever had to face that kind of phenomenon when I'd lived there.

I'd been under her watch when she disappeared. But I didn't remember.

Ma said I hadn't known her when she came to take me away. I'd been waiting for my great-aunt to come back. I was born in Taiwan, but I had no memories of it. Still, sometimes I had flashes of experiences I couldn't explain. Riding strapped to someone's back as we zipped through narrow streets on a scooter. A feeling of being too hot. The taste of sticky rice with garlic. My mother would never have made that dish—cooked short grain rice in all that sesame oil. But when I tasted something like it later at yum cha once in Toronto, my mouth remembered it.

I suddenly longed for more of those flashes.

It was hard to tell what was a dream and what was real, what were stories I'd heard often enough that they seemed like my own memories. Trying to puzzle it all out removed it from the texture of real life.

I shook my head and turned off onto the road to meet with my next client, Paige St. Clair. Twenty-seven years old and a first-time mother. The baby, Tyler, was four weeks old. If all went well, I wouldn't be seeing them much longer, not that I minded. Paige's husband wasn't my favorite. Luckily, he was also generally never there.

Tyler was cranky, but healthy.

"He hasn't slept well lately." Paige looked listless, her hair matted.

"Which means you haven't been getting any rest, either."

She nodded.

"Are you able to sleep at all? Have you had any time to go outside?"

"It's hard. He's feeding a lot, and it's so hot. I don't want to leave the house."

"How about your meals?"

Paige looked away. "It's all my fault. I can't get it together. My husband, he doesn't really cook, and he's busy. I should be able to . . ." Her voice trailed off.

I shook my head. "You can't blame yourself for not managing to do everything. Life is difficult with a baby, and when you're not getting enough sleep on top of that, it can feel impossible."

"I worry," she said.

I glanced around. Paige lived in a wide, ranch-style home with an open concept. It was mostly neat except for the family area where we were sitting, with its easy chair and boxes of diapers next to a changing table. I got the feeling that Paige didn't move from that spot much.

"Do you have any help? Maybe a sibling or a parent who can come by and check on you sometimes?"

"It's worst at night," Paige said seeming to disregard my words. "I'll be sitting here feeding him, and I close my eyes, but every time, it's after me."

I tried to keep my voice neutral, but I didn't feel detached at all. "What's after you, Paige?"

"The thing. It's so bright. With teeth. I want to run but then it catches me and I can't move anymore. My limbs stop working. I wake up with a start and my heart is still pounding, and I hold the baby tight."

I shivered. I couldn't help thinking of my own nightmares. But weren't all bad dreams kind of like that? Well, except for the high-school-exams-while-naked ones.

I looked down at my tablet. Paige's screening indicated she was a likely candidate for postpartum depression. I was going to have to talk to her primary. She'd need more follow-up.

I swiped on my tablet, and that's when I noticed the faint glow from my hand.

This time, instead of panicking, I took a deep breath and thought hard. I looked up. Paige's eyes were closed. She hadn't noticed—though even if she had, I doubted she would even register it. She was that tired.

I looked at my hand again. *The Wus have magic.*

"I'm going to examine Tyler," I said.

She didn't react when I took the baby. Didn't notice when I put him gently in a nearby crib and drew nearer to Paige instead.

I didn't know what I was doing. The idea that I could end up hurting her with my unproven powers made my heart squeeze. Except . . . how could I describe it? A kind of certainty rang in me, as true and pure as a glass being tapped that my touch would not do harm.

What should I do? Should I mutter a spell or do some sort of chanting? I couldn't believe I was even thinking this.

Maybe I should make up a couplet, I thought, casting desperately around in my mind for a rhyme for *healing.*

Appealing? Stealing?

I heard my mother chime in my head, *Limericks are for white people.*

Right. The sound of Dr. Shu-ling Wu was enough to chase the poetry out of minds stronger than mine.

Instead, I took some deep breaths. It was time to make a quiet space in my mind. I focused on the conviction, the pure resonance I felt in myself. And in the end, all I did was put my hand over Paige's as she lay back and tried to rest. A moment of connection. I felt something like sympathy, something like a vibration, a song. My hand flared briefly then settled into a barely there glow.

It felt good and right to hold her hand. I felt myself growing warmer, as if I were truly doing something other than being there.

But what did Paige do? She conked out completely.

Wait, this *was* sleep, wasn't it?

To confirm, a small snore escaped her.

I blinked for a minute then let her go. That was . . . far less spectacular than I anticipated. To be fair, it hadn't been the first time a client had ever dozed off on me. It was possible Paige drifting off had nothing to do with me and my so-called Wu magic at all. I examined my hands. No more glow. The skin looked the same as always. Maybe a little dry despite the oppressive humidity. I wiggled my fingers and glared at them. Now that I actually wanted something to happen, nothing did. Had I been expecting sparks? A demon chained in fire appearing to do my bidding? A shock running through my own system that caused my hair to stand on end?

None of those sounded appealing or conducive to healing.

Damn, that should've been my rhyme.

Paige snored again.

Well, at least she was getting the rest she needed now. I nudged her gently into a safer sideways position on the couch and covered her with the small quilt that someone had probably made for the baby. (Despite the fact that babies shouldn't be sleeping with loose blankets or pillows. But I'd told Paige this already, and I wasn't about to wake her up to repeat my warning.) I would still have to chat with her primary about her suspected postpartum depression—a few minutes of shut-eye wasn't a long-term solution.

The baby snuffled, and I recalled myself and went to give him the promised checkup. As he wiggled and stared at me in that confused and slightly outraged way that newborns had, I concentrated on trying to be the calm, collected clinician I usually was. I was not the type who went for all that supernatural stuff. Not someone who believed in the laying of hands, strange bodily glowing, and instant cures. Despite the reputation that midwives had for herbs and folk songs, we were trained, modern professionals, and I wasn't about to cast aside the things that worked for a few moments of hand glowing.

"Have you ever heard anything about this?" I asked baby Tyler silently. Despite the glaring, or maybe because of it, he was a good listener. Very healthy. I tested his limbs and admired his grip, but he didn't answer.

I had many good years ahead of me, people kept telling me. I could take up parasailing or sit in a restored clawfoot tub in my backyard along with the life drawing. I could probably even schtup a thirty-year-old if I wanted to. All of these were great items to add to the empty nester to-do list. First I'd have to make my fence higher, and clear out the garden, and also find and restore a tub and figure out how to get plumbing outside. But the point was, I theoretically had plenty of time and energy to do these things because my child was moving away and, wow, instead of an empty hollow shell, I was about to embark on *the best years of what was left of my life!* I was supposed to want these things.

But it made sense if I got a little weird, followed my (or someone else's) dreams, added hot water plumbing to my backyard. It did not make sense that my hands, and my mother's and daughter's, had suddenly turned into night lights.

It's the Wu magic, a seductive voice whispered to me. *The Wu woo.*

But I hadn't done anything. Paige had fallen asleep *because she needed to.* I had a glow, I could admit that now. But useful powers? I wasn't so sure.

The more logical part of me reasoned that if any of us were going to develop powers, it would be Lulu. Wouldn't it? To be young, energetic, and exploring her identity, to be able to access all the magical blood that still pumped vigorously through her veins, to be able to direct it somewhere useful, or, I don't know, use them for evil—all of this should be happening to Lulu.

I was setting myself up for disappointment thinking that this thing happening with my fingers, this strange weather, and these memories and dreams of my great-aunt meant anything about me.

I looked over at Paige, still asleep.

The point was, I already had an identity, and it didn't include being a superhero or curing people with magic.

But it couldn't hurt to see if I could do it again.

I tickled the baby's belly, and he wriggled accordingly. At least babies made sense.

⋆ ⋆ ⋆

I turned up Joni Mitchell for the drive back into town—okay, so the midwives and folk music connection did hold up—and sang loudly to "A Case of You." Everything was completely fine. I wasn't going bananas. It was such a normal day, in fact, that I decided to go to June's for takeout, something I often did after home visits.

Totally normal.

June's was a little bit outside town limits, and when I arrived, it was packed. There would be a wait. After putting in my order, I said hello to Harjeet Kohli, whose daughters I'd delivered, and Sarah McCaffrey, who I'd gone to high school with but never talked to much. Then I stepped outside into the parking holding my phone to my ear so no one would try to start a conversation with me.

I'd had enough of people, especially grown-up people, for today.

Lulu had texted. Feeling ok. Got some sleep today. Can u bring home chips? Fries? <3<3<3!!!

Apparently, my mother had cooked her lunch, which was nice, but knowing Lulu, it was probably the only thing she'd eaten all day. I moved to a shady spot and thumbed out a message about making sure she ate some more of my mother's lettuce soup or something before I arrived home.

Kids.

I wanted to be back with my daughter. I don't know why I thought my mere presence could protect her, but maybe with my highly skilled radioactive hands I could illuminate any bad guys—or make them fall asleep.

Be home soon with potato products, I wrote. Love you.

Then I screwed up my courage and scrolled down to Kenji's text from this morning.

Hope you're all right. Heard there was a major accident yesterday.

Then: I miss you.

Ugh. He wasn't supposed to worry about me. What made it worse, though, was that I'd had twinges of wishing he were around so that I could talk to him about how terrified I'd been last night, and then how odd and unsettling and yet how strangely peaceful it had been to sit in the kitchen with my mother and daughter later.

Below those texts he'd sent a picture of himself holding Rose. I sent a smiley emoji in response, then finally checked my voicemail.

Parisa had left me a long, gossipy message—she hated texting—about one of the new Obs at the LaValle Clinic, and I listened to it, chuckling. I texted back some laughing emojis and she called me back right away.

Without saying hello, she started, "The world has gone completely bananas. I've been working here for almost 30 years, and I've never seen such a strange year. Reports of postpartum depression through the roof. Combative clients and partners."

"I've had a lot more, too," I admitted.

"I've had to call security so many more times than usual this year."

I shuddered. "I heard."

She sighed. "And speaking of babies, my husband's hardly getting any sleep either. He's so busy. Turning into a real grouch about it."

"He *is* the new chief of neurology."

"I'm declaring a public health crisis. Everyone needs to prioritize getting at least 9 or 10 hours at night."

"I'll alert the papers and inform all the newborns about these rules."

I could picture Parisa stalking around the office gesturing with her hands as she kept talking. "I knew his taking the position would mean more work and meetings for him. His department is run off its feet. They had to extend the hours of their migraine clinic, and all sorts of sleep disorders are on the rise. Emergency and Psych are swamped, too. And I'm so tired keeping up with my own work."

Something niggled at my brain. But like everyone else, I was too exhausted to chase it. "I'm sorry."

"I ran the numbers, Leeann. You may be logging more cases of postpartum depression than usual, but in follow-up your clients are reporting better rates of recovery. That's always been the case for you. But this year it's more pronounced. What I'm still trying to figure out is if there's something you're doing that we're not. And right now it seems more important than ever."

I thought of Paige who'd let go and fallen asleep when I held her hand. I thought of Cato relaxing in the clinic after my glow began.

It wasn't nothing.

"I don't know what to tell you. I've definitely been doing all the screenings and following up on people who are at risk." I shifted uncomfortably.

"You're the only common denominator, though." Her voice abruptly shifted out of work mode to friend mode. "You have real a gift."

She'd told me this before. But now her words hit a different way.

I took a breath and said, "I learned that my great-aunt was a midwife, too. Apparently, I come from a long line of people delivering babies."

"*Oh.*" Parisa said as if she'd grasped the situation when *I* didn't even understand it. "It's in the blood."

"What—what do you mean?"

Parisa paused and I heard a small thump. "Part of it is the same way the number one predictor of whether someone is going to go to medical school is if their parents are physicians. But part of it is what you get used to in the family. I come from a long line of midwives, too. I think that if you grow up with those stories in the house, you're more likely to be interested in it, to not be afraid of it. Because you and I both know there is a lot to fear in birth."

"But my mother isn't a midwife. And she didn't exactly regale me with stories."

"She does deliver babies, though," Parisa said cheerfully. "Listen, I've been tearing my hair out so much I've been giving serious thought to quitting. And I think you should consider applying for the position as chief of the clinic."

"Wait, what?" The clinic without Parisa. I couldn't imagine it.

"Just think about it," she said, still sounding serene.

I groaned. "I'm not going to be able to sleep tonight."

"Get it anyway."

I laughed. That was how we had to do the job.

She hung up and I flipped through my phone again, restless. I looked at the book I'd started, read a page without absorbing the contents, and turned back to the message Kenji sent me this morning. I miss you.

It was ridiculous. I'd known him for what, a couple of weeks? I was becoming as foolish as Shu-ling had warned.

I was a grown woman. Maybe I was even going to be head of the clinic someday. And I was thinking soft, pastel-colored thoughts about a boy.

My cheeks were red but I could put that down to the heat. I pushed a hank of hair off my neck and thought about cutting it short. If I did that, I'd look like my mother. I stared out across the parking lot to the trees and the horizon.

I had to reply to him, something more than an emoji. So I wrote, Been having the most vivid, weird dreams.

It sounded like a bit of a come-on—but I wanted to keep it on that level anyway. Light, sexy. Not too deep. As long as we didn't get into psychoanalysis, we'd be fine.

At least I was also telling the truth.

I stared at my message screen. No response. Well, I'd waited most of the day to say something to him. Only fair that he wouldn't jump to reply right away. Besides, he was probably busy. Making dinner, like he said he often did for Andrea. Maybe he was standing in that old-fashioned kitchen rinsing lettuce, looking out the window into the backyard, gazing at the spot where we'd spoken.

No, I was the one staring.

I blinked. I was barely taking in the scene outside June's spread out in front of me. The evening had a strange light. It was still bright out, but the sky had a gray tinge. Maybe we'd finally get some rain. But the air didn't feel right. It smelled almost metallic.

My body hummed. I stretched my hand out experimentally.

This time the light stretching from my fingertips wasn't only a glow. It was a spark. It seemed to call to something in the air, gathering the heat in visible waves that seemed to be coming toward me. My hair seemed to stand up on end.

A bird cawed. A warning.

Go inside.

But my body was too fascinated with its newfound skills, and I found myself reaching forward again. It wasn't until I walked to the edge of the porch that I realized the danger I was in.

I turned and ran.

A flash tore the sky in half followed immediately by a deep *BOOM* I felt more than heard. I felt it through me, in my heels, my heart, my throat.

If I screamed no one could have heard it. I didn't. But the sound ground raw in my throat.

It felt like forever before I came back to myself.

When I did, I was still standing, clutching the wall of the restaurant. Sarah McCaffrey appeared beside me. "Jesus, Leeann, are you all right? What the hell was that?"

Her voice sounded tinny and distant. So did mine when I replied, "I think it was a lightning strike."

I flexed my fingers. I was aware other people were there, babbling in the background. Someone was asking if they should call an ambulance.

"Did it actually hit her?"

"Of course it didn't. Does she look like someone who's been struck by lightning?"

"I have no idea what that would look like. She screamed loud enough."

"Probably like the bride of Frankenstein, you know? All her hair straight up with one white streak."

"Shut up, Kent. You're an idiot."

Sarah was still beside me. She handed me a glass of water that she must have taken from inside the restaurant. "The whole building lit up like it was on fire. But there wasn't any thunder that we could hear. Except the cups all began to rattle at once and you . . ."

I'd heard something. Or had I? My lips didn't want to form words properly. "It must have struck nearby," I croaked.

"But the sky is clear. It wasn't even raining. I don't understand what happened."

I closed my eyes.

"Are you going to pass out?" Her voice was shrill. I was glad I was still having trouble hearing. "Maybe we should get you a doctor."

"No," I said. I was all right. Except for my ears. And my heartbeat. And my dangerous hands. I didn't even want to look at them.

Someone helped me into a chair.

"We'll have to call her mom."

Oh, for fuck's sake. I had to get it together. "Do not call my mother. Please. I was just startled, and it was close by. Maybe we should make sure that lightning strike, or whatever it was—" *It was me. Oh gods, it was me!* "Let's check to see it didn't start a fire somewhere."

"Wayne Letts is having a look. Maybe I could drive you home, though?" Sarah said, still hovering anxiously.

June Wong herself came out. She thrust a mug of tea at me. I realized I was shivering despite the heat. "Your order will be ready in a few."

"June, thank you, but I'm fine. Nothing hit me."

"That thing shook the room around and it looked like it set my place on fire. For a moment I thought we were burning in hell. My eyes sure aren't going to recover any time soon. But we were all inside—unlike you." She raised her voice. "Everyone's getting a free coffee or tea or whatever on the house. I think we have a few boxes of wine somewhere. Drink up."

People started filtering back into the restaurant.

I felt foolish, and even more silly when Sarah, still lingering, said, "I'll drive you home. It'll be no problem."

But it was a problem. The car would be stuck here at June's, and we only had the one while Lulu's was in the shop, and I didn't want my daughter on the road anyway. Not after she'd been in an accident. But what was almost as bad was that I wouldn't have that much to say to Sarah on the way back. I was used to making conversation with people as part of my job, but right now Sarah would probably want to ask me a million times how I was really doing.

I was fine.

I simply needed a little quiet time to myself.

Sarah was only trying to be nice.

You could zap her, an insidious voice whispered.

My phone rang. It was Kenji.

"I need to take this," I mumbled to Sarah, ashamed at how relieved I felt.

I headed out from under the long awning, took one look at the sky, changed my mind, and had to come back closer to Sarah, who wasn't even pretending that she wasn't interested in my conversation.

"Hi, Kenji," I said very quietly. Sarah cocked her ear toward us. I turned away. "I'm at June's."

"Oh, is she a client?" His voice slightly out of breath.

"No. It's a restaurant out by Lower Cormier Road."

"Oh, I think I know the place. Big painted sign that says something about best burger in town?"

"Even though it's not really in town."

He snorted. "You like your old school, out-of-the-way places."

"Nothing is out of the way in Reineville."

My voice must have been a little louder that time because Sarah laughed.

God, did she have to listen to every word?

I turned away from her and heard the swooshing of wind from Kenji's end.

"I was just calling to check on you. We had some weird storm action just now," he said.

"Yeah, I was outside. It struck really near." I shivered again.

He must have heard the strain in my voice because he asked, "Hey, are you okay? Did something happen?"

"I'm fine. I just want to get my food and go home. Where are you?"

"Not too far from Cormier—"

Lower Cormier, I automatically wanted to correct him like the obnoxious townie I was.

"I went to pick up some diapers at the big box store. The lights flickered for a good minute. If you can sense a storm while you're in a warehouse stacked sky high with extra-absorbent diapers, you know it's a huge weather system. I thought I was going to get run down by a woman with a cartful of frozen peas. She looked like she wanted to dive into the breads and stay there forever."

"The bakery section is where I'd go if I needed shelter." Impulsively, I said, "Hey, if you're not that far away, maybe you could swing by here and we could throw your bike in the back. I could drive you and your groceries home.

Actually, you'd be doing me a favor. I could use a ride to my place."

Sarah was gesturing at me, but I ignored her.

"That'd be great," he said. "I was worried it was going to rain, and these diapers would bloat up and get home only to find the Michelin man strapped to the back of the bike."

The air was heavy with humidity, but the sun was shining again; it was unlikely to rain, but he'd said it so smoothly I wanted to close my eyes again over how relieved I felt that he'd given me an out. I asked quietly, "You sure you know where June's is?"

"Yes. Getting on my bike now."

He sounded so lighthearted and normal. I couldn't help smiling, despite the fact that even my face felt tired. He was happy to get to see me.

I glanced up again and saw Sarah hovering. "Guess you don't need my help," she said.

"Thank you. It was really kind of you to offer," I said, feeling awkward.

She sighed. "It's no problem."

My food came out, and she went back inside. I was relieved again, but this time it was because I didn't have to answer any questions.

♦ 7 ♦

"WHO WAS THAT PARKED outside with you?" Lulu asked.

I should have expected Lulu to be up and about and, apparently, peeking through the window.

I dumped the food bags on the kitchen table and adjusted my shirt before I turned away to wash my hands.

She wouldn't have been able to see inside the car. I knew it wasn't really possible, but still. I made out with him only a little bit because we were in my driveway, but soon that wasn't going to be enough for me.

Lulu had probably watched Kenji take his bike out of the back and say goodbye.

I dried my hands and was proud of how casual my voice came out. "It was Andrea Hartell's brother. We were helping each other out. He only had his bike and a huge box of diapers, and I had my car. So he drove me here."

"Why? That sounds unnecessarily complicated."

You said it, kid.

I sighed. "It was a long day. How are you feeling?"

"I'm fine," she said impatiently. Her face was still reddened and scratched, but her energy had returned. "Why was he driving?" She started taking the food out of the bags.

"I . . ." How to explain it? "I was outside when the lightning struck. It seemed really close. It rattled June enough that she gave everyone drinks on the house."

Lulu looked up in mock horror. "My God. *June* giving out free stuff?"

"A once-in-a-million experience."

"I saw a flash of something, but no thunder." She said it like it hadn't been a big deal. Maybe it wasn't. But what had been that deep vibration I'd felt?

"Did it look like it struck anywhere around there?" Lulu asked.

"Maybe. I didn't see anything burning or anything like that. Someone from the fire department went to check."

Again, my brain stuttered at the thought that there hadn't been any rain. There wasn't any trace or smell of it in the air. In fact, if we hadn't all heard it, the only way I would have known was from the ringing in my ears. Uneasily, I thought of the scorch marks across the university bell tower. I'd been dreaming of lightning that night.

"So you wanted to drive Andrea Hartell's brother home because of the lightning? And then you let him bike home from here? Why not drop him off? It's not that far to Andrea's place."

She crinkled her brow. Up until now, her tone had been determinedly cheerful. She was probably trying to erase last night from her head. But now, she sounded worried again.

I thought of lying, of letting that explanation pass, but Lulu was smarter than that.

"They wanted someone to drive me home because I was shaken by the storm."

Lulu snorted. "You're never afraid of things like that. You love storms."

"It felt too close," I muttered.

"Mom! Were you kidnapped? Are you feverish?" She stretched her hands toward my forehead, as if expecting me to have a fever. That Wu family medical prowess was such a scam.

"The lightning felt too close," I repeated stiffly.

So close I could still taste the heat and metal on my tongue, despite how Kenji had tried to soothe me with his mouth.

We sat down at the table. I knew Lulu was watching me, trying to figure out my strange behavior. There was a long pause as we both took bites out of our sandwiches.

"Sarah McCaffrey almost called a doctor. She offered to take me home, but I felt weird with her. I mean, we were never friends—"

She raised a brow. "But you felt comfortable with . . . what's his name?"

"Kenji, his name is Kenji." I took a big sip of water and willed myself not to blush.

"Was he the one that A-mà was warning you about?"

"She talks about all cis het men that way. You can't listen to her."

"Almost all of them. But you felt comfortable enough with this person you met a few weeks ago that you let him drive your car instead of Sarah McCaffrey who you've known since high school?"

I put my sandwich down. "Lulu, do you have something you'd like to ask me?"

Lulu put her hands up. "I'd just like you to consider dating sometimes, okay? You seem interested, and this guy looks—"

I started to laugh. I couldn't help it. The past twenty-four hours had been strange and draining, and my daughter still looked like she'd been beat up. If tears leaked out in the hilarity I wouldn't stop them. "He looks like what?" I gasped. "Bipedal? Breathing? Is that your criteria?"

Lulu did not join in my spiraling giggles. She handed me a napkin and watched until I exhausted myself and set my head on the table.

She said quietly. "This guy was nice enough. He helped you with your stuff. He watched you the whole time while you got on the porch. He didn't put that huge box on his bike or ride off until the door closed. And even then, he stood there for a while and made sure you were okay. I couldn't see him very well, but I'll bet he was cute."

I shrugged and stared at the table. "He's patient."

And hot. And kind. And he knew how to listen to me.

"I'm just worried about you, is all."

I could hear the threads of anxiety gathering in her voice. Last night had been a lot. The accident, the injuries, the magic. And now here I'd appeared shaken, driven home by a strange man.

"What are you going to do after?" Lulu continued.

After she was gone.

"You think a relationship will get my mind off the fact that you're leaving?"

She made an impatient movement. "I know you. You act so cool and make jokes to try to pretend like you don't care about anything except me and your clients. Even then sometimes you go behind, I don't know, this facade of being apart from it all and cynical. But who's going to take care of you?"

This patronizing little woman I'd raised. My fries were cold. I was tired and drained. Now my own child, who had been in a car accident just last night, was wondering who'd take make sure I was safe and secure, when I was the one who should've protected her.

Immediately I retreated into the sarcasm she'd accused me of using to keep people away. "So you think I should just go wild once you're gone? Maybe do some topless sunbathing on the shores of Lake Ontario. Rob the bingo hall? I'll add that to my list."

Immediately, Lulu went into her shell of calm. "No, I think you should consider expanding your horizons."

I nodded. "Making a plan."

"Yes, sure. A list." She brightened. She really believed she could control everything if she were organized enough. No wonder she was having trouble stomaching the Wu magic. "I mean, Mom, you don't have to take care of me anymore. You don't have to be obligated to me. I've been taking care of myself for years anyway. I know you gave up a lot for me."

"You feel guilty."

"I do," she agreed.

I didn't give birth to you because I wanted to burden you with guilt. I wanted to yell, but I kept my voice steady. "It wasn't that every moment was a pleasure. Of course it wasn't. But Lulu, you have to understand I don't consider having you a sacrifice. I wanted you, and I'm happy with the life we made together. I am grateful I didn't marry your dad. I'm doubly grateful that because of you I finally found the work I really wanted to do. We have a home, friends, food, warmth. I have loved getting to know you for every single day you've been with me. Watching you find out who you are has been a privilege."

I gestured with my sandwich, which honestly I didn't want to eat anymore.

Lulu said, "But it can be overwhelming sometimes to think that I'm responsible for all this."

"What do you mean? If anyone should consider themselves responsible that should be me."

I looked around the kitchen. Okay, it was messy. The linoleum counter tops had lost their original color and had dulled to a scuffed looking gray. A lone, shriveled apple lay in a fruit basket where I'd also deposited some mail—I should probably look at those bills. But we owned the place. I hadn't taken any help from my mother. We cleaned it occasionally.

"You know, A-mà's always saying you could've been a brilliant physician."

My mother had never said anything like that to my face, though. I snorted. "So now's my chance to shine and that's what I get to be? Instead of, say, a unicorn? I never wanted to follow her path exactly."

Lulu considered that for a moment. "I think what A-mà fears is that you made her mistakes."

And one of her mistakes had been having me.

"All errors are my own. She's free and clear. So are you. I own it, like I own this sandwich."

"That you don't want to eat."

"If I throw it in the compost that's my business. Listen, I tried living the life that my mom wanted for me, but when I found out I was pregnant and became fascinated with pregnancy and what it did to my body I got an inkling of what it was that was important for me." I paused. "I always wanted to have you, more than I wanted anything else."

"But a different future—"

"I knew I had a choice—just like you always have a choice, and you can come to me if you ever become pregnant. I'll help you get the morning-after pill. I'll take you to any kind of doctor you'd like to see. I'll hold your hand."

My darling daughter, my reason for being, grimaced. "Is this your version of The Talk before I go to university?"

"Yes. Should I give the STD one while we're at it?"

Lulu shuddered. "We've already had that conversation, too. Besides, you're avoiding my questions."

"You're avoiding thinking about last night."

"Don't you want something else, Mom?" she pressed. "Not that I think you're a failure. But this is an opportunity for you."

It was frustrating talking with someone young and full of life and ambition and energy sometimes. "You mean do I want a handful of man butt and a new degree under my arm? You want me to live my young undergrad days all over again? Follow you to school. Get drunk and make out in the library? I think there's a movie with that premise. Maybe you should be giving *me* The Talk."

I reached over and grabbed her hand to take the sharpness out of my words. But maybe I was the one who was feeling the sting more.

"Mom."

"You're right. You wouldn't do a lot of that—you've always been responsible and have always volunteered and sat on committees and gotten good grades. But some things don't fall into neat categories, like love and magic."

"Magic isn't going to keep you company when I'm gone!" Lulu almost shouted.

We stared at each other.

Lulu pressed her lips together. "I'm sorry, Mom. It's not real."

I held her gaze. "You saw it, Lulu. We all did."

She shook her head. "It was a one-time thing. I was injured and we were all tired."

I sighed and closed my eyes and tried to think about all of the strange phenomena, all of this change that was about to come. "Listen, I know you're worried about what will happen to me after you're at school. And I have not been a perfect mother. God knows, I understand that. But damn it, Lulu. You should not need to—to feel responsible for me or what happens to me, or this house, or my future. Part of me understands that you've been so grown up all your life because you didn't want me to worry and stress over you. But I should have been taking care of you better so that you wouldn't have to feel that obligation to me. So you could've had some more freedom. But I'm going into this with my eyes open."

Lulu was smart and poised and driven. She'd done well in school, she had friends, and people adored her. She worked hard. She was the magical one, not me.

It should have been me telling her to go and make out in cars.

"I know you're good at things—at your job and keeping things together," Lulu said. She started clearing the table, putting the leftover food in the correct-sized containers. She was already completely self-possessed again. "You've been a good mom, too. I just . . . You seemed dazzled last night by the idea of, well, magical power. Of course, I was too until last night—"

"Until you actually felt it."

"I don't know what that was. But I didn't like it. Anyway, but there are different, *real* things. And that guy—Kenji, you said his name was?—it looks like there's something there if you want to pursue it.

"I don't want you to, I don't know, drift after I've left. Emotionally, I mean. And yeah, maybe that means traveling, or leaving yourself open to relationships, not necessarily just sexual ones—"

"Oh, good gravy."

"But also relationships with the community."

"And not stay at home stirring a cauldron? Lulu, I get out all the damn time. The reason I stay home when I can is because I'm out there in people's bedrooms and living rooms and generally with my face in people's reproductive business."

"But that's a job," she insists. "What about the other parts of your life?"

"Lulu, this kind of job, it isn't so easily cordoned off from life. If you want to go into medicine, you'll find that's true, too. It becomes a part of how you deal with your town, or wherever you live. Obviously, my job isn't the only thing I've got going on, but I have to be careful, especially in a smaller place like Reineville."

"Well, that's one reason to get out of here more often," Lulu said.

We were quiet for a bit. I guess I'd always known she wanted to leave, but I'd never heard her put it so baldly. In my mind, maybe I'd expected her to go away for school and then come back and do . . . what? Live in our house again? Lip-sync in the kitchen to bad music while making cookies and then putting on her white doctor's coat to go to work while I watched her, smiling?

I reached for her, and she let me take her hand. I turned it over and thought about the power we'd all shared last night, the thing that scared her now. "When you were a baby you used to point at planes or helicopters in the sky and then point to yourself and say, *Yeh,* which was your way of saying, *Me!* You were going to be on that plane, traveling off into the sky. I don't know how you knew the difference between a bird and something you could fly in, but you knew. Even then, you got that that is what you'd be able to do one day. You never wanted to stay here."

She tried to take her hand away. "You don't have to either."

"Lulu."

This time she succeeded in escaping my grip. "I'm serious. There's nothing stopping you from selling this house, ditching your clothing, and going across the country. Or driving around in a camper to visit craft fairs, or . . . I don't know, going to New Zealand."

Kenji had gone to New Zealand.

"We could take a vacation before you start school," I said.

"We already talked about this. This is a great internship, and you're so busy this summer. Anyway, I want to spend more time with A-mà before I go. Plus, I'm only going to be a few hours' drive away."

I swallowed. My own hands, with nothing to hold, tightened into fists. It was true, and I'd told myself that very fact several times. "We could go to the Southern Hemisphere together. Sleep in a park! Have experiences we've both never had."

"I didn't know sleeping in a park was part of the dreams you had for me."

"No. I don't want that!" What was I even saying? "I mean, I want you to have your own goals and wishes."

"Good, because these ones sound like they belong to a member of a Fleetwood Mac cover band."

"Look, my point is I've never tried to put my own stuff on you. I've always told you to do what you want. And I'm telling you that I'm generally happy with the way things are, and I'll figure it out when you leave. I don't want you worrying about me."

She rolled her eyes. "I can't help worrying."

I tried to joke. "Well, it's not like you have to be anxious that your dad and I will get divorced once you've left the nest."

"That's not funny."

"Other people think I'm funny. Maybe that's what I'll do—find people who laugh at my jokes."

Kenji laughed at my stupid cracks, but there was no reason to tell Lulu that right now.

It was one thing for her to say she wanted me to have a relationship right now, but if she knew I was already kind of dating him—well, that wasn't information I needed to share with my daughter whether she was grown or not. It wasn't good parenting, not that I'd ever been picture-perfect before.

She was the one whose footsteps I should follow.

But there I was again, putting that burden of perfection on her. She shouldn't have to be a role model for me any more than I should have to be ideal for her.

"What if I told you that I was sort of interested in seeing that guy from before? You know the one on the bike. Kenji."

Lulu smirked. "You almost couldn't say his name out loud to me."

I closed my eyes. Kids. They didn't really let you get away with much. When I opened them again, she stood wiping her hands with the dishcloth and watching me with open amusement. "You li-i-ike him," she said in a singsong.

"Lulu. I love you very much. And I am asking you to please not do that."

"He seemed very into you, judging by the fact that he helped you out and how he watched you. What's wrong with admitting you may be interested?"

Somehow it sounded too exposed to even agree to Lulu's statement. Why then, did I feel a small jolt of pleasure to hear that to her relatively objective eye that he'd showed an obvious interest in me even when we weren't together for naked reasons. "You know he's younger than me, right?"

"Oh, I guessed that."

"Yeah. Thanks."

* * *

I had to wait a few days for Lulu's car to be repaired and for her to be safely out of the house before I could try to summon the magic.

I decided the basement would be my best option. We didn't come down here unless we had to, and if lightning really was attracted to my glow, then, at least there would be cement and brick to protect me. One time, when Lulu was still little, there's been a tornado watch throughout the Tri-Cities and we'd hidden down here eating crackers and reading with flashlights.

I sat cross-legged on a yoga mat on the floor and tried to remember what I'd been feeling each time I'd seen my hands glow. I couldn't think of the connection: during an accident, a couple of client exams, making a cup of tea. It made no sense. "Maybe I have to start this manually," I said to the basement air.

I spread out my fingers and stared at them. I pointed at things. I sat very still and imagined light bulbs, the sun, the moon, disco balls. I tried rubbing my hands together like I was making a fire.

"Just work!" I said frustrated, gesturing at the air like a conductor.

Nothing.

Of course there was nothing. I lay back and let out a big sigh and closed my eyes. It was a little cooler down here, so at least that was nice, and there was less sound. If I didn't have a middle-aged back, I could fall asleep right on this mat.

I hate to say it, but instead of practicing whatever magic may have been in my veins, maybe I did half doze off for a while. I circled that state between being asleep and awake and my mind drifted to Lulu and my mom, then strangely, to my great-aunt, my Yi-beh.

I could almost picture her, reaching for me as I began to glow, and I couldn't move because I was pinned down by her hungry stare. But I was only half asleep. I should have been able to move, but my limbs felt drained of all energy. With great effort I looked away from her and tried to move my arms, my legs, anything, then I sat up slowly and opened my eyes.

And immediately was blinded by the pop and fizzle of the basement's only light bulb burning out.

What the hell?

I was panting and creeped out and strangely exhausted sitting in complete darkness. I had to get out somehow. With weak arms, I patted the floor beside me and found my phone. My fingers were wet with sweat and it took a while for me to swipe the phone enough for it to shine its comforting light at me. I found the flashlight and heaved myself slowly up the stairs, leaving my yoga mat behind.

I'd retrieve it and change the light bulb another day.

Back upstairs, with shaking fingers, I called Kenji.

* * *

We met at the Caravan because Kenji knew where it was, and I couldn't think of the names of any other places in town.

He was waiting for me in a booth. There was a slice of cherry pie on the table.

He slid it in front of me, and a waitress, a different one from the afternoon after the accident, came over and poured me a steaming hot cup of coffee.

"How did you know I needed this?" I asked shakily.

"You sounded a little off."

"And you came just like that?"

"Yeah."

He didn't say, *I always will.* Or *I can't stay away.* But there was something in that single syllable, that soft finality, that made me look up.

"Eat your pie," he said after moment.

I did as I was told, and after a few bites, I began telling him an abbreviated version of events: no attempts at summoning magic, no glowing. But I did say I'd been in our creepy basement and thinking about my aunt. I did say something about the light burning out and panicking and not being able to move.

"Sleep paralysis," he offered helpfully.

Maybe. But it had felt worse. I could still feel the drain of it, as if my soul was being taken from me.

"Well, that's the last time I try to do something around the house," I said, trying to play it off as something silly.

The pie and coffee were helping. I didn't feel as drained as I had before. Kenji's quiet energy helped, too.

"I could do that for you," he said, taking my free hand. "At least change the light bulb. There's a joke in there somewhere."

"How many Kenjis does it take to screw in a light bulb?"

I didn't know how Kenji's name combined with the word *screw* would sound until it came out of my mouth.

The air between us changed abruptly. My heartbeat sped up again, my pulse moving frantically even as exhaustion still pulled at me. Kenji's hand tightened around mine as he glanced down, red staining those sharp cheekbones.

"Kenji," I said after a moment. My tongue felt slow. "I know we haven't . . . Do you want to . . . ?"

"Yeah," he said again.

Yes, we haven't. Yes, I want you. Yes, I always will. Yes, I can't stay away.

We stood up at the same time and he dropped money on the table. He pulled me outside and we were leaning against the warm brick of the diner, kissing. My limbs still felt heavy and languorous, but the taste of coffee and cherry mingled in our kisses and every time his mouth left mine, I found the energy to chase him.

I let him do the thinking. We couldn't go to my place or to Andrea's. So we stumbled our way across the Caravan parking lot to the motel.

I still felt strangely heavy, but whatever I was doing made him groan and stutter, even as he almost carried me those few last steps to our room. I'd wanted this for so long, and if I couldn't have magic or power, at least I could have this.

The door closed, and I didn't stop to think of what Lulu had said to me yesterday, or about the failure of any magic that was in me, or about what lay ahead of me in the coming months. I could only think of now, of how good it felt when he pulled roughly at my shirt, dug his fingers under my skirt, and rubbed his body up into me.

He stripped off his own shirt and as I ran my hands slowly along his sides before I tugged at his shorts. I stared at him in the dim motel room, the shadowed valleys of his arms and chest promising power, before he pulled me close again and we tumbled onto the bed.

I didn't even have time to think about my own forty-something body, because that body wanted to feel good now. He kissed my cheeks and collarbones, the stubble on his chin scraping its way pleasurably down, down as he sucked on my breasts and the skin of my belly button, down between my legs before hauling them over his shoulders. I cried out at the first touch of his tongue between my thighs, the thick, luxurious licks gaining strength, until, panting, I pulled him up and told him I wanted him inside me when I came.

He turned away for a moment to put on a condom, and at once, I pulled him down on top of me, into me, and I curled into his chest as he held himself still for an agonizing moment, staring into my eyes, before starting to move.

And oh, everything swelled up inside me in pleasure. Newly energized, I rolled against him, enjoying the feel of his muscles bunching under my fingers, the hairs on his chest, the pressure of him between my legs. I urged him on, grasping him, making him work and sweat and moan.

The light began to emanate from my skin, at last I'd summoned it, but I didn't care, as I pulled Kenji up and over with me.

♦ 8 ♦

A WEEK LATER, I WOKE up with a start in the backyard wearing my pajamas, or rather my tank top and underwear. I was leaning against the tall fence, my face plastered against a stout post, and I was gripping the wood as if it were the only thing anchoring me to the earth.

It took me a moment to recognize my own yard at night. Probably because usually when I got home from a delivery, I wasn't gazing fondly at all my magnificent property. I was heading straight for my bed.

Where I should have been now.

Especially since I was in skimpy underclothes—and although it was dark, any one of my neighbors would have seen my thighs flashing whitely in the night.

My heart skittered too fast, and I ran inside and closed the door. I put the chain across the rarely used bolt as if there were something out there waiting for me, instead of me being the night interloper. I'd never sleepwalked (sleptwalked?) before. The idea that a foreign compulsion, even my own subconscious, had propelled me out of bed, out of my house, was disturbing.

I checked the pantry to make sure I hadn't eaten anything strange. A few years ago, there had been all these news stories about people who took sleeping pills and would proceed to consume entire bags of flour, and of course that was the only fact I could remember about somnambulism.

Then again, I wasn't sure how much flour we had to begin with, but since the pantry wasn't dusted with white, and my scanty clothing seemed clean enough, I felt relatively confident I hadn't been downing handfuls of Bob's Red Mill products.

I didn't remember food in my dreams. All I had were fragments, as always: an old woman reaching for me, trying to take something essential away from me. Sadness and grief. Then lightning coming from my body.

I slumped on the floor of the pantry feeling suddenly drained. Even just the memory of the dream sapped any energy I had left. Maybe I should get checked out by the doctor. Again.

Lying on the floor of the pantry, I closed my eyes and I wondered briefly what Lulu's dad Paul would think of this. As she got older, Paul's mother went to the doctor more and more frequently. She never consulted her son about anything because he'd grown too used to her complaining and never took her seriously. But despite the fact that she didn't seek him out anymore, he thought her illnesses were a bid for his attention. If I said something similar, he'd probably conclude I was becoming one of *those* women.

Paul's mother had never liked me. Of course she didn't. I'd gotten pregnant and nearly derailed her son's life. She'd never taken to Lulu either.

I clambered slowly back to my room and drew a sheet over me. I was exhausted and inexplicably teary, but my brain was too keyed up for rest. I pulled my phone off my nightstand and read more about perimenopause. Stress and sleep disturbances, a predisposition to anxiety, hormone fluctuations—these could all exacerbate symptoms. But somehow my sleepwalking didn't feel like that. Neither did my glow.

It felt like magic.

It was still hot out, despite the fact the sun had gone down, and the air felt heavy and wrong. I had occasionally tried to tap into my own glow after that first time with Kenji. We'd started seeing each other almost every day, and we usually ended up at the motel.

I didn't delude myself that it was simply sex, because I was emotionally involved—and so was he. I could tell by the way he sounded so happy just to talk to me. The way he sent me pictures of things he thought I'd find funny. The way he looked at me sleepy-eyed and affectionate after we'd made love.

But I did think of what we did together sometimes as magical practice. Because I glowed and glowed when we got together. It was the most reliable way for me to call on that power. Once or twice afterward, he tried to say something, but I'd always rush off or change the subject, or distract him—usually with more sex. And every time, I felt energized afterward. I should have felt exhausted leading my double life of being there for Lulu and my clients, eating dinner with my mother, and seeing Kenji in the moments in between. But I avoided worrying about the sleep I wasn't getting, because I had this. When I did find time to try to summon my glow outside of sex, it came a little more easily now. It manifested as a weak light, but at least it was something.

Of course, I still didn't know what the glow *did.*

When I told Lulu about the sleepwalking episode the next morning, I tried to underplay it, leaving out the part where I was out in the backyard in my underwear. I was probably too successful. I could tell she didn't believe me when she patted my shoulder, and suggested I fasten a little bell to my toe.

* * *

In the light of day, my nighttime adventure didn't seem very important to me either. I told myself that dreaming of sad black-clad figures draining me of energy didn't mean it was true, that it would really happen.

I soon discovered other things to worry about anyway, because somehow between the sleepwalking, the sex, and the glow, somehow I'd lost track of the fact that I'd missed my period. I hadn't been this late since I found out I was pregnant with Lulu. Then again, I'd never had this much sex since before I was pregnant with Lulu. Sitting in my car in the late afternoon after my client visits were over, I poked my belly. Sure I was exhausted and restless—so was everyone these days. But I didn't feel like I was carrying anything. And yes, as a midwife, I knew that was a ridiculous statement.

Kenji was making me lose track of the summer. Which was what I'd wanted, because at the end of that time, Lulu would be gone.

I did what any sensible person would do the day I realized I was late. I avoided answering Kenji's texts, and after work I drove to the next town.

In the parking lot of the big box drugstore, I made some calculations on my phone. There was no way I could be more than a couple weeks pregnant. A test might not be accurate this early. Besides, what were the odds of having two condom accidents almost twenty years apart? Then again, I'd almost been struck by lightning recently because of, oh yes, my glowing hands. Unlikely events were piling up.

I lifted myself carefully out of the car as if my center of gravity had already shifted and laughed bitterly to myself. Was it a baby I was dreaming about, or some sort of future with Kenji?

I managed to find the right aisle in the pharmacy. But, of course, as I stood there deciding between two pregnancy tests, I heard someone call my name.

It was my old classmate Sarah McCaffrey, the one who'd offered to drive me home the other day. "I thought that was you."

As she spoke she craned her neck to see what I was buying. Hiding the thing in my hand would've been too obvious. Besides, I was standing right in front of the pregnancy test section under fluorescent lights, the pink boxes as bright as toys.

Her eyes widened. She looked at what I held in my hands, then at my stomach. I resisted the urge to cup it protectively.

Not a subtle one was Sarah.

But judging by how horrified she looked I'd given her as much of a scare as she'd given me.

The less-panicked part of me laughed. It served her right for being nosy. But instead of asking me questions, Sarah turned three shades of red and put down the basket she'd been holding.

"How are you *feeling*?" she asked, and, if possible, her skin turned brighter.

I sighed. What were the chances that there'd soon be rumors about my out-of-town trip to the drugstore floating around? Sarah wasn't a gossip, as far as I could remember. But she'd seen me with Kenji the day of the lightning, and she'd been curious about it. She could put one with the other and come up with a pregnancy. Of course, there was the possibility that she could think that I was buying these for Lulu.

I peeked at her face again.

Nope. She definitely knew the tests were for me.

I smiled blandly. "I feel good," I said. I picked up another test and studied the back, willing my hand not to tremble.

I took in a surreptitious breath. But Sarah didn't ask the obvious question, and when I looked up again, she dropped her eyes.

I knew right then she wasn't going to say anything to anyone.

My heart slowed from its frenetic pace, and I felt the vibration of something go through me. Was this power or just relief? There was definitely something edging around my vision, making me feel bigger than I was.

"I—I just remembered, I have an appointment." Sarah turned around and fled.

I watched her go before calling, "You forgot your basket!"

But she was gone.

I took another deep breath. The feeling had receded, and I felt almost normal again—well, as normal as I could under the circumstances. I peered inside Sarah's abandoned basket. Two could play at this game. A couple of ready-bake pizzas and ice cream from the freezer section, a box of tampons. That would've been my haul too, if I had my period.

Instead, I grabbed a box of Plan B and put it in my own basket. If I couldn't use it, then I could give it to Lulu as a nice dorm-room housewarming present.

Hysterical laughter bubbled inside me, but I paid for everything calmly. I even made small talk about how debit and credit sounded too much the same to the cashier.

When I got inside my car I burst into tears.

Did I want a child right now? No. I was as certain about it as I was when I'd decided I wanted to have Lulu. Did Kenji want to be a father? Probably, but I couldn't imagine he'd want that responsibility at this particular moment.

I'd seen him cradling his baby niece the day she was born. It was easy to be an uncle from a distance, and yet, he'd come here in order to help his sister out, and he showed no signs of leaving. He'd be good at it.

I had to admit to myself, a small part of me briefly weighed having a baby Kenji so that I'd feel young enough for him—young enough to keep him. What was happening between us was more than magic practice—I was falling in love with him.

But none of that was reason enough for me to have another kid.

The day had been a strain, and meeting Sarah McCaffrey in the drugstore had put it over the top. I didn't truly want a baby now, not even if it meant keeping a man—not that it would. I knew that from experience. I'd been telling the truth with Lulu—I'd wanted her badly, and she was the right choice. But now? Even though I was better off financially than I was when I was an undergrad, and my workplace was sure to be supportive, the big, real part of me didn't want this. I was supposed to feel empty after Lulu was gone, but I didn't need to fill it with another child. I didn't have to make the same choice I'd made almost twenty years ago, because I was different now too.

I reached into my bag for tissues and mopped at my face. I was going to be all right, no matter what happened. I'd lived through worse, and I'd thrived.

By the time I got home I was calm again. Lulu was back at work. A friend would drop her back here later. I had plenty of time to myself.

I locked the front and bathroom doors anyway, as if expecting my well-mannered daughter to barge in Kool-Aid Man style while I peed on a stick. I took long, deep calming breaths.

The test was negative.

I felt lightheaded. I squinted under the bathroom light to make sure I was seeing it correctly. *Negative.* The sensible part of me planned to repeat the test at the clinic after I'd waited a bit longer, but I wanted these results to be true, and I grasped at any relief this result would get me.

I washed my hands, and took the trash and recycling outside, and came back in and washed my hands again.

But if I wasn't pregnant and I hadn't gotten my period, what did this mean?

Lulu breezed in, and I spent the rest of the day pretending to be a calm, together person, asking about her day, making popcorn on the stove. The bruising on her face had mostly cleared up in the weeks since her accident, and after our fight the other week, Lulu was herself again. It was exactly how I'd wanted my summer with my daughter to be. All the normal beautiful things.

But after I climbed into bed, I tossed and turned. I needed sleep, even though I was afraid I'd have that dream and wander out at night again. Tomorrow would be a tough day. Irini Vlassapoulos was due soon. I'd have to take a pregnancy test at work at some point and somehow get it past all the prying eyes, and I had to break it off with Kenji. I was in too deep—my mixed feelings about this pregnancy scare had proven that—and there was no way we wanted the same things out of life. It wasn't fair to me or to him.

⋆ ⋆ ⋆

"What if next time I take you to a real dinner? Within city limits. We dress up. I, uh, borrow Andrea's car. I meet your daughter. What are some of the fancier places in town, anyway? I guess I could ask Andrea."

Needless to say, I had failed to break up with Kenji.

I paused with the cheeseburger halfway to my mouth, then put it back down on the wrapper.

We were at the Caravan, our food spread out on the bed. Kenji, of course, naked, which was his preferred state.

Or rather it was my preferred state for him, and he liked to oblige me. Often and enthusiastically. *Ah, youth.*

My period had arrived the morning after the pregnancy scare and had gone away after just a handful of days like an irresponsible houseguest who had no idea how much uproar her lateness had caused. After that I'd been so relieved, and so busy and . . . what were my other excuses?

Maybe it was better if I simply told myself I was waiting for the right moment to talk.

However, it was always the right moment to grin at one of his texts. To daydream about him, since I wasn't having much luck sleeping at night. And it was always a good time for sex and a cheeseburger and sitting cross-legged across from him in a motel room.

But now I'd delayed it enough that he was asking for a date in public when I'd been planning on less. I didn't want to let go of him. Of the sex, of the long, bladelike strength of his thighs, his teeth and lips, all that golden skin. The low laughter of his voice when we talked.

But as I looked more closely at him, he seemed not quite as relaxed as I'd thought. He had a fry in hand and was casually studying the sheets of the bed. They were not fascinating. In fact, unless you were a forensic investigator, it was probably best not to think too hard or look that closely at the sheets at the Caravan Motel. His questions to me had come out in quick succession, too. As if he were nervous.

Meeting Lulu.

"Is that what you'd like to do?" I asked carefully.

"It's what I wanted from the start. But I took anything you offered, and I respect that you've been gun shy. Although, I feel like that's changed a little now?"

The pregnancy scare had made me feel softer toward him. It should have done the opposite—reminding me of what risks I was taking. But instead it had been freeing.

Still, a fancy public date. Why was that different?

"I'm not keeping it a secret on purpose," I said, maybe feeling a little defensive. "I mean, we're sitting here eating together. Lulu and I have talked about you. People have seen you with me when you picked me up at June's. Or the eye doctor's. And Sarah McCaffrey knows about us."

Even as I spoke I realized I already had a little life with him. It should have bothered me how easily I'd fallen into calling when I needed someone—him.

Kenji said, "I know you want to be cautious because you have a daughter. But she's an adult, and I was also hoping . . ."

For more.

I took a deep breath and tried to calm the intoxicating rush of want. *Hoping.* The word throbbed, the two syllables of a heartbeat, proof of a life we could have if I'd let myself.

But could I open myself to it? When I became pregnant with Lulu and dropped out of my last year of university and hadn't gotten married to Paul, I'd given people something to talk about. At least that's what Ma said. I was too busy being pregnant and trying to figure out where to live and getting on with things to care much. But she was an eminent ob/gyn, and her own daughter had slipped up on birth control. I hadn't known anyone here gave a damn about me until she told me her colleagues had mentioned it.

Ma worked so hard to be exemplary. Now I could understand why: She was a single mother and she wasn't white. And I, the child she'd almost left behind in Taiwan, had done this to her, struck at the heart of what people knew about her: her work, her standing. Without it, what did she have here? No friendships, no family, no ties. Except flawed me.

But that was a long time ago. I had a job that I did well and my own reputation in the community, and Lulu was her own person forging her own path.

A few people might talk—they always did. It's why I told Kenji that I'd wanted some privacy when we started. But that wasn't the issue. The issue was that the one or two other people I'd dated after Paul hadn't mattered much to me. Kenji did.

Didn't that just make my stomach twist?

It was like I was afraid that people would see I cared. I'd have to admit to other people that I might have feelings for Kenji. That I'd been hoping for more this whole time, too.

I took a deep breath. "Okay," I said cautiously. "Let's try this. I am scared. Even though she talks a good game, Lulu will need time to get used to it. It's been a while, and I don't remember how to do any of this stuff." I gestured between us.

"You've been doing fine," he said, his voice low. Pleased.

My whole body blushed. I ducked my head. "But as for that date, I'm not a fancy kind of person. I don't want to have to, like, wear opera gloves or something."

He glanced around our motel room as a brief, illuminating smile came over his face. He was like a boy. It was both charming and alarming. But all he said was, "I will try to avoid making plans for us that involve you putting on gloves in summer as long as I don't have to wear an ascot." Kenji laughed at his own joke, bounding up energized and then seemed to remember he should play it cool. *God, he was so young.* He sat down again. "Should we try to see a show or a play or a movie or something?"

"I don't know what would be going on right now."

"Oh, Fontaine has a repertory theater festival going on with all these actors from Toronto. I don't know what repertory theater means, but it sounds classy and summery."

"Like the people who come out here to their cottages and go on wine tours."

"We could do a wine tour."

I finished putting on the rest of my clothing. "You're telling me the classy, nice things in town are the imports?"

"I'm an import."

"You're a real luxury."

I couldn't help myself, I moved the food to the night table and crawled right into his lap. Immediately his arms came around me, one hand splayed across my breast.

"I thought you'd try to fight me," he murmured, stroking me. I shivered. "I was prepared to play dirty."

"You're playing pretty dirty now," I said, squirming because of the things his hands were doing, but also because I felt guilty. For a minute I'd wanted to refuse him. I wanted to hide out and not have people comment on my life like they had before. Not have to worry.

I wish I could control what people thought of me.

The stray thought arrowed across my brain. Mind control was certainly more useful than glowing. Or even calling on lightning.

Kenji managed to unbutton my shirt and reach under it to cup my breast. We'd just had sex. More than once, if we were counting, but my body was clearly ready for another go. Unexpectedly, he pulled off the rest of my clothing and set me on my hands and knees on the bed. And then he put his face right there in my ass. I felt his teeth graze the soft undercurve of my butt and trail up. I whimpered, unable to move. "I don't understand what this is," he said, almost to himself. "I want you all the time. I'm so tired, I've slept so little I can't see straight. But I think of you constantly. Your face, your eyes, your ass, your breasts, your shoulders, your legs, your neck, your smile, your laugh. You. It's nothing but you and how much I want to be with you all the time."

I heard the swearing, then the crackle of a condom wrapper. In another moment I cried out as he pushed himself inside. And gods, I wanted it. His voice was close to my ear, more breath and heat than sound. I braced myself back into his thrusts, arching so he could go deeper. My wrists hurt from holding myself up so I let go and buried my face in the pillow. One of his arms came around to clasp me. I felt trapped—but only for a moment.

I pulled myself away and, still on all fours, turned my head to face him. He held his hands out, then up. I sat on my heels, conscious of how wet my body was from sex and lay him flat on his back and climbed on top of him.

His face looked young, overwhelmed. "This is what *I* want," I said before I positioned myself on top of him.

I'd spent so much time worried about his youth, how he wouldn't want me one day. How he could tear up my little heart like a piece of paper. But it wasn't that at all. *I* could break *him*. I could drain the life right out of him. Not that I wanted to, not that I ever wanted that to happen. I wanted to cradle him with my body, to feel him hold me. I wanted to cry at how he hadn't protected himself from me—how he should have guarded himself. But he hadn't, and it made me feel strange and wonderful at how generous he'd been to me.

So this was power. I was never sure I'd had it like this before. But from the way he watched me, from how he shuddered and gasped, I felt the power pulsing under my scalp, in my heels, in the tips of my fingers. I was wild with it, the pleasure and the joy, the furious fierceness of it.

I glowed with it, and he opened his eyes and saw it.

I could see him taking in the outline of it around me, the reflection of it in his eyes. Worse, I didn't want to deny it any more.

He knows.

I'd doubted it before, but now I knew. This could be nothing but magic.

Afterward, when I collapsed on top of him, sweaty and tired, ready to sleep even though we probably both had to go, he stirred.

"What was that?" he asked.

I rolled aside, shivering a little at the damp trail left by his cock sliding out of me and across my thigh.

"I don't know what's happening to me," he said.

I didn't say anything. *I* was happening, not only to him, but to me.

I got up and he groaned. "I don't know how you're standing after that," he muttered more to himself. "I don't have anything left in me. But to look at you is to want more and to see that light coming out of you again."

"It's my magic," I said, the words feeling strange in my mouth.

"Okay." He scrubbed his face with his hands and closed his eyes.

"That's a lot to take in. I thought something was just wrong with my eyes, especially since it was always during sex."

I laughed almost hysterically. "That's why I got my eyes checked."

Kenji blinked, still looking dazzled.

I said more gently, "Believe me, I know. I can barely believe it myself. But no, I don't know what it does or where it comes from. If I knew . . . well, I'd tell you."

He nodded. "I need to think about this," he said.

Like Lulu and Ma, and me, he wanted time to absorb it. Or maybe he was so drained that he couldn't think of anything at all. He seemed to nod off, so after some hesitation, I went into the bathroom to clean up.

Before I closed the door I heard him murmur sleepily, "So I *am* bewitched."

Bewitched. That was such a funny, old-fashioned word. I thought of old TV shows with blonde women and brooms and cartoon characters and sparkles. There was something so benign and rounded about the image that had nothing to do with the spiky power I felt scraping my insides raw.

I washed my hands over and over. No light emanated from them.

And yet, over the course of one orgasm I'd gone from skeptic to believer. Call it what you want: call it healing, call it wild, call it power. But there was no denying something was there. I was bewitching because I had a glow. It was inside me, and Kenji had seen something. It was powerful, and it was growing.

I looked in the mirror and said out loud again the words I'd had trouble with before. "It's *my* magic."

♦ 9 ♦

POWER CHANGED ME.

It made me sit up straighter when I was driving. I strode down the street instead of walking with my head down. In the guest chair in an office at the bank for a meeting that I'd put off for at least three months, I listened for a while to Gordy Maclaren, the mortgage specialist, and I thought, *I could zap him*, while he droned on about interest rates.

I swear I felt my fingers tingle.

Gordy had been two years ahead of me at school. He'd played defense for the school hockey team. My best friend, Jen, had a crush on him, and he was handsome enough in that blocky sandy-haired, white boy way. I had never entertained any hopes, because it seemed too ambitious to like a star hockey player. But today, I leaned forward and cut him off just as he was about to launch into another paragraph. I watched him gulp nervously as I made him agree to refinance my mortgage at a much lower rate and smile dazedly at me as I rose to leave, having signed the paperwork.

When I went to the grocery store late that night after a clinic delivery, I flat out turned down a man when he asked for my number without saying I was seeing someone, without trying to soften the blow, without blinking once. He started to protest, foolish idiot, and I thought, *I could turn him to stone.*

As the curse left my mind, he stopped talking, stopped moving. I plucked a box of cereal off the shelf and left him there.

I filled my cart with ice cream and thick cuts of red meat and green vegetables and energy drinks. I couldn't explain what was happening, because maybe nothing was happening. The week had passed without accidents, or electrocution. But I could summon the power or snuff it out, and I knew it. I was always swirling with energy. I was causing turmoil. I was powerful. I made a young cashier blush when I briefly touched his warm hand when he gave me my change. I made the shopping carts behind me crash. I caused the wind to whip up suddenly so that I could free my hair from its ponytail and let it rise electrified in the air. I slept badly all week and woke up from dreams of calling down lightning.

I didn't need rest anyway.

Lulu was still up when I got home from the store, sitting at the kitchen table writing something on her phone. She was so absorbed in it, she hardly looked away from her writing as she got up to help me put away groceries.

When her eyes finally did come up, she blinked once or twice. "You look different."

I *felt* different. Maybe I should have been more worried about the changes in me.

"Your hair's a mess," she added.

Ah, nothing like your children to make you feel less goddess-like.

"It was windy. What are you writing?"

"Notes and lists of things I have to get done." Her voice became absent-minded again. Then her eyes jerked up. "Wait. Something else is going on with you. You've been acting strange for a while. What is it?"

I hesitated. But I'd always tried to be honest with her. "I started seeing someone. Kenji. I started seeing Kenji."

Lulu looked astonished for a moment. When she finally did speak, her voice was a little tight. "Well, good for you. I really didn't expect you to—I didn't think you'd do anything about it until . . ."

Until after she'd left.

I shifted a little in my seat. She had pushed me to date. But as with her excitement about the healing magic of the Wus, the reality of my dating was probably different from the idea she'd encouraged, especially since a few weeks ago I'd seemed so reluctant. I got up to get the cereal and poured myself a bowl.

Apparently, I wasn't so powerful in face of my daughter. Maybe the Wus canceled each other out.

I crunched hard on the flakes.

"Well, I think it's cool, Mom!" Lulu said, a little too cheerily.

"We're going out to dinner next week," I told her.

"Great!"

"Somewhere nice."

She nodded and put her eyes on her notebook.

Then, mostly to change the subject, I said, "Lulu, we haven't talked a lot about the magic. What do you think of the powers our branch of Wus are supposed to have?"

She looked surprised and maybe a little relieved that I didn't want to gush about my new boyfriend. "Well, all families have their stories and legends. Like my friend Stacey's family always says they're distantly related to Russian royalty. Or Eliza's mom says all the women in her family have a sixth sense."

I swirled the cereal around. "For me growing up, the legend was always Taiwan. This was before Internet. We received letters in thin blue envelopes and got up in the middle of night to receive long distance phone calls."

"Long distance?"

"You had to dial 0 to get the operator and—anyway. So few of my friends knew where Taiwan was—or, if they were from mainland China, a lot of them tried to claim it was the same country, which made A-mà mad when I told her. If we were told to do a group project about where our family was from I always had to work alone, drawing that red and blue flag with the sun on it. So it felt like a legend to me. We never did visit, although Ma used to promise me we'd go when I was a teen."

Before I knew it, I was older, and I had a child.

Oh, sometimes Ma told stories about her childhood, especially when comparing hers to mine and Lulu's, but she'd rarely called her mother or her older brothers or even the sister who'd sent us the photographs.

"She's like that about my father, too," I mused. "And of course, every time I'd tried to ask about my dad, she'd gaze at some point beyond my shoulder, as if he were standing right there, and grimaced. In fact, until the photos had arrived, we'd almost never talked about her life in Taiwan."

Or the magic. Even now, we weren't discussing it. Or maybe we were.

"I've seen that look on her face. It's a little creepy. Do you think . . . he did something to her? And that's why she left?"

I blinked. In all my years of wondering about my father, I'd been so focused on trying to finding out why he'd left *me* that I had never considered that maybe he'd hurt Ma.

I sagged, any high I'd felt now gone. Maybe I'd been too self-involved to see what was in front of me. Maybe that's why Ma was the way she was.

Lulu rinsed her bowl, and when she turned back to me, her eyes were calm again. Detached. "I guess you could learn a lot more about Taiwan on the Internet now," she said, seeming ready to move on. Let her old mother stay in the kitchen bathed in nostalgia. "But the best person to ask about more family stuff would still be A-mà."

"It's hard for me to ask her questions about that. She never answers me." I heard the childish whine in my voice.

"If you really want to know, I don't see how you can avoid pushing it."

"But then she'll ask questions about me." About Kenji. "She'll sniff it on me, like she sniffs out every secret," I muttered.

But Ma didn't say anything unusual when we arrived on Friday—well, nothing worse than what she usually said. I wore a skirt and a sleeveless blouse, because it was hot. It was always hot lately. My mother had always warned me against baring my arms because she thought too much flesh and muscle in the arms of a woman was unseemly—*ugly*, she said in English.

But if she didn't want to see my guns, she'd have to turn on the air conditioning. I wanted my shoulders out, my skin free. I was tired of feeling warm and overheated. And I really wanted to discuss the Wu powers.

Instead of telling me I should cover up my unsightly arms she crinkled her brow. "You look . . . nice," she said.

That managed to completely derail me. I didn't know how to respond to that.

"At least it's not jeans again," she added.

Belatedly I remembered my manners. "Thanks."

It turned out it was my daughter, flesh of my flesh, who ended up betraying me.

"Mom's started seeing someone," Lulu said, all sing-song-y as Ma reached for more greens.

My mother's eyes darted at Lulu, then me. "Who is this?"

I did my best not to glare at my daughter. It would have been nice to have waited until after our meal—and maybe a few months later.

"His name is Kenji."

"The brother of the vice provost," Ma said flatly. "The younger man."

Wow, her memory was sharp. Maybe that was another Wu power I'd get? Probably not.

"I told you this would be a mistake. But you had to go and get together with that boy."

"Ma."

"And your daughter's not even gone away to school yet."

"We can't all be like you and wait until our kids are retired and possibly dead before we start dating."

She sucked in a breath. "This is not funny, Leeann. I don't want you making another mistake."

"Well, I'm not likely to get pregnant again seeing as I'm apparently in perimenopause."

That stopped Ma for a moment. "That's early."

"It's what my doctor thinks. When did yours arrive?"

She glowered at me. "You aged me prematurely. You and your recklessness."

Lulu stood up. "Stop it."

My mother looked at her, and realized what she'd said. "Lulu—"

"I am not a mistake."

"You aren't," my mother said, chastened. Her eyes darted to me as if asking for help. I didn't feel like giving it. "But your mother—"

"Is a grown woman. She was an adult when she had me."

"And I can fight my own battles," I said quietly.

Lulu bit her lip. "Mom, I'm sorry. I shouldn't have brought up your boyfriend." She turned her shoulder away from my mother. "I just . . . I didn't expect A-mà to be so . . ."

I understood. She'd wanted to tease me—maybe needle me a little, too. Maybe she'd sensed this thing with Kenji was different for me. But my baby had gotten hurt. I pulled her long body into my arms and tried to cradle her the way I had when she was tiny.

"I never said you were a mistake, Lulu," Ma said fiercely.

"Stop talking, Ma. Stop it."

"She has more than once," Lulu mumbled, her voice muffled. "Over the years, so many times in so many different ways. I don't want to hear it anymore."

"Lulu, this has nothing to do with you, and everything to do with your grandma and me. C'mon, kiddo," I said. "Maybe we should go."

"How can you separate it out, though?" She turned to my mother. "What you wanted for my mom and my entire existence are not two independent things that you can pack up in two boxes. They're part of the same whole. I am so damn tired of this."

For the first time, Ma looked almost stricken. Her hands opened then shut again. She looked like she was trying to summon a magic that wouldn't come.

I stood up with Lulu and took her hand. It was funny. I'd wished often enough that my mother would feel remorse for her harsh words, and that I'd be able to witness it. I had wanted to make her regret all the digs about how I could have finished medical school, how much more money or job security I'd have by now. But now that it had happened, now that I could see her features twist with regret, I didn't feel good about it. Especially because I knew Lulu was also taking deep breaths so she wouldn't cry in front of my mother.

Ma turned her own face away because she didn't like her own tears to be seen, and I thought about how they were very much alike.

I sighed. The argument between them—between all of us—had been simmering for years, but something had tipped the balance. Maybe it was me. Maybe my power had protected me from a confrontation about Kenji, but I didn't like this alternative very much.

I should probably try to be mature about this. "Lulu, your grandmother loves you very much, and even though it does seem like it's about you, it really is about me. And Ma, Lulu loves you too. Which is why you saying this hurts her, right now especially. It isn't long before Lulu moves. Maybe we should . . . try to make the most of our time."

I sighed. The words came out stiff, and neither of them would look at each other.

"Let's take a little break, and we can see about next week."

"But—" Ma said. She opened her mouth and closed it. "We haven't finished dinner."

I looked at the leafy ribbons of greens on my plate. We'd probably be getting takeout on the way back, but I didn't mention that part. Oddly, I didn't want to make her feel worse.

Ma said desperately, "I have another box to open. Some of my aunt's things."

I could see Lulu's shoulders loosen a bit. In truth, I was desperate to see that box myself. But Lulu's posture straightened again. "No, thank you," she said, her voice icy.

Whoa.

"Thank you for dinner, A-mà."

She stood up and went to the door for her shoes. After a minute, I followed. My mother did not.

Lulu took the keys from me and sat in the driver's seat. "Don't try to defend her," she said. "She has no right."

I didn't know what to say. Maybe for all these years I should have fought harder and first, but I'd always figured it was just me that Ma was sniping at. My mother always praised Lulu. She was proud of her granddaughter. Their relationship had always seemed so much easier, so much less fraught. But of course, I had neglected the fact that I couldn't just absorb all of my mother's disappointment like a sponge and wipe it all away, leave the table clean for my daughter to eat at it.

"She was raised differently from us," I said.

"She's lived here for 40 years!"

"I know it's not an excuse. It's just she has a different idea of what she can expect from me and what she can say. You're not a mistake, baby. You are the best thing that ever happened to me—and to her. She isn't lying when she says that."

"Aren't you the best thing that ever happened to her? You'd think her own kid would be."

I probably wasn't. I had no idea if I'd even been wanted. Probably not, given I'd been left with a relative so long ago. The possibility that my father had hurt my mother also festered in my brain. Ma could have had a better career, a marriage, better, cleaner, more obedient, more intelligent children if she hadn't had me.

But then neither of us would have Lulu.

I didn't doubt Ma loved me on most days. But we'd both made that love hard to earn and hard to hold.

"I think as you get older things get more ambivalent," I said cautiously. "Even your biggest joys are a little shot through with sorrow. It's not that she doesn't love you. Her life has been complicated."

And I hadn't bothered to ask about any of those parts except the ones that related to me.

I could see Lulu rolling her eyes in the reflection of the windshield.

"Sometimes I don't like how you talk to each other," Lulu said quietly.

Not just how Ma spoke to me, but how I responded to my mother, too. My gut hurt a little as I thought of how long I'd been making Lulu uncomfortable, all because I was stuck in time being a surly teen around my mother.

Lulu continued. "It worries me because when I go you won't really have each other. A-mà will have no one."

I was silent. Lulu was right. My mother didn't have friends really. She had colleagues and patients and respect—and probably fear. I had all that and friends.

And I have Kenji now. The thought sparked, a small filament in my head. "You'll still talk to us," I said uncertainly. "You'll text and we can Zoom. It's not that far away. I'll visit you so often your roommates will give me a nickname, like Cool Asian Mom."

"Stop joking. Don't you get it? You need each other! We all need each other! I know you want the magic, but it's not the point. It's nothing without all of us together."

"I'm sorry, Lulu." She wasn't wrong. "I'll try harder to be . . . civil around A-mà when you're around. And after you've left for school. Not just because of the magic."

Lulu sighed. "I wish you could just be kinder to each other and not dwell on the past, but that's impossible. At least find things to talk about. I know it's not that simple, but you should have so much in common."

I shook my head even though I knew she was right. "Honestly, Lulu, that may be part of the problem."

10

"CAN I ASK YOU something?" I said to Parisa.

We were sitting in the shade on the campus lawn. We'd both brought our laptops but neither of us had bothered sliding them out of our bags. I had paperwork to fill out. Parisa had classes to prep for. It was too hot to move, and both of us were picking at the salads we'd bought at the cafe.

Work had resumed on the clock tower. It made me a little nervous to see it. The air shimmered with heat, appearing to make the limestone bend. Too easy to imagine the whole structure toppling.

Maybe I could do it.

I banished the stray thought as soon as it came. *The Wus are healers*, I reminded myself sternly.

But I made sure I sat facing away from the sight of scaffolding and workers traipsing along the narrow paths of wood and work even though I could still hear the shouts and the occasional startling bang.

Parisa's eyebrows went up. "It's been a long time since you've needed any advice from me."

"It's not about work. It's . . . personal."

"Must be a doozy if you're giving me such a lead up."

This was the point where I should have told her about Kenji. I wish I had. After all, it was his questions that had made me wonder if I could talk to people other than my own family about the magic. But for some reason, talking about my relationship with him still felt too private, too hopeful, too . . . foolish. So I shared this instead. "I think I may be entering perimenopause."

She considered that. "That's a little early but not ridiculous."

I nodded. "Yeah. But I'm not completely sure that's what it is. Did you . . . have any unusual symptoms?"

Parisa looked at me thoughtfully. "I felt unusual—no, I *feel* unusual, present tense. Because I'm still not quite in menopause."

"You aren't?" She hadn't been able to stop herself from talking when she'd first begun. The hot flashes, the irritability, the inability to sleep. Even her sense of smell seemed to have heightened.

"I can't say for sure, but I think it's been nine years."

"Nine fucking years!" I yelped earning me reprimanding look from one of the construction workers walking down the path.

"And that's why I stopped talking about it around year five. I finally decided to resign myself to feeling like I was coming out of my skin until I was done with this. I mean, obviously it's different for everyone. But I haven't felt normal, like myself, in a really long time. I've been forgetful and on edge and . . . I don't know. This summer has been especially terrible." She fanned herself ineffectually and tried to smile, but when I looked at her more closely, I realized something was off.

"I can't believe you haven't said anything more! We could have commiserated. I would've bought you chocolate chip mint ice cream for the office freezer. And a spoon! A really sturdy one."

She looked directly at me. "Honestly, some of the things happening to me at this point seem almost hard to believe. Besides, it's not like you tell me every single thing happening to you. We're alike that way. We need time to process."

That was true. I thought guiltily of Kenji. Still. "I tell you everything that counts. Eventually."

She nudged me. "So, what's up with you, then? Are you getting the usual fun stuff associated with *the change*?"

"Maybe? I was late last time." I hesitated. "I haven't been getting hot flashes, per se."

Parisa waited. She was used to clients circling around telling her their symptoms.

So was I. I should have known better.

"I went to the doctor about this already." I stared at my hands, which were not doing anything magical at this moment, but it helped to not look Parisa in the eye as I said this next part. "I seem to be . . . glowing."

"Oh, I've noticed that look about you. I just thought maybe you'd started seeing someone," Parisa said.

I stopped. "No, that's not what I mean." Even thought it was true. Oh gods, I really needed to talk to her about Kenji. But this was more urgent. "I'm being literal. I'm causing light to appear. Like from my hands. Or at least I think I am."

Parisa regarded me steadily for a moment.

That was it. She thought I had finally gone bananas, just like I'd always threatened. Her best friend's brain boiled in a stew of hormones. Such a pity in one so almost-young.

"When does the light appear?" she asked after a moment.

"What?"

"The glow, the luminescence, the light saber force thing. Is there a pattern?"

I tried to think. "I don't know. I don't control it. It's sometimes when I'm working. Or . . ." I was going work up to the sex, and the time with Lulu and Ma around the kitchen table.

"Anything else?" Parisa pressed.

I exhaled. "The other night, I started sleepwalking. I woke up in my backyard. And I've been having nightmares about lightning that comes from my fingers." I swallowed. "I dreamed of it the night before it hit the tower."

Parisa thought for a minute. She didn't seem to be reaching for her phone to call the hospital to admit me to the psychiatric ward though, so I concentrated on breathing.

"Is there any of this in the family?" she asked.

"You mean . . . dementia?"

"No. Like unexplained things."

I thought of my great-aunt. "The other night, Lulu and my mom and I all started to glow. Together. But Lulu's in denial and my mother's keeping closemouthed for now. My mother said that the Wus may have—" I dropped my voice to a whisper. "Magic."

I held my breath because for a while, Parisa didn't speak. Then she nodded. "I had a feeling about you."

I blinked. This was not the reaction I'd expected. I'd been braced for fear, pity, even laughter. But Parisa calmly accepting my announcement unnerved me. I licked my suddenly very dry lips. "You don't sound surprised."

Parisa slanted a look at me. Then she glanced down at her own hands. "Why do you think I encouraged you to go into this field all those years ago? I don't go around befriending all my clients, you know."

I opened my mouth and closed it again. Parisa laughed softly.

"You told me last time that you come from a long line of midwives, and you know that I do, too. There are always funny stories in families like ours passed down from the women, especially the older ones."

"Not my family."

"No. Not in yours. And because my boys are more interested in video games than anything else, I suppose that will be what happens to my family stories, too."

She paused. Parisa, her grandmother and mom and aunts and uncles had all immigrated here from Iran, and she was close to them. It wasn't always easy, keeping up with a large family like that, but part of me envied her connection to her history and culture.

"We aren't observant, you know. But we still had to be careful when my grandmother whispered blasphemous things among the women, like that we were descended from a water goddess from Persian mythology."

I looked at my longtime friend again, trying to see the traces of it in her. She was sitting on the lawn wearing a cotton blouse and divided skirt. She looked like an ordinary woman. Tired, pretty, with big, pensive eyes.

"There's a lot that can't be explained through medicine," she said. "I'm sure you've seen it. I know I have. I mean, okay, I'm a nurse, and my husband's a neurologist, so I'd also recommend you get your eyes checked—"

"Did that."

"Good. And maybe ask for a referral to make sure you don't have other health issues. But if you can rule those out, then maybe there's something more to this." Again, she regarded me steadily and I could swear I glimpsed the goddess in her.

I breathed out. "You're not worried about me? About this? I come to you with a strange story about things that could be in my head. And you're like, *maybe you're magical*?"

"I trust my intuition," Parisa said. "Okay, maybe I'm a *bit* worried, but you're hardly the only one who may be having a breakdown this summer, so the way I figure it we're all screwed no matter what."

I snorted. "You're a comfort."

"My clients say so." She gave me a beatific smile.

I nodded. "A Persian water goddess, huh?"

"What?" Parisa said, finally giving up and balling up her napkin to chuck into her uneaten salad. "You aren't the only one who's magical around here."

♦ 11 ♦

THE CURRENT RUNNING THROUGH my body was not the only strange thing happening this summer, but I couldn't figure out how to control it, and what it all meant. I didn't have time to figure it out, because one of my first-time clients went into labor unexpectedly. By two the next morning, I regretted that I hadn't gotten more shut-eye, even if the fear I'd sleepwalk again and have those oddly draining dreams kept me from resting easily.

As Amira's baby's head was delivered, I allowed it to extend. A quick check indicated the cord wasn't around its neck.

Aside from the baby's slightly early arrival, things had gone smoothly, if slowly. We were at the birthing center with plenty of backup. It should have been a nice, calm night.

"Is this normal?" Amira's partner practically shouted in my ear.

"We're just waiting for the delivery of the anterior shoulder," I said, wincing. "I know it's been a long process, but you'll see your son very soon."

"I've had a lot of energy drinks!" the father-to-be said loudly.

"You've mentioned," I replied.

I hoped his jitters would calm down enough for him to cut the cord without stabbing his wife, me, or himself.

"Had to stay awake for this. Been having trouble sleeping."

You and me both. "All right, Amira. Are you ready?"

Amira huffed, her brow sweaty and nodded, teeth gritted.

"You're doing amazing. The baby's coming out."

"I see him!" Amira's partner screeched. "He's out! He's all the way out." Then, quiet for the first time since I'd met him, he said, "I wish my mother was alive to see this."

The baby bellowed almost immediately. The dad started yelling again. Amira cried. I waited a short time before clamping the cord to allow more blood to transfer from the placenta to the baby. In that few minutes, I managed to create that small space of quiet in my head. Amira had a healthy baby. I'd done good work.

Maybe the extra few minutes would calm the new father down. But he came at me a little too quickly and I put my hands out instinctively.

That's when the glow came out. Even then, he didn't seem to see it. He stared over my shoulder as if he'd seen a ghost behind me. Then he began swaying suspiciously. He said something that sounded a little like *You're not real*, or maybe *Unreal!,* but I wasn't sure. All I know is even I felt something for a moment before he hit the floor.

I put my hands down and breathed hard.

Had I done that?

But this wasn't the time to stand around and analyze everything. At least when the new father had crumpled he had the courtesy to knock his head on the wall instead of on the bed, or Amira or me. I pressed the call button, cut the cord myself, and put the squirming baby on his mother's chest. Amira cried harder, but it was hard to tell if it was because she was happy about her son or worried about the blessedly silent but unconscious man on the floor. Probably a little of both.

"You have a healthy baby," I said. "And as for your partner, this happens a lot. We're just going to deliver the placenta."

Almost immediately she and the baby quieted. There was nothing except Amira's shuddering breaths, the beeping monitors, and the shuffling of a nurse coming in and out as he dealt with Amira's unconscious spouse.

Still, I told the nurse quietly that it might be a good idea to run some tests on the husband in case it was something more than nerves.

I finished up with Amira, made sure she was settled, and headed home in the early morning to take a nap.

Had I done something to that man?

I couldn't even think. I'd never felt this tired before in my life. To top it off, this evening, I was supposed to go out to a fancy dinner with my boyfriend. With sluggish fingers, I set my alarm for an hour before I was set to leave, closed my blackout blinds, turned on the fan, and settled myself down for what I expected to be a couple of hours of tossing and turning.

Instead, I fell deeply and darkly into a dream.

At first it felt good to be burrowed in this vast cocoon. But I kept hearing sound, waves of voices swirling together, a thick aural layer pulling me down, murmuring, lapping at me. Sometimes a word or sentence would try to reach out to my ankle, my hand, like water, a sudden advance, a retreat. I tried to ignore them.

I felt the touch on my shoulder, warm yet somehow insubstantial. A breath. I opened my eye. It was my great-aunt, the one in the mysterious photograph, the one who I'd thought I'd caught a glimpse of in Andrea's yard on that day I finally decided to give in to Kenji.

"Yi-beh?" I asked slowly, the title coming to my lips easily. My voice was a little girl's. I was small. And I knew the woman in front of me.

"They want to leave," Yi-beh said. Her voice was so full of love and doom.

"Who?"

"The dead."

I shook my head and tried to stretch myself to my full height, but I was practically a baby.

I felt so weak. Being beside her as she absorbed more and more of my essence made her stronger. She was becoming more real and bright in front of my eyes.

Now there was too much light coming from her. I couldn't see her clearly even when I shaded my eyes and blinked. Was she speaking English? Was I speaking Taiwanese? I didn't even care. Because the more I tried to see her, the more my vision was obscured by grief, the shine of tears that couldn't seem to fall from my eyes. My throat felt full and heavy.

This is another dream.

I tried to say it, but I couldn't open my mouth. But as if I'd spoken aloud, Yi-beh said, "Yes, you're dreaming now.

That's where we can travel. That's where we can come to your side."

The light grew bright and terrible. I cowered from it. I couldn't see Yi-beh's face anymore.

"Mei mei," she said—that was me. *How did I know that?* How could I remember her with such an ache when I hadn't even known she existed for so many years? I needed to hold her hand. She'd always kept me safe. She couldn't leave me now. "Mei mei, we want to get out. Help me get out."

As she drained me with her light, I felt loss, infinite loss that I hadn't known her, that I didn't remember how it felt to be carried by her, her thin arms tight around my chubby body, that I didn't recall how it felt to touch her face and ask why she had so many wrinkles, that I didn't remember the laugh she always tried to cover up because of her crooked teeth. I'd never been to Taiwan to visit her gravestone.

I'd always thought I was one of the lucky ones: I didn't know my relatives enough to mourn them. I'd never felt their loss. But now the grief, not only for the dead, but for all I'd never know about them, pulled and pulled at me. It intensified until I could feel the hollow ache of it in my bones.

A part of my mind was screaming at me to wake up, and I felt my physical body struggling as her face twisted for a moment as if in anger. But the rest of me was frantic to keep her there. Tears pulled at my whole small body. "Yi-beh," I said in my little voice. "Don't leave me again."

But she was becoming too bright again. I screamed with the force of a child being torn from the only parent she ever knew and wrenched my eyes open only to find myself sobbing and out of breath.

I was in my bedroom.

I'd fallen asleep. I'd had that dream. But it wasn't dangerous, like I thought it was. I'd seen my great-aunt, and I'd felt an inexplicable love and yearning for a ghost.

I breathed in trying to calm myself. But my heart leapt when my alarm started ringing.

No. Oh gods. I was supposed to go out with Kenji in an hour. How was I going to settle?

I scrambled out of bed and caught a glimpse of myself in my mirror.

I did not glow. I felt drained and wan, and my throat still ached from all the tears I'd cried in my dream that hadn't been released in real life.

Even my bones hurt, as if I'd suffered a real loss, when it had only been a dream of someone I didn't remember.

I stumbled to the shower, hoping to wash away the heavy feeling, but it didn't help. I couldn't get my mind off the fact that Yi-beh had been here, I'd seen her, and I'd forced her to leave by waking. It was my fault. She was gone, and I couldn't remember her. I hadn't for so many years. I'd abandoned her ghost.

I'd betrayed her.

I heaved another shuddering breath. Tonight should have been exciting. I was going out with someone who made me feel like I was fascinating and sexy and magical. I was powerful around him.

But right now, I felt like a child overwhelmed by recognition and loss. This was the connection I'd always wanted, that feeling of knowing something about my past.

My hands were unsteady as I applied foundation and powder. I dropped the brush in the sink and saw the white porcelain take on an almost human blush before I dashed it away with water and soap.

I stared at myself in the mirror. I usually didn't wear makeup—long and strange hours didn't make for much opportunity. By the time I was done, I gazed at myself, and I didn't seem like me. I looked like I was trying too hard.

"Mom?" Lulu knocked on the door before opening it. "Are you getting ready for your first big date?"

I nodded.

She took in my grief-ravaged face. "What's wrong? Are you worried? Mom, it's okay. You look festive!"

I burst into tears.

"Oh my God, Mom. You're fine! Gorgeous. I swear. I . . . don't think I've seen you cry before." She cleared her throat. "You're going to spoil your makeup."

"It looks terrible anyway," I said. Somehow admitting it made it a little better.

"Stop! We'll wash your face. It'll be okay."

Lulu sat me down on the toilet lid and scrubbed my cheeks and nose hard. And I just let her. Then she pursed her lips and started to do something to my eyes.

"Not too much," she muttered. "I don't want to make you feel weird and anxious."

"It's too late," I said holding my stomach. "I'm that way no matter what anyone does."

"It's just one teeny date," she said, mistaking the reason for my unease. "If you don't like being out with him, you can call me. Or just leave. But I know you haven't gone out with anyone in a long time. Look how happy the idea of it made you last week."

"You noticed that, huh?"

She put down the eye pencil. "I'm not saying that you never had confidence before, but lately you've seemed able to bust through walls or leap over buildings. Call down lightning." Lulu flinched at her own choice of words, but she tried to continue. "Which is awesome. But remember, you're great no matter how he is."

I attempted a smile. "Thanks, kid."

"Have fun, you know. Get to know him a little before you let things happen."

Oh, well. Too late for that.

I was pretty sure she was this close to asking me if I had condoms. I had to stop her. "I had a weird dream just now," I said. "I saw my great-aunt. The one in the picture."

She cocked her head as she picked up some lipstick.

"Not just a strange dream. An—unsettling one. I talked to her, Lulu. She said—"

I blinked. What had she said? Why couldn't I remember?

I took in a deep breath. Yi-beh had been trying to tell me something important and I'd already forgotten.

"Mom?"

I jumped up and nearly got lipstick in my eye as Lulu pulled her hand back. "I need to remember, I need to write this down." I streaked out of the bathroom and plowed through my room looking for a piece of paper, or my phone. Anything.

"Mom."

Lulu was standing behind me as I tried to get it all down. The murmuring, the dead, the fact that I'd known I wasn't awake the whole time. Yi-beh. "She told me they were trying to get through. They can travel in dreams."

"Who can travel in dreams?"

"The dead."

Lulu stared at me.

I looked up and saw myself in the mirror. My eyes were huge and dark, making my face look pale. At least Lulu managed to cover up the fact I'd been crying. My hair stood up wildly. My upper lip had a dark streak of red but my lower hadn't yet been done. It looked like I'd taken a bite out of something and left it to bleed.

I'd strewn clothing and hair brushes around my room in my search of something to write with. I wasn't dressed.

The doorbell rang.

"Dammit," I said. "He's early."

"Mom, I don't think you're okay. You're acting weird. Maybe you should postpone."

"No, no. I'm all right. I just have to get this down and finish my hair and my lipstick and get myself organized. And into a dress."

Lulu watched me. I'd distressed her. I hated that look—hated that I'd had cause to make her anxious about me.

"I'll go down and get the door," she said.

"No." I didn't want her to meet Kenji this way. But what choice did I have? I swallowed hard and took a breath. "I'm sorry, Lulu, I was really unsettled by the dream. You know how it can be to wake up like that. Especially in the middle of the evening. I'd appreciate it if you'd let Kenji in and tell him I'm almost ready."

There. The fact that I managed to string together a series of coherent sentences reassured her. I gave her a wan smile.

Lulu went downstairs. I heard her answer the door, and I looked again at the notes I'd made. A mess. Just like this room. No wonder my kid thought her mother was losing her grip on reality.

I slunk back into the bathroom and finished putting on the lipstick. I combed my hair out and went back to my closet. Over the past few days, I'd run through my limited choice of outfits. I picked out a navy blue sheath that I wore everywhere remotely fancy: New Year's parties, weddings.

But now, I grabbed a yellow sundress I'd bought on impulse. It was brighter, much more colorful than my other clothes. It felt light in this hot weather, probably because the straps were mere wisps, and it dipped low enough to show a hint of what little cleavage I had. I pulled it on and checked myself in the mirror.

No puffiness, no red eye. Lulu had wrought a miracle. No outward signs of my earlier . . . disturbance.

I went downstairs and found Kenji and Lulu in the living room.

Lulu appeared serene, although the worry still twitched at the corner of her eyes. Kenji, with his elbows on his knees as he sat on the couch, looked solemn but respectful. I could imagine him listening to his students that way, taking them seriously because they deserved it.

But then he glanced up—stood up—and his eyes warmed to something more.

I still felt nervous and oddly bereft from my dream, but it did me good to be able to see him, to be reminded of my real life, of real feelings and not this strange disorienting time I'd been having lately. Kenji kept staring and my chest loosened a little with the warmth of it. I understood why people sometimes grabbed their skirts or put their hands in their pockets. It was to keep them from reaching out and holding too tightly to things that made them feel too much.

I drew in a slow breath and gazed steadily back at him, handsome in slim pants and a crisp shirt. His dark hair was a little tousled as if he'd been running his hands through it. As if I'd been running my hands through it.

I could let him ground me.

We stood looking at each other in silence as if we'd never seen each other before. Perhaps we hadn't. These were different versions of ourselves than we were used to.

Lulu cleared her throat. "Well, have fun, you two," she said.

She made a shooing motion with our hands to get us to move. No doubt it was uncomfortable to watch her mother and a strange man ogle each other. She peeked at me again to make sure I was all right. Satisfied, she started pushing us to the door, pausing only to let us collect our shoes. To Kenji she said, "No drinking and driving. Have her back before midnight because she needs her beauty sleep. Hurt her and I'll hurt you worse."

She stood on the porch and waved.

Kenji opened the door for me then slid around to the front. He seemed to come back to himself when he slammed the car door. "She meant every word, didn't she?" he asked, his voice rueful.

"Yep."

"I like your kid."

"I do, too."

He shifted gears to back out of the driveway. "That's a great dress. I've never seen you in one before."

I took a deep breath to relax myself and inhaled the scent of warm car. My heart still hurt from before—I kept rubbing the spot—but I had to put it out of my mind. Dream or no dream, tonight would be fine despite the sense of loss that had washed over me. I wanted it to be good for Kenji.

"I fancied myself up for our big night," I said, trying to keep it light. "Speaking of new, is this car Andrea's?"

"No," he glanced a little sideways. Was he blushing? "I bought it. Figured I should have some wheels if I was going to live in town. Andrea's been doing a lot better since your last visit, so I'm going to get my own apartment, too—or rent a house. Once I get more settled."

The word *settled* hung in the air between us. I'd never wanted to trap someone into taking care of me. I had enough of that feeling with my mother.

He glanced over at me once again. "Are you all right?" he asked carefully.

"Why wouldn't I be?"

"You seem to be not quite yourself."

I tried a smile. "Nerves," I said. "It's not often I live the high life."

He let that pass.

A few more minutes went by in silence as we made our way slowly downtown. "We're here," Kenji said with some relief.

A parking spot seemed to magically open up right on Main Street. Kenji once again strode around to get the door and helped me out. I swayed into him a little and his eyes kindled once again as his body seemed to close around mine. "I don't mean to freak you out more, but you look beautiful," he whispered.

"So do you," I murmured back.

He laughed, and I suddenly felt a little less off-kilter.

He slid his hand to the small of my back, his fingers dipping low briefly, just enough for me to feel that tingle of awareness before they came to a more correct position in the middle of my back. Not that it stopped my skin from transmitting signals to my knees and breasts. My breath quickened. If I could concentrate on this moment, then I could at least forget about the dream, the draining feeling of loss that seemed to settle in my bones like the cold on a winter day.

He led me into the restaurant and murmured his name to the hostess, and we were led to a table. I tried to take in my surroundings, chiding myself that I should at least remember so I could tell Parisa about the place. I'd never been taken anywhere as fancy as this before. Sprezzatura was new-ish, with glamorous dim lighting and sparkling glass and silverware. All the customers seemed to speak in discreet voices, like they were whispering *Money, money, money* to each other.

Suddenly my sundress seemed flimsy and overbright. I wanted to be a small child with Yi-beh, back in the soothing light of nowhere.

As I shrank back, I recognized a few people at the tables, some university types, one of the ob/gyns from the hospital. No one I knew well. I felt like they were watching me, like they could see all the power and weird residual feeling from my dream that I wore so badly.

Kenji touched my back and looked at me inquiringly.

Right. I should relax, have a glass of wine, enjoy the food, try to have a good time so that Kenji, who'd gone to all this trouble, would have a good time. I shouldn't be longing to be sucked back into a dream.

After we sat down, our server Kelly came to our table. "Leeann!" she said delighted. "Oh my goodness, it's wonderful to see you."

Kelly had been one of my first clients. I remembered everyone from that overwhelming, strange, and wonderful rookie year. I'd helped deliver both her children.

"Heather'll be doing her first year of high school, and Jonathan's going into grade seven now. I can't believe how quickly the time passes."

"Which school?" Kenji asked.

"Prince Edward."

"Oh, I'm starting there in September. I'll be teaching English. Maybe he'll be one of my students."

Kelly looked back and forth between us, delighted. She put her hand to her heart and breathlessly asked what we'd like to order.

It probably wasn't the romantic dinner Kenji had imagined, but we were showered with all the nurturing that Kelly could muster for people who had been and would be responsible for her kids. She came back with a tuna carpaccio amuse bouche and a complimentary glass of wine for me—Kenji had taken Lulu's warning to heart and kept to seltzer. Kelly had evidently told the other staff, too. The chef, who was Kelly's sister-in-law, came out to meet us. A smattering of extra small plates arrived at our table. Fried olives, two ravioli light and delicate as clouds, cauliflower bites crisped in a spice blend that had me reaching for water with one hand and another helping with the other.

In between courses, Kelly showed us pictures of Jonathan, a gangly, mischievous-looking kid who was obsessed with his bike, and Heather, who cast a knowing, very almost-done-with-junior-high look at the camera. Kenji held my hand and beamed at me with something like pride.

I couldn't help but melt a little at that. Between Kelly's attention, Kenji's smile, and the generous glasses of wine, I began to feel calmer. It was easier to ignore that last aching remnant of my dream at the back of my throat. To think that before today, I'd worried about the gossip. People were talking about us, but these weren't whispers coming from the tables. The staff kept up a low background murmur, polite and warm and anxious to please, curious enough to gawk. They weren't doing it because I was dating the vice provost's brother who was younger than me, but because they knew me and were ready to like Kenji.

If the other guests noticed the hum of activity around our table, and the extra dishes being sent, they didn't crane their necks. The only person who found this all strange was me. So I ate out of relief, and kept drinking, letting myself get a little tipsy. And as I looked around, I reminded myself that the glow was from the candles and not because I was weird and radioactive and *different*. Kenji seemed delighted at how the evening was going, not because I'd bewitched him, but because I seemed . . . loved and that love had slopped over onto him.

When we finally left the restaurant calling goodbyes to all our friends, Kenji said, "That was not how I thought that would go."

I giggled then put my hand over my mouth. I never giggled. "How did you think it would be?"

"First of all, I never expected to be stuffed with food, especially at such a fancy place."

I snorted and patted my stomach. Had this dress seemed flimsy? Now it was stretched tight and sturdy over my belly. "Me neither."

Kenji gave me a lopsided smile. "You seem surprised at how many people like you and appreciate you. You've carved out a place in this community."

Well, maybe that was the truth. I wasn't quite the outsider I always thought I was—or maybe needed to be. I shrugged uncomfortably. "I've lived here almost all my life."

But Kenji continued. "I like hearing the funny things you say under your breath when you're with other people, except tonight you were muttering them to me."

"I do not mutter. I murmur sexily."

"That's a given."

"You young people and your sharp hearing."

He laughed lightly but watched my face. "You've mentioned it before. It's something that bothers you a lot—the fact that I'm younger."

"It didn't tonight," I answered evasively.

It wasn't fair of him. I was a little tipsy, I was wearing a dress, I'd had a strange and terrible dream a few hours earlier, and I was relieved that I'd gotten through the evening and even enjoyed myself. I shook my head to clear it, which made me a little dizzy, and I stumbled into one of the men crossing behind me on the sidewalk.

"Watch where you're going, bitch!" he slurred.

Kenji was between us immediately. "Hey, there's no need. It was an accident."

The guy sneered at Kenji. He was one of those preppy white university boys who were usually vomiting outside pubs in fall and spring.

"I'm sorry," I said quickly.

"She's cute," the other one said into the sudden silence.

They both gazed at me bleary-eyed.

"Kenji, let's get out of here," I muttered, suddenly wishing I hadn't had three glasses of wine.

"He should apologize," Kenji said.

Of all the times to dig his heels in. "I don't care." I grabbed his arm and started propelling him toward the car.

"We aren't done yet!" one of the drunk guys yelled.

The first one turned around and slammed his fist into a lamppost. The impact of his action—but not his punch—was diminished when he started crying and rubbing his knuckles.

His buddy stared at him befuddled.

Kenji sighed. "Idiot's probably broken his hand." After one agonized moment in which he silently checked with me, he went up to the guy to make sure he was okay.

The other one sidled up. "You look radiant," he said drawing out the long "a." It sounded how I imagined Templeton the rat in *Charlotte's Web* would pronounce the word.

"Thank you?" I stepped back but he swayed toward me getting a little too close, and I put my hands out to keep him away.

It happened fast. One minute he was smiling in my face, the next I felt myself flare.

Everything flashed with light, and he turned white, his eyes widened in recognition, seemingly seeing something or someone beyond my shoulder, the way Amira's partner had that day at the birthing center.

Then he collapsed.

He fell right at my feet, and I screamed.

Kenji and the other guy turned around. "Did you see that? She tased him or something! Dude, get up."

There was no answer. I took a deep breath and knelt. He was breathing, but unconscious, and smiling with a goofy grin he hadn't had on his face before collapsing. I didn't know what had happened.

Kenji came to my side. "Are you all right?"

"I'm fine."

I was not fine. *He'd seen something.* They'd all perceived too much.

Kenji pulled out his phone to call 9-1-1 while I stayed down with the unconscious man. But aside from loosening his collar I was afraid to touch him. I'd done something to him—I didn't know what it was, although I suspected, and I didn't know how to control it.

A few people had come out of the restaurant by now, including Kelly. The guy who had injured his hand pointed at me and yelled, "She zapped him! She did something to him."

I couldn't even deny it. I wanted to hide. But Kenji was saying, "You tried to assault us. And an ambulance is coming for your friend."

Luckily, the paramedics arrived just as the cops did. Kenji said, "That one's unconscious and that one may have broken his hand punching the lamppost."

"What has gotten into people lately?" the EMT said.

I recognized him. "What's going on, Dan?"

Dan grunted as he strapped the unconscious guy in. "People acting weird, getting into fights. Kids mixing energy drinks and alcohol and freaking out, you name it. We always get this kind of thing in summer, but this year it's been off the charts."

"But she did something to my buddy!" the first guy wailed at a police officer. "Check her for a taser."

"I don't have a taser," I said calmly.

"Leeann, you don't have to tell them anything," Kenji started to say, but I showed everyone my tiny purse and opened it. "And my dress doesn't have pockets."

This was probably the one time when that was an advantage.

The police didn't even bother searching me. They took our information, but it seemed like it was a busy night for them, too. Everyone suddenly seemed weary. "Unless you want to press charges, you're both free to go."

"I'm telling you, she did something!"

Kenji bundled me into the car. The night hadn't gotten very cool, but I rubbed my bare arms anyway.

Outside, things had begun to disperse. The ambulance had taken the men away, people had gone back into the restaurant muttering about university kids overstaying their welcome. The police were still standing in front of their police car poking at their phones.

Kenji took in a deep breath and breathed out again. Then he turned to face me. "I saw the light coming from you, too. You looked a little like you did those other times." He said the last part carefully: "Glowing."

I glanced down at myself. The light was dissipating, but a hint of it was still there in my hands if you knew to look for it. I took a deep breath. "Kenji, if you're ready, we need to talk."

* * *

We ended up parking in an empty lot. I tried to explain some of the strange things that had been happening, the flashes from my hands, the dreams. I told him reluctantly about my week, how I'd felt like I could influence people and things around me, although of course, I was never sure. I stumbled through an explanation of how energized I'd felt sometimes, despite the weather, despite the lack of sleep.

He remained silent, letting me talk, nodding along with the parts he recognized, that he'd been there for.

But when I tried to admit that maybe I'd done something to him, he laughed a little.

I protested, "I don't know what's happening to me. No one seems to have any answers. But I don't want what's going on between us to be because I'm ensnaring you."

"Is that what you think this is?"

"I don't know. I don't know anything. My daughter doesn't want to talk about it. My mother can't give me any insight. I can't control whatever it is that's causing me to glow. I feel guilty because—because . . . I don't want to trap you into something that you might regret when you wake up from whatever this is that I seem to be doing."

"Leeann."

I looked down. "I'm sorry."

"Leeann." He leaned forward and touched my face. "You haven't bespelled me, or hexed me, or whatever it is you think."

"Because you don't think I have powers."

"No, because I don't think *I'm* being magically influenced. Well, not in the cauldrons and woo-woo sort of way. I wanted you. The first time I saw you, I was attracted to you. I know you felt the same. That's some kind of magic or chemistry, or what have you, but I've gotten to know you, and it's deepened."

"That's exactly what a bewitched person under a really strong spell would say," I muttered.

"If it were something else, don't you think the minute you confessed it, I'd start to look back and wonder why I was acting out of character? Wouldn't I at least be a little confused or unsure? I've had time to think and to examine my actions, and I'm acting exactly how I want to."

"Maybe it's a really good spell."

"That you just happened to throw at me because you needed me? Except no, you fought it the whole way."

I threw up my hands. "I don't know. I don't know how any of this works. The tension between you and me and the magic stuff. It's all very new to me."

Kenji leaned forward to touch my face and pulled me in for a kiss. "I'm the one who feels powerful every time I'm with you. Every time I talk to you and you trust me with another piece of your life. Every time we laugh together, every time I touch your hand, every time I'm inside you."

His voice had dropped to a husky whisper, as if he didn't want the rest of the empty parking lot to hear what he had to tell me. "I've been walking around thinking I've managed to fool you into thinking I'm a good bet. I mean, to you I'm probably some silly kid. I get around town on a bike, I don't even have a real house, a real life. And here you are, utterly competent, strong, beautiful, and complete. And powerful. If anything, I've been trying to snare *you*, to bespell you. I want to lure you to my bed and into my life all the time."

I kissed him before he could say any more, drinking greedy kisses from him, because I knew the feeling. The sex was heady and powerful, and maybe it was its own kind of magic. Maybe it had nothing to do with . . .

I had to keep my head. I dropped my head and took in a shaky breath. "You don't think I'm perimenopausal and losing it?"

Kenji played with my hair a little more before he let go. He shook his head, trying to clear it. "There is the fact that other people have witnessed the events. Objectively speaking, something *is* happening. You—and I, and your family—have seen things about you that we can't understand. I think you're trying to find an explanation for it with the tools you have available."

"Which isn't much."

"No, there isn't a lot to go on yet. But answers are out there, and I'll help you find them, if you'll let me."

♦ 12 ♦

Ma's voice came frantic over the phone. "What's wrong? Did something happen? Did Lulu get in another car accident?"

This is what I got for doing something twice in one summer that usually I almost never did—call my mother.

"We have to talk about my great-aunt, my Yi-beh. And about that night of Lulu's accident. When we all glowed."

A pause. "Why now, Leeann?"

"Because." My voice dropped to a whisper even though I was downstairs by myself. "I dreamed about her. She knew I was dreaming. A few other things have happened recently too. People saw me glow. And they were asking questions. Are you sure . . . are you *sure* we come from a line of healers? Because I've done some things. Not healing things."

There was a long pause. I expected my mother to deny it all, to hang up on me angrily. She didn't do that. "Your hands lit up again?"

"Is it so hard to believe?"

She didn't answer that.

When Ma finally spoke, her voice sounded distant. "It's past midnight, Leeann. We can talk about this when you come over for dinner on Friday."

"I know you're up, Ma. You never sleep."

"Well, you should be in bed, too, if you don't have a delivery." Her voice had none of its usual snap. In fact, if anything, she sounded . . . concerned.

"I don't think anyone is sleeping well these days." I hesitated and added, "If we wait till the weekend, we'll have to talk about it in front of Lulu."

Another pause. "She'll have to deal with it sooner or later." She ended the call.

I pulled the phone away from my ear in disbelief. Even when Ma was willing to give me the information I needed, she still managed to be galling.

I also didn't expect Lulu to balk at returning to my mother's on Friday.

It was early evening. Lulu was already in her pajamas. I, on the other hand, was getting ready. By which I meant I was pre-snacking.

Lulu pouted and stole one of the crackers from my box. "I don't want to see her. I think we need a cooling-off period."

"You're leaving in four weeks. We don't have time for cooling off."

"Why are you so eager to see your mother all of a sudden?"

"I have questions she should have answered years ago. Just get dressed."

Lulu grumbled. But she never complained too much. Because my child was an adult in all situations. Of course, she was ready to put on her shoes before me, and even had time to help me brush the cracker crumbs from my clothes.

Ma was trying her best to appear welcoming, even attempting some sort of smile when I got to the door and treating Lulu with painful attentiveness. We all managed to crunch our way through the meal without too much conflict. Or conversation. In our family they were often the same thing. It was after dinner, when Ma brought out a slightly different package from the others, that the protests began.

"These aren't the pictures that āyi sent," Lulu said, tugging on a corner.

"No, we've had these for longer. They're your Yi-beh's writings."

I pressed my fingernails into my palm and breathed deeply.

That hollowed-out feeling returned. Ever since dreaming of my Yi-beh, I'd yearned to know more about her and about all of my family history. Now, here finally was something.

The package gave off a slightly medicinal smell, as if what was inside had been too long confined.

The dead wanted to leave, Yi-beh had said.

The cardboard was different from the usual bland, tan stuff I was used to seeing from the other boxes my Aunt Shu-chuan, had sent. This was shinier, a little more yellow. The tape, which had been retaped once or twice was cracked with age. Ma had clearly not touched this box for years, even though she knew what it was.

My mother paused a long time before slitting it open.

"Ma," I nudged.

She opened each flap one by one, sending a puff of that scent out each time. Flap. Flap. Flap. Flap.

Unable to hold myself back, I stood up and looked inside. There were papers. Scraps, some of them. A couple of notebooks. I flipped through them, hoping to at least see something I recognized.

"These aren't in Chinese," I said, half frantic.

Ma nodded. "Your Yi-beh was educated in Japanese. Before World War II, Taiwan was under Japanese colonial rule, so that was the language she was most comfortable writing with. But I was born under Chinese nationalist rule. That's why I learned Mandarin."

"So why do we speak Taiwanese sometimes, A-mà?"

"Because we are Taiwanese, no matter who's in the government."

I shook my head. I'd thought my mother would finally tell me something, and instead, I'd hit another dead end. "You knew you wouldn't be able to read them," I said slowly. "What are we going to do now?"

I stared helplessly at the notebook in my lap, willing myself to be able to understand the stuff written on the thin pages.

Lulu looked back and forth between us. "Mom. Is this about that dream you got so worked up about?"

I avoided her eyes. "Yes."

She turned to my mother. "A-mà, you're a physician. Do you believe Mom is communicating with someone who's dead?"

"I understand science. Which means I know we don't know the explanations to some things. And I see things I can't explain."

Lulu turned flopped back on the couch. "I can't believe this is happening. You've both been possessed."

"You saw it, too, Lulu. We *need* to talk about this." I turned to my mother. "Why haven't you told me more about our background and what all of us are?"

At least Yi-beh was trying to help me. Or, at least, I thought she was.

"I try all the time to get you to listen to me."

"No, you try to tell me who you want me to become, not where I came from. And now I think I might be a danger to people." I flung up my hands.

I gave them the story of the sleepwalking episode, trying to keep my voice as neutral as possible. I recounted what happened yesterday with the kid outside the restaurant, the father in the delivery room, and about the other times I seemed to have light emanating from me.

I finished my whole talk by saying, "After last night, I don't know that what we Wus have is entirely for healing, and now I can't even read these papers she left." I gripped one of the pages for emphasis. "You should know the most about this. But Ma, can't you tell me about Yi-beh? Isn't there *anything* you can say about what—what this power is, or why we've turned into human glow sticks?"

Ma shook her head, frustrated. "All I know is the little she told me. She said that the most we could actually do in this life was soothe people's hurts, that healing wasn't a real thing. Hurt always left something behind. I always thought it was funny, because she wasn't a calm, peaceful woman. She was abrupt, and she could be harsh, and sometimes even mean and impatient. But not with the people whose births she attended."

"Did you ever see her do something extraordinary?" I persisted.

"You mean like throw a fireball at someone?" Lulu asked snidely.

"If it's an awesome healing fireball, then yes, I want to know about it."

Ma ignored us both. "It was all extraordinary. Your Yi-beh didn't have equipment like us, or a fancy birthing center with a pool, or a team of people to help her in case something went wrong. Every household she went into, she didn't know what she might expect. Would there be clean linen if it was washing day? Would a mother-in-law try to interfere and manage the birth? Would a patient hemorrhage, and how could she deal with it with minimal drugs at her disposal?

"Once, I remember, after she'd retired, we were called out to a family. Wealthy people—for the countryside. I don't think she expected to be summoned there, but maybe the doctor or the district nurse wasn't able to come. I don't remember. The delivery didn't take too long, I don't think. There were a lot of people around to help. I remember the baby was a boy. The father was pleased. But for some reason, my aunt stayed there. Someone said something like 'The baby was already delivered why is the midwife still around?' And someone else joked that maybe we were hoping we'd be adopted.

"They were so rude. I didn't want to stay there. My house in Taichung was very nice and it wasn't in the middle of the country. My father had owned a Japanese motorcycle—one of the first in Taichung. I told my aunt we should leave, but she shook her head and stayed right where she was, in a chair, by the woman's feet. Then the patient hemorrhaged."

I drew in a breath. "There were no signs?"

Ma shook her head. "I didn't know at the time. Afterward my aunt explained to me to look for heavy bleeding and signs of shock, nausea, pale skin, pain, and swelling in the area around the vagina and perineum. I didn't think much about these things at the time, but she told me as though I should care. And now I remember all the details, every word she told me.

"But I still don't know how she saved that woman," Ma said. "Your Yi-beh performed uterine massage, but it was still so much blood already. I don't know how—I remember that. I didn't know much about medicine, but I remember I thought the woman was going to die right there in front of us."

Ma sounded lost. I'd never heard her that way. Her English was always crisp, unaccented but inflected with the rhythms of Chinese. Always, her voice was clear and tart, the same tone used to quiz her students about the symptoms of obstetric cholestasis as she did when she told me over and over that she was disappointed in me.

But now, her voice wavered, uncertain. I squeezed my eyes shut at the thought of how sudden and terrifying it must have been for everyone—even as a professional, that sudden drop deep down in the gut that accompanied the first gush.

Then she whispered, "I may have seen a light." She paused. "The problem is, I hadn't been looking because I didn't want to witness any of it. But your Yi-beh didn't lose one patient the whole time I was there. At the time, I thought that was how it was. But now, I realize it's remarkable. By the time a doctor came, your Yi-beh had stopped most of that woman's bleeding."

My mother's voice was steady again.

It wasn't much. A terrible yet hazy memory of something that Ma had seen long ago. It could have been explained by my great-aunt's long years in the field, by her knowledge, by tricks of light. By the desire to believe. I wanted a grand revelation, thunder and lightning, ghosts, prophecies, and magic visibly shooting out of people's fingers.

At the very least, I wanted to think this thing inside me could help people. But we were never really going to know.

"A-mà, I don't know that this proves anything," Lulu said quietly. She sounded almost reluctant after her desperate attempt at logic earlier. To me, she said, "I'm sorry."

We all sat silent for a moment.

I asked my mother, "Do you remember anything else?"

"I don't have much else to tell you," Ma said. "She didn't pass anything down to me."

"But she told you about the signs to look for—" There *had* to be more information.

"Anything I do is through hard work."

"But she knew that you were going to end up delivering babies. That's why she told you about the signs to look for."

"How much is what she knew and how much is because she believed it?" Lulu interjected.

"She believed she had a gift," Ma said slowly.

"But did she ever zap someone with her hands like Mom apparently does?"

"It's not like I'm staticky, Lulu. I prefer to think of it as engulfing people with a gentle glow." Except for when I almost fried that guy after the date with Kenji. And maybe the annoying father in the delivery room.

Ma wasn't listening to us though. She was lost in a memory. "A few times I thought I saw her with her plants at night. There was a light coming from her hands. And I didn't understand how that could be. She wasn't carrying a lantern. This was when I was even younger, a little girl. But when I asked her about it, she laughed and told me I must have dreamed it."

I could almost hear my Yi-beh's voice. I couldn't remember her face, or *her.* But the words rang clear.

My mother shook her head, her eyes still far away. "I hadn't thought of that in years. But as you say, I have no proof."

"Plus it was a really long time ago."

That remark made Ma come back to herself. "Yes, Lulu," she said tartly. "I realize I'm so old, how can my memories be trusted?"

Lulu looked a little ashamed of herself. *As she should be.*

I couldn't believe I was taking Ma's side in this.

"Maybe I'll clear some of this up," Lulu said, picking up her water glass. And A-mà, maybe you'd like some tea?"

Ma nodded even though she probably wasn't going to drink it, but she seemed to understand it was Lulu's way of apologizing to her this time. She watched Lulu go, and when she was out of sight, my mother sighed and her straight posture sagged.

"Ma, are you feeling all right?"

She waved at me irritably and blew out a breath. "I'm frustrated. Because we are losing knowledge, as a family. When you were growing up, I vowed I'd teach you Taiwanese and Mandarin, but here we are, speaking English."

"Hey, I can sort of get by in both."

"But not well. And even then, what use is it? Your Yi-beh's journals are in a language I don't even know." She paused. "Even when we know the same language, I have never understood how to talk to you. When you were a little girl, and I brought you here, and you weren't speaking, I was afraid we'd never be close each other. When you finally said your first words, I was so relieved. But it goes deeper than that. The way you grew up, and the way I grew up is so different. The way Yi-beh lived is even further removed. I don't know how to tell you about any of these things, because there is something more than language that separates us. It's about what we see."

I could have reached out to take my mother's hand at that moment. But soft touches were not what we did. "But you witnessed it, the glow. We all had it."

"I did," she admitted.

"And Yi-beh gave you all these papers. It must mean she thought you'd be able to do something with them."

Ma looked at me for a long time, as if I'd missed another thing I was supposed to know. "No, Leeann," she said finally. "These are for you. The photos my sister sent to me, but the box was for *you*. I opened it a long time ago, when I brought you here with me. I thought there might be something in it that would help me . . . help me reach you. You missed your Yi-beh so. She was the parent you knew. You cried and cried for her, and you wouldn't speak to me for a long time. But you were still a baby. You wouldn't have been able to read anything in the box. I couldn't."

That bitterness again in her voice. But for the first time, I understood that the feeling wasn't about me. It was for herself, for all the things she'd lost—we'd lost—somehow along the way. My gut squeezed, and I remembered the hollow feeling I had when Yi-beh left me in the dream. I was bereft.

"I wanted a message, Leeann. I wanted something from her, anything, a note, a sign that she was proud of what I was doing. But in the end, she didn't pass anything onto me. She didn't say goodbye."

She drew in a breath, and suddenly I realized my mother was still grieving in her own way all these years later. "She knew I didn't have the power. I tried again and again after that night after Lulu's accident when we all seemed to have it. I'm still practicing, but I can't do anything, not without you. But your Yi-beh knew you had this gift."

★ ★ ★

Lulu drove us home, her hands tight on the wheel. She was talking to me like I was someone she needed to calm down. Maybe I was.

"Look, I know it's been a weird summer with all the lightning strikes and heat and general strangeness, but I can't have both of you falling apart especially now that I'm leaving."

"At least Ma and I are sort of in agreement," I pointed out. "The other week you were worried that we weren't going to get along without you, and we'd both be completely alone, isolated except for ten cats each."

"I didn't say anything about cats. A-mà hates cats. I just want you both to be normal and not fighting."

"Not fighting isn't really our normal."

"Everything is changing," Lulu said. "You've never been this way, talking about strange powers and phenomena. When I was little and I was afraid of a thunderstorm, you told me about rain and moisture in the air. If a person asked you out, you never got this excited about it. You didn't wake up and try to tear the house apart because of a strange dream or think you had electricity in your fingers. You didn't date. You didn't wear gold dresses and go out with younger men."

"It was yellow. Daffodil at most."

"If something strange happened, you asked me to think of why it might have occurred. You're practical. Logical. You helped me sleep when I worried at night. And now I can't sleep—*no one is sleeping anymore!*—and you and A-mà have teamed up with all this talk of Wu woo and powers you've both turned it into a folie à deux."

"A what?"

"A folie à deux! A shared delusion!"

"That's very fancy-sounding. Are you sure your grandma and I didn't make a folio adieu on purpose? Because that sounds great." My voice was light, but inside I felt twisted up and uncertain.

On one hand, I didn't want Lulu to worry. On the other, I couldn't help coming back to the fact that my mother had believed—known—all along that I was gifted in some way. All that time, I thought she'd been perpetually disappointed in me.

But that wasn't it.

Ma was angry she didn't have the Wu gift. When she admitted that those papers were mine, I recognized that look on her face because maybe I'd felt it myself at my lowest points. That frustration, not with the universe and all its fickleness, but with myself.

My mother was jealous of me.

What an odd feeling. Because even though we disagreed on so many things, I felt like she could have used whatever powers I had more effectively than I did. There was never any doubt that she was determined and hardworking. Think of all the cures Shu-ling Wu could enact with light in her fingertips!

But no, I reminded myself. I was just as energetic and important as she was. But we were different and our talents were different. Maybe I'd gotten into the habit of believing my abilities were a pale imitation of hers when we hadn't been the same all along.

"I just want things to be back the way they were!" Lulu said.

"Back the way they were when? Last week? Last month? Two years ago?"

Lulu pulled into our drive. We stayed in the car.

"You're the one who said I should try to have a life outside of work and being a parent. Get some hobbies. Date."

"I meant stable, dad-like men with the beginnings of male pattern baldness. I meant pottery, maybe a little cross-stitch. Not weird mysticism and visible sexual tension!"

"You encouraged me to go out with Kenji," I reminded her. "You said he was eyeing me."

"For fun once or twice. You weren't supposed to fall in love with him right away!"

I swallowed, ready to deny it. What did Lulu know? But the words wouldn't make it past my teeth.

Lulu got out of the car. I followed her into the house, still trying to speak. At last, I said weakly, "That's not really fair. We just started going out, of course we're going to look giddy. But, I admit, you're right in a way. I need to figure out what I'm going to do when . . . when the house is empty. When I don't have you to talk to. I'm not trying to fill that silence with another person." Was that a lie? I wasn't sure. The vast Lulu-sized space in my heart was somewhere else, a different place than the slowly growing corner devoted to Kenji.

Which was also in my heart.

Focus on Lulu.

"It's just that I need to be able to figure things out. What works in my life, what doesn't. What I am." My words echoed in our hallway, as if it were empty, as if Lulu were already gone and not there looking at me.

A small surge of frustration rose in me even as Lulu threw up her hands. "Fine. But why suddenly believe you have latent magical powers?"

"You saw them! You shared them!"

"And why the—the *intensity* of this relationship you already have with this Kenji guy? Is he the one who's telling you about some sort of witchcraft? Is that what you did on your date? Draw pentagrams on the floor and burn candles?"

I ignored my guilty blush at the thought of the other ways I'd summoned the glow. "We're not white people or witches, as your A-mà keeps reminding you! We have a totally different history and set of traditions, not that I know anything about them."

I thought of my mother's words. *I don't know how to tell you about any of these things, because there is something more than language that separates us.*

"If I could explain what is happening to me I would, Lulu. But I don't even understand what it is myself."

"It's fake," she insisted.

"It's us!" I yelled.

I never raised my voice at Lulu, and we both jerked back in shock.

She drew in a breath. "This Kenji guy might not know about the direction you're taking, but he's making you believe other things."

"Like what, Lulu? That I'm special? That I'm interesting as a person? Because that's all it is as far as I know. Maybe this other part of myself is waking up because it's time, and he's the first person to see something new in me for a long time. I don't know, Lulu. I keep telling you I'm feeling my way through this, and I wanted to get answers from your A-mà, but she doesn't know either, and I only have more questions."

Lulu's lips were tight. "Mom," she said. "I can understand that you want to feel powerful and interesting and that there's something important about you."

But there isn't.

The words hung there unspoken. Still, they burned right in my chest as if she'd branded them on me. I knew it wasn't that she didn't understand I was important, but there were ways to be something and someone, and in her eyes, there was only one way for me to exist.

I wondered if my mother felt that way with me, sometimes wishing I could see her as a person rather than an overbearing parent.

"I'm sorry," she said. "I love you. You're a great mom, and a competent, caring midwife—"

"You think I'm a fool. And my *mother* is the one who believes I've got some sort of talent," I said.

"Mom."

I shook my head and tried to ease my hurt heart. When I finally spoke again, my voice sounded like a croak. "I thought I'd seen all sorts of strange things over the years, but this reversal is the strangest."

♦ 13 ♦

I DIDN'T EXPECT TO SLEEP that night. As Lulu said, no one was sleeping these days. Not well, anyway. I thought I would end up replaying everything my daughter had said to me, all the hurtful things made all the worse because I feared on some levels she was right. But she was going through a lot right now, too. She'd be leaving me. We'd hardly ever been apart for more than a few days.

Lulu thought that what she was telling me was the truth. A few months ago, I would have agreed with her.

But as I felt myself sinking down, down into layers of rest, it was my mother's words that came back to me. *She left this for you.*

I dozed and thought of that box, old and still sturdy. I could smell it, that mix of herbs and medicines. I saw the almost-translucent papers in front of me, the writing that I'd never be able to read, being riffled by invisible fingers. I began to see words that I could understand.

Dreams.

Sleep.

The last was said in Yi-beh's voice, but even though I wanted to see her, to feel that strange, hollow sadness she gave me, something kept my body on alert, as if danger was near, and I could never quite fall deeply into rest.

But Yi-beh had said something about dreams, too, not that I could remember. The sense of it drifted away from me the harder I tried to sleep.

But she didn't appear, and I wanted to cry in frustration.

"What are you trying to tell me?" I pleaded until my eyes were open, and I was in my room again, staring into darkness.

Lulu had sneaked out early to work the next morning, but she left me a bowl of steel cut oatmeal that she'd cooked despite the heat.

It was her way of saying she was sorry she'd hurt me—although probably not sorry for her actual thoughts, or words, or beliefs.

I stared at the sensible portion of healthy breakfast and tried to be grateful for her thoughtfulness. That she cared for her old mom. But it was a warning.

Maybe Lulu hadn't meant it that way, but the oatmeal was what I was supposed to be. Sensible, unexciting. I should carry on eating these kinds of things, being this kind of well-adjusted person. Getting enough fiber. Sleeping. Working. Dating appropriate men. Not glowing.

I picked up my phone and texted Kenji.

Are you up?

Making a bottle for her royal poopyness. What's going on?

Can I see you tonight?

A pause. I'm going apartment hunting. If you'd like to come.

I smiled. Tell me when and where.

I arrived early after work and waited outside on a side street just off Main. I could see Kenji living around here near the bookstores and coffee shops where students usually sat at tables arguing over group projects, and cottage-country summer people bought big bags of bagels to feed their friends and families brunch on weekends. If I'd had a different life maybe this could have been me.

I watched Kenji swoop in on his bike. He locked it up and grabbed me and kissed me. I felt myself relax into his arms. It had been a good idea to meet him. I didn't have to worry about who I was or who people thought I should be. I could just feel his lips and hands and tongue and enjoy my body. We stood there for a while making out against the side of the building until someone cleared her throat. I pulled away reluctantly, giving Kenji time to shake that dazed look from his eyes, and turned around and saw it was Sarah McCaffrey.

Of course. I remembered a little too late that her family owned a few of the buildings in the neighborhood.

She'd seen us together at June's. And who could forget she'd been there when I bought the pregnancy test? If the news hadn't come out when Kenji and I went on our first public date, it was bound to come out now. I made a mental note to catch Parisa up.

Sarah greeted us both brightly. "Kenji said it was important to get your approval on this place," she said. Her tone attempted blandness, but she'd turned a little red, and her eyes were curious. Despite the grown-up business lady pantsuit she was wearing, she seemed uncertain. She kept looking between Kenji and me and (not very subtly) at my stomach, as she fished keys out of her purse and led us up the stairs.

In summertime, it was easier to rent apartments in Reineville because the students were away. It was smart of Kenji to get a head start.

But part of me quailed. Why was my opinion so important? Was I going to be spending much time here? Was Kenji planning to settle? Was he pinning too many hopes on me, or was it the other way around?

Sarah threw open the door on a small but pleasant room. Wood floors, big windows to let sunshine in, an old-fashioned steam heater that would probably clank and whistle in winter—but some people found comfort in that sound.

"It's a bit stuffy in here," Sarah said. "Let me open up some of the windows." How was she not dying of heat in that suit? She moved to the bedroom and left me and Kenji standing there.

"What do you think?" Kenji asked.

"So far so good."

"Come on, let's go to the kitchen."

He pulled me gently. I hadn't even noticed we'd been holding hands the whole time. He pointed out the nearly new appliances, the stacked washer and dryer tucked in a corner, the window over the sink that faced the brick of the next building. But it was pleasant and bright. When we got back to the living room, Sarah was on the phone, so he led me into the bedroom.

"It's not that far from the school," he pointed out. "So I could walk or bike there every day."

"I know you're very energetic—" I began. He waggled his eyebrows at me. "But it's a decent walk. It does get snowy here. You might not want to bike in winter."

"I have a car now."

"Right. I almost forgot. Is there parking?"

"One spot. You can see it from here." I dutifully looked out the window at where he pointed, but he was too distracting. "What do you think?" he asked, slipping behind me. He pressed himself lightly against me so that I felt the line of his strong body. His warm hand caressed my waist and hip. "Not the greatest view, I know. But I could fit a queen-sized mattress in here. I'd get nice sheets. I could cook you breakfast in the kitchen, and then we could go outside for a walk along Main, or anywhere you wanted. Or go back to bed."

I let my head drop back into his chest. I guess I could have pointed out that my own house would be empty soon enough, that I didn't always have time for breakfast, that I'd be getting up in the middle of the night to get to a client's house or the birthing center, and that the life of sunshine and leisure wasn't always possible here in this rainy climate.

Not that it had rained the whole time he'd been here. I drew my brows together.

But Kenji misinterpreted my frown. "Or I could find another place? Maybe this one's too small."

I shook my head. "No, it's perfect."

His arms tightened around me, and he started kissing my neck.

I heard another cleared throat.

Sarah had poked her head into the room. She smiled brightly. "So, what do we think?"

The question should have been directed at Kenji, but her gaze was on me. So was Kenji's.

Was I comfortable having the final say in this? I guess I'd have to be.

I took a deep breath. "It looks great to me," I said, trying to put enthusiasm into my voice.

This was too much power. Last night I'd been cautioned against turning into some kind of megalomaniac who thought she was magical. Today I was being made responsible for the course of my boyfriend's life—or at least his living situation for the next year.

Without waiting for Kenji's answer Sarah beamed. "I'll get the lease agreement, then."

She flitted out of the room again, and I took the opportunity to turn around and press myself against Kenji once again. My hand crept to the waistband of his pants. I felt strange, reckless. Electric. "Does this mean you get the keys right away?"

"Yeah, pretty much."

"I want to have sex. Here. When she's gone."

I felt his immediate response. Ah, the bodies of young men. He blew out a breath. "Okay." His voice came out a little strangled, but his hand slid up sure and strong to trace the underside of my breast.

Footsteps.

Sarah came back in and presented Kenji with the papers.

I stepped back a little to give them some room. Plus, it would help calm me.

Kenji managed to smile, and soon he was scribbling away at the window seat.

Sarah watched for a minute. "Sooo," she said. "How long have you been seeing each other? Since before that weird lightning strike, I guess, huh?"

It was finally time for Sarah to give in to the curiosity that had probably been eating her alive over the past couple of weeks. To her credit, she tried not to stare at my stomach this time.

I made a sound that was supposed to pass for an answer.

"I think it's great," Sarah blurted. "You dating someone younger."

Oh boy.

"You always seemed braver than everyone else, destined for cool things. Like you didn't belong in this small place." She had the decency to blush. "Not because you were Asian or anything. Although it made you seem—"

Don't say exotic.

"Sophisticated. But you always did your own thing. Never paid attention to the cliques at school and stuff like that."

There was envy in her voice, and I had no idea what to do with this feeling she'd apparently nursed about me since high school. "It was a while ago," I said cautiously.

But Sarah wasn't listening. "My family's all so . . . *normal*, you know?" I had no response to that either, but luckily it didn't seem required of me. Sarah forged on. "I'm even still working for my dad even though it stresses me out. It's gotten so bad that I can't sleep at night anymore."

"Everybody's been saying that lately," Kenji said handing Sarah the sheaf of papers. "My excuse is my baby niece. Good thing she's cute."

Kenji grinned, and Sarah smiled back dazedly. She hadn't paid that much attention to him before, but she was captivated now. I couldn't really blame her. He had dimples. The man was ridiculous.

She gave him the keys as if hypnotized and blushed when he told her he'd walk her down to her car. "Leeann said she'd stay up here and—"

"Take some measurements," I supplied.

Sarah didn't check to see if I had a measuring tape. Of course, I didn't. "Oh, sure. That's great." She looked over at me vaguely. "I'm so happy for both of you."

When I was alone, I took the time to stroll through the rooms again. Kenji would be back up soon, and we'd make love. Maybe it was that physical ache inside me, the emptiness of the rooms, the silence, that made me feel like a ghost. I stood in the middle of the living room and stretched my arms out and closed my eyes breathing deeply in and out.

Leeann.

Who was calling me? I didn't want to be summoned.

"Leeann."

This time I heard it. My eyes opened. Kenji was at the open door. He was looking at me strangely. "Do you want to talk?"

We ended up cross-legged on the floor, ordering takeout sushi, and I explained what had happened at my mother's.

"I could take a look at the journals," he said through a mouthful of cucumber-avocado roll. "If you want."

I blinked. "You read Japanese?"

"Some. My mom wanted me to learn. She thought it would be a way to be closer to my heritage. I took some courses in undergrad to keep it up. Because we're not sure what kinds of papers your great aunt left you, I'm not saying I'll understand all of it, but I may at least be able to flag things or give you the gist of what she may be trying to say."

"Did it work? Getting closer to your Japanese side, I mean?"

"Yes and no. My mom's parents know each other from their internment."

My throat tightened, but Kenji continued, "She speaks less Japanese than I do. So, when I'm reading, or if I manage to make myself understood, I get that that's an accomplishment, but also like I'm missing something. I don't know what it is, and I don't know how to describe the feeling. I feel like I should be part of the culture—I've been told I'm not white enough—but I'm not part of this either. It's like a feeling of loss for something I don't know I ever had."

I got that hollow feeling in my chest from when I dreamed of Yi-beh. "I'm sorry. It's a tragic history."

We were quiet a moment. Kenji clacked his chopsticks. "Yet, here I am, and I'm not suffering. And now we're eating sushi."

"Sushi prepared by a Korean Canadian family business, not Japanese," I pointed out.

He gave a short bark of laughter, and we both started to eat again.

"I think that's what's been so frustrating about this," I said. "Our family histories are very different, but they've both got these traumas and triumphs. Whatever is happening to me is connected to the Wu side of the family, to my background, to my heritage, but I don't know enough to understand or control my ability to interact with it. Even my mother—*especially* my mother—can't help me. It's like all the knowledge is fragmented into different languages that we speak, into the different cultures and histories behind us. I'm here as a product of all of it, and my family exists, but there's so little I can do to connect all these things together except be and . . . glow. I can't make the different parts talk to each other, let alone understand each other."

I leaned against the wall and straightened my limbs in front of me gingerly. I wasn't able to sit around cross-legged for long periods of time anymore, and my back hurt. I was too old to find myself and my roots. Weren't mine already down? At this age, people were supposed to finally start getting comfortable with who they were. Your forties were supposed to be about not giving a fuck. Instead I yearned for the acceptance of a relative I didn't recall, worried about a childhood I didn't remember, and was plagued with inexplicable incandescence, sleepwalking and making people faint and fall asleep.

"What do you say to having me take a look at your aunt's things?" Kenji asked.

I thought about the box that had been sitting in the trunk of my car for days, ever since we left my mother's house. Somehow it felt safer that way, a box locked within a box.

But Kenji had seen my light, and he hadn't pushed me when I didn't know how to talk about to him.

"I'd appreciate it," I said. "I could probably find someone to translate it at the university. But I don't want a stranger looking through it and judging it."

I hugged my arms even though the apartment was hot. "My mother says my great-aunt might not have been herself around the end. Her mind was wandering. I must have been around to see it. For some reason, though, I'm sure she took good care of me. I just know it, and I don't want to think of her losing her faculties. I don't even remember her, and yet I don't want that to be how a stranger thinks of her, an eccentric old single woman who used to go around delivering babies."

"I'll try not to judge her," Kenji said gently.

"I know."

He stood up and started to put the lids back on the containers and started to take things to the kitchen. I made a motion to get up to help him, but he waved me back down. "Let me enjoy my first evening hosting an event in this apartment," he said.

"This isn't the enjoyment part," I called.

He stuck his head out of the doorway. "I know. I was promised sex." He shot me a grin and ducked his head back in.

Oh, no.

I was in love. And I was pretty sure he loved me back.

♦ 14 ♦

"But I don't want to go to the hospital!" Emory Andrews's white anguished face stared at me.

"I know this isn't what you planned."

"You promised."

I'd done no such thing and neither had Fiona, the midwife whose long shift had preceded mine, but seeing as Emory Andrews was in the middle of giving birth, it didn't seem the time to bust out a transcript. "We need to do what's safest for you and the baby right now. At the moment, there are some complications—"

"You said it would be fine."

"Emory, you know that the unexpected can happen. We have to make sure you get to the hospital so you can deliver safely and your baby can receive medical care."

"But I don't want a cesarean! I want a natural childbirth. It's right there in the plan."

Her partner glanced between us, clearly wishing that his involvement could cease. I gave a little laugh. It was only going to get worse for him as time went on.

"Emory," I said. "I've already called an ambulance. You and your baby will be safer at the hospital. Let's call this plan B, okay? Plan A isn't working right now. We need to focus on what will."

"But I don't know plan B. I don't know the steps."

"Emory, look at me, please. Look at me."

She squinched her eyes and screwed up her face. "You're going to hypnotize me. You're going to convince me to do something I don't want to do."

Could my powers do that? Too bad I had witnesses.

"I wouldn't take this step if I didn't think this is the best course of action right now. We've been at this for a while and your labor isn't progressing. Trust my instincts on this. It's time."

She opened one eye and glared at me suspiciously. She opened her mouth. Then a wave of another contraction hit her. She screamed, loud and ragged, and I held her hand and got her to breathe through it. "Okay, okay," she sobbed.

The time before the paramedics arrived was a tense blur. Luckily, Emory's spacious Victorian on Lake Drive wasn't that far from Reineville General, and it was early evening.

We sped off into the darkness, the EMTs oddly tense. "It's been a busy night," one of them told me.

"Glad you could get here so soon."

A car honked as we sped by. Emory breathed hard. The dispatch radio crackled continuously, and when we pulled up, a hub of activity surrounded the entrance. It really had been a tough night.

"Let's get her out and to labor and delivery stat."

The EMTs had unloaded Emory's stretcher into the entrance when another ambulance came wailing at the entrance. We all turned as one. The ambulance wasn't slowing down enough.

I didn't think. I threw myself over Emory and pushed the stretcher toward the entrance, even as she screamed again.

Metal and metal screeched as the vehicles collided. I felt an object hit my leg, causing me to lurch forward. Something heavy seemed to be attached to my limb.

Emory raised her head. "I thought you said we'd be safer at the hospital."

I gritted my teeth and kept moving despite the reluctance of my lower muscles. Nurses and orderlies sprinted out the doors. At least if anyone had been injured they'd have a lot of medical personnel on hand. "We're all taking care of you." To the EMTs, I said, "Let's get her inside."

"But Leeann, you're—"

"Never mind me."

I limped forward—why was my leg still so heavy?—but I was determined to get Emory in safely just as I'd promised. It wasn't until we were in the elevator that I glanced down. My pant leg was dripping blood. I'd been sliced with chunk of taillight or some other debris. "Oh shit," I said.

Then, for the first time in my life, I fainted.

⋆ ⋆ ⋆

I was a little girl again.

"Listen carefully," Yi-beh said, taking my chubby fingers. "Do you hear them? Do you hear the resonance? Feel the vibrations?"

I squinched my eyes.

Yi-beh laughed. "No, you can open your eyes, Mei mei. Spread your hand like this. Now, do you feel them?"

I sensed it. It was like my hand had become a tuning fork. I felt it deep inside my bones, but radiating out, too. The glow wasn't in me. I was just the transmitter. As I watched fascinated, my fingers elongated, the pudginess smoothing then wrinkling as I grew older and older, my skin outlining knuckles, veins coming to the surface.

I looked up. Yi-beh was gone, and she'd taken something from me again.

I felt so heavy.

An obnoxious light flashed across my vision.

I shook my head trying to escape it. This couldn't be happening so soon. I wanted Yi-beh back. But someone was holding my chin.

"Can you tell me your name?"

I shook my head free. "Leeann Wu." I recognized my questioner. "Dr. Dao, I'm fine."

I was in a hospital bed, narrowly curtained off. Parisa, in scrubs, was just beyond Dr. Dao's shoulder. "Where's Emory?" I asked sitting up. I winced. "Where's my client?"

Parisa spoke. "She's doing well. It's good you brought her in when you did. You mom's sectioning her."

"Did she put up much of a fight?"

"Emory? No. No one fights Dr. Wu.

"Except you," Parisa added.

I glared at my best friend, but she only grinned at me. The hubbub of the hospital ebbed and flowed beyond the curtained walls. Dr. Dao checked made me turn over and checked my wound. "Well, Leeann, except for the cut in your leg and being exhausted, you'll be fine. Someone will be here to clean you up and put in stitches."

My leg. Now that I thought about it, it throbbed as if it were twice its size.

"The accident. Something hit me right in front of the doors. I can't believe it."

"Freak accident. Good thing it was so close to Emergency and you all weren't still in the ambulance. Or unloading your patient," Parisa said.

"Was anyone else hurt?"

Dr. Dao shook her head and turned to leave, still absorbed in her notes, but Parisa said, "The nurses say they think the driver's sustained a concussion, but you're the only one who got bloody. It's a mess in the ER right now, though, even without the collision."

Parisa slumped in the chair beside my bed.

Exhausted or not, I needed to make sure my client was all right. I started to get up, but Parisa cut me off. "Don't get any ideas. You'd been up for hours. Your leg needs to be stitched. Knowing you, you probably haven't eaten or slept."

I hadn't slept. No one had been sleeping.

"Parisa," I clutched her arm. "After I talked to you, I had a dream about my great aunt, the midwife. Two dreams. Maybe more. She's trying to tell me something."

Parisa looked at me for a long moment. She did not say anything like, *Did you get a knock on your head when you fainted?* Her eyes held speculation. But one of the residents bustled in before she could respond.

We all watched quietly as the resident administered a topical anesthetic before leaving and returning with a suture tray.

When she finally finished, I told Parisa, "I know I sound unhinged. But I feel like Yi-beh's telling me there's something I'm supposed to do. But whenever I talk to her, I'm even more tired than before."

Parisa sighed and started to get up. "We'll discuss it later. But if I told you this wasn't even the most bananas thing anyone has said to me lately . . . I don't know what to think honestly."

"Are other people talking to the dead?"

"Oh, Leeann. Some of us are barely alive at this moment. I'd join your aunt if I could. I just want to sleep."

I looked at my friend, at the pansy-colored circles under her big eyes and worry stirred in me. She was thinner. Why hadn't I noticed how gaunt she had gotten recently? I thought of how she'd kept her perimenopause symptoms from me for years. "Are you all right?"

Was there something else she wasn't telling me? She had been the one to see the potential in me no one else had. She believed I might have some sort of real power when I was worried everyone might think I was losing my mind. But today her whole being seemed turned inward as if to protect herself.

She stood up to leave. "We'll talk," she said.

But we never did.

⋆ ⋆ ⋆

"I've thought about what you said," Lulu began.

She'd arrived at the hospital shortly after Parisa left. After making sure I was all right and almost threatening to hijack a wheelchair despite the chaos in the emergency room, she decided I was well enough to limp my own way to her car. She'd also brought me some shorts and a new shirt. I had a pair of leggings in my locker at the hospital birthing center, but those would probably be too tight around my stitches.

My hulking SUV was still parked somewhere on Lake Drive. My leg hurt, and I was hungry and tired, and I needed a shower. Everything—the long session with Emory ending in the accident, the dream, the abrupt conversation with Parisa, wondering if I should have called Kenji—had left me feeling itchy and restless and unsettled. But I couldn't do anything about it now except rest. I didn't tell Lulu about any of it, and it felt strange.

"Hmm?" I said, distracted.

"You know? That stuff about our great-aunt?"

My eyes slid toward her. "What about it?" I asked, my voice probably coming out more surly than I intended.

I slouched down in my seat and tried to shield myself from the overbright sun. I hated the light. It was too strong, too hot. And it reminded me of the dreams of being pulled away from Yi-beh. I shielded my eyes.

"I was thinking that maybe you're having anxiety."

That woke me up. "What?"

"It would explain a lot. You're in a high-stress job and you don't get enough sleep. Plus perimenopausal women like you are more prone to anxiety attacks than normal."

I groaned. Not this again. "Last time I checked, the symptoms of anxiety didn't include glowing hands and calling down lightning."

"You're not breathing properly, and it's causing you to see weird flashes," Lulu said confidently.

"That's not how it works, Lulu. I am not having anxiety attacks in the middle of my sessions. And we were not hopped up that night around the table when we were all drinking tea. Your hands glowed that night, too."

Lulu pressed her lips together. It wasn't often that I contradicted her ideas, but come on. By now I'd made up several better explanations than anxiety for what happened. *Warmed my hand in front of a microwave too much. Got bitten by a radioactive pianist.*

"I've been trying to practice," she admitted quietly. "The glow. But it won't come to me. Not by myself. Sometimes I get little tingles, but that's probably researcher bias."

She sounded frustrated, but I knew how Lulu worked through things. I had to be patient, so I held myself very still . . . until I couldn't.

"When things don't come easily to me," she continued, "then I work on it, and it's better. But this . . . this isn't like that."

That was true. The magic wasn't usually an act of willpower. I didn't command it. I let it come to me. That wouldn't work with my daughter, though.

"There's got to be an explanation," she said, almost to herself. "I'm getting our water tested."

I suppressed a sigh. "You go right ahead."

"I didn't want to say this before but there could be an environmental cause. It could be a public health emergency."

"How delightful."

"It would explain a lot."

My phone rang. It was Ma.

"Your patient's doing well, and the baby is fine," she said before I could even ask. "Seven pounds, ten ounces, Apgar 9. I wanted to check how you are."

I made a face she couldn't see. "Eight stitches."

"I saw you, you know, when the elevator door opened to labor and delivery. You were on the floor with an EMT holding a towel over your leg. Your patient was wailing and you were on the floor covered in blood. I thought you'd severed an artery." Ma was quiet for a minute. Then she said, her voice still strained, "I'm coming over."

"What? No. Ma, I'm fine. It looked bad, but—"

"I'll be there in five minutes." She hung up.

I stared at my phone, then looked over at Lulu. "Your grandma is threatening to beat us to our house."

Lulu did not "step on it," like I told her. When I pointed out we'd have to clean and get food, she shrugged and told me to order something.

"But your A-mà is so picky."

"You're the one who got hurt today. You eat whatever you want."

I stared at her. I didn't know how I'd managed to raise her to have such healthy expectations of . . . well, anyone.

"We're getting Indian," I said. "Chana saag and murgh makhani, a biryani, samosas, and lots of naan."

I pulled out my phone, and by the time my mother actually arrived, dinner was well on its way. I thought of calling Kenji, too. Maybe Lulu was right. I should take advantage of the fact that my mother had almost seemed vulnerable enough for me to introduce them.

But I'd had some painkillers and was not at my sharpest. And I was tired, so goddamn tired. Besides, while it would have been nice to curl up like a ball in Kenji's lap and have him feed me samosas, I didn't think anyone else would appreciate my dining arrangements.

But I did text him to let him know what had happened.

"Keep the leg elevated," my mother snapped as soon as she got in the back door and saw me at the kitchen table. She didn't bother knocking. Evidently, any fuzzy gentleness about my injury had hardened into a bludgeoning rock of maternal feeling on her way over.

I put down my phone and took a deep breath. "Food will be here in a few minutes."

"I can make something."

"We already ordered."

She crossed the kitchen to wash her hands as Lulu thumped down the stairs. We gazed at each other for one tense moment, and it seemed as if we all remembered the last time we'd been in the kitchen together.

Ma suddenly decided she needed to fill a pot with water, even though food was coming. The doorbell rang, so Lulu went to get it.

What a relief.

My phone pinged. I looked down to see a message from Kenji. Are you sure you're all right?

Again, I was tempted to ask him to come over. Maybe he would be able to shield me from the tension simmering in the kitchen. What did it mean that I thought his presence might actually make this easier for me? I reminded myself of all the passive aggressive (from Lulu) questions and the aggressive aggressive (from Ma) statements he'd have to deal with. So, I turned the phone over and didn't answer. I didn't know what to say anyway.

Ma frowned when she saw all the bags fragrant with the food we'd ordered, but she didn't say anything. We all sat down. I gestured at Ma to start. She was the oldest, after all. She took some rice, no doubt muttering under her breath that it wasn't sticky enough and scooped a little chickpea and spinach into her bowl.

Lulu and I tore in and for a moment I didn't mind the silence. I was roaringly hungry. But my phone pinged again. I ignored it. It sounded again.

"Aren't you going to get that?" Ma asked frigidly.

"Later."

"Maybe it's a patient."

"It's personal. Mom has a different ringtone for her expectant parents," Lulu said.

I wanted to glare at her, but she was trying to be helpful. Or was she? They turned both their gazes on me.

I sighed. "It's probably Kenji. He's concerned."

"You should answer then," Ma said stiffly.

I picked up the phone and thumbed in a reassurance that I really was fine, even though I was probably going to be ripped into by my family faster than this food if he called once more.

But I'd no sooner put the phone down again than Ma and Lulu decided it was time to lay in.

"I want to meet him," Ma said.

"We need to talk about the magic," Lulu said.

I held up my hands, and a samosa, to defend against the two of them. "I'm exhausted. My stitches hurt. I don't need this from either of you."

"But we're all here," Lulu said. "We can try this out. An experiment."

"Eating," I said, pointing to the samosa. "Tired. *Stitches.*"

"Don't you want to know if we can light up again? Don't you want to see if it was a fluke? Or are you afraid it's not going to happen because you need it to be true?"

A pit opened in my stomach. Kids, they really knew how to slide the knife in. It might prove something to Lulu if it failed. But I didn't know exactly what it would prove to me. Yes, I was afraid, but it wasn't that I might lose faith in the magic; I might lose faith in me.

Lulu was right. I needed it to be real.

"Fine," I said pushing my plate away, suddenly unable to swallow the bite I'd taken. "Let's do this."

Ma glanced between us. Then she said firmly, "We should look through the papers first."

"That might be a good idea. Maybe there's something that we missed that we'd be able to read. Or some drawings, any sort of clue. Or I could bring up Google translate," Lulu said, her voice warming.

Now I had to tell them. I closed my eyes. "I don't have the papers."

Ma put her fork down. "What do you mean you don't have them?"

"I gave them to Kenji. To translate."

"You talked about this with your boy friend?"

The way she said *boyfriend,* the two syllables not even touching each other, made it sound like he really was a small child. I tried to put that out of my mind, but I knew that from now on when Kenji rode up on his bike my mother's voice was going to pop up in my head.

"How much does he know?" Lulu snapped. "He supports this?"

I winced. From her tone, I could tell that she considered Kenji's agreement to translate Yi-beh's things a mark against him.

"How could you give the family papers to a stranger?"

"He's not exactly unknown to me, Ma. He can read Japanese. I didn't see the harm."

"Didn't see the harm? How much did you have to tell him? You can't pass Wu secrets to some—some person you're *dating*."

"But that's the point of dating, isn't it? To find a person you can talk to?"

I was too tired for this conversation, too exhausted for logic and argument. I wished I could let them understand my feelings, but that was the thing about Lulu and my mother—they would never allow that.

"She trusts him," Ma said, and it was a terrible thing.

"It's us you don't have faith in," Lulu said.

I shook my head, my anger starting to take over. "You're one to talk. Do you think I would act like this if there were no reason? Do you think I'm doing this because I enjoy it?"

"You're doing *him* because you enjoy it," Lulu said.

There was a short pause where a gasp should have been. Then Lulu covered her mouth. She was going to apologize, I knew it from how red her face turned, from the hunch of her shoulders. Suddenly, inexplicably I felt a bitter surge of love for her and all her obnoxiousness, for all the parts of her that were like me.

I looked her straight in the eye. "So what if I am?"

Ma glanced between us. I wasn't sure if she'd caught all of what Lulu said—her English always sounded fine, but she wasn't always certain of slang terms. But she'd felt the undercurrents.

"Let's just try this," I muttered, rubbing my face. Suddenly I wanted to defuse everything. "We'll try to see if we can call the light, clear the air, and then I can go to bed."

"Fine."

I didn't think I'd have the energy to do it. That vision I'd had of Yi-beh while I was unconscious had drained me. All of the times I saw her made me feel like a husk of myself. But Lulu stacked the takeout containers in the fridge, put the plates in the sink, and wiped down the table.

"Should we try to replicate what we did last time?" she asked.

I didn't remember the order of everything, but Ma pointed to the pot she'd filled with water. "We made tea. We all added something to it. I can't remember what."

"Honey," said Lulu.

"Maybe cinnamon. All this sounds really cozy."

Of course, it was all wrong for hot weather.

When the water boiled, we cast our ingredients into the water. Ma poured it out for us, and we stared at our cups. I cleared my throat. "Should we join hands again?"

That was the thing about having three people, I realized. You could hold everyone's hands at once if you were part of the circle.

I thought of the dream of my great-aunt, how firm yet gentle her touch had been on my fingers. But under the calluses and the strength and bone there was something seething and hungry.

I held on to my family. What had Yi-beh said to me? Feel the vibrations. Hear the *resonance.*

I closed my eyes and spread out my senses trying to tune myself in to the humming I could sense under everything.

It came to me—no, *they* came to me. My mother and my daughter's energy, feeding my depleted stores, connecting me to a larger harmony. I felt it falling into place, a pull in my pinky finger that went like a silver line through me, through wrist and bone, lighting my nerves like a highway at night.

Ma gripped me hard, to the point of pain, but was silent. Lulu made a sound like a whimper. But through that, I could feel them, their essences, so familiar and powerful, and it was wonderful.

"Mom," Lulu said.

I opened my eyes. And looked right at Kenji who'd just walked through the door.

"So, I guess you're all right, Leeann," he said. Through the glow of our hands, I saw his face moving from relief to humor.

"You could say that."

I was already smiling at him—I had been as soon as he came in. Maybe the room seemed bright—brighter—for a moment.

But then someone—probably Lulu—coughed, and we suddenly became conscious of our audience.

"I'm sorry for interrupting your, uh—" Kenji seemed to search for an appropriate word for whatever we were doing and clearly found none. "It's just that Leeann wasn't answering my messages, and no one heard me knocking on the front door."

"You're seeing this, too?" Lulu asked him. "You aren't surprised. She's done this in front of you before."

"Yes."

"How are you managing it?" Ma demanded of me. "Why aren't we all glowing? We tried all the things we did last time."

"I can feel your energy," I said. "Can you feel me?"

"No."

As if to echo her word, the luminescence of our joined hands faded slowly and completely.

We all stared at where it had been, our eyes wanting to find something left on our skin. With it gone, it was easy to say that it might never have been there, that there was nothing special about us.

Except Kenji's smile never faltered.

I got up and stumbled, forgetting about my leg. Apparently, I hadn't healed myself.

Kenji was around the table and holding me before my family could move. "Can you walk?"

"Yes, it's fine. I just pulled on my stitches."

My mother cleared her throat. "You must be Kenji," she said.

He settled me into my chair and flashed a charming grin at her. Ma did not bother smiling back. "May I get you more tea since I'm up?" he asked.

Oh, he was really pulling out the stops to try and please my mother, but I had not prepared him adequately, because if I had he wouldn't have bothered.

"They're nice to you and your family until they marry you," my mother said to me in English without bothering to modulate her voice. She turned back to Kenji. "Do you have the papers Leeann gave you?"

Kenji's smile didn't let up. If anything, his voice sounded more amused than usual. "They're in my trunk. I haven't gotten through many of them, though."

"We want them back."

"I could get them, but they're Leeann's, so unless she says, they stay," Kenji said firmly.

I could see how he would be good at managing middle schoolers.

Lulu at least had some manners. "Kenji, do you want to sit down? Have you eaten? We ordered Indian food."

He smiled at her. "No, thanks." But he moved to get himself a mug of tea, grabbed the spare chair in the corner, and took a place at the table.

We rarely had more than three people in this kitchen at a time. I wonder why I never noticed this before. But we all saw the ease with which he moved right into that place, though he'd only been in this house once. It was as if he belonged here. He wasn't showing off, not asserting a right. It was already his.

Sneaky.

"Did you make any progress with Yi-beh's writings?" I asked.

"Not much. I did put them in chronological order, though. It's a set of journals first, mostly notes and fragments about the people she treated, so I don't understand all the terminology. We can work through them together."

I touched his hand. "Thank you. I really appreciate it."

Ma watched us. "How old are you?"

"I'm thirty."

She glanced at me. "He's going to want children."

"Ma!"

Kenji said, "There are a lot of ways to make a family."

I turned to him. "You don't have to tell her anything." Too bad I also wanted to know his answers.

"He could change his mind about kids."

"Or Leeann could decide she wants to be with someone more ambitious and worldly," Kenji pointed out. He turned to me. "Someone who has a car."

"You have a car!"

"*Now* I do. Or someone who doesn't live on a teacher's salary and has never slept in a park. I keep waiting for you to realize that you could get someone more successful, more ambitious."

I shuddered, thinking of Paul, Lulu's dad. "It's not like that for me."

He held my gaze. "For me either."

Ma ignored us. "If you adopt, they won't have the Wu blood. They won't have that power."

Kenji turned back to her. "What should that mean to me? From what you said when I came in, you don't have it without Leeann anyway."

Ma drew her head back. She was expecting him to cower. She hadn't expected him to have answers—and frankly neither had I. But Kenji regarded her mildly. He hadn't meant it as an insult. It was a statement of fact.

It was too early to have this discussion—everything was too much all at once. I'd been in an accident! We'd just been glowing, for Pete's sake! But maybe that was something I needed to consider, that whatever this was, it wasn't a gift or a burden so much as it was simply a heritable characteristic. Whatever it was, it seemed Kenji had already given some consideration to what a longer-term future with me might look like.

Lulu had been mostly quiet, and I flushed guiltily remembering what she'd said about watching my mother and me fight.

"Ma, we're going to leave this discussion for another time. We should talk about something else."

"Yes, like how we lit up like lamps just now," Lulu finally piped up. "Although apparently some people see Mom do it all the time. You reacted more to her limping than to her shine. Like you expected it. But this isn't my mom! She isn't like this. She's funny, and practical, and she doesn't go around lighting up like a jellyfish! And here you are making her do it."

"I'm not making her do anything. She's actually been trying to hide it from me, but I think your mother has had this all along. This is just Leeann."

Ma and Lulu both glared at him, not me. I looked at all their faces, and maybe I should have wept to see all this anger, but I only wanted to laugh and cry.

So, this was love. All three of them loved me so much in their own ways, all of them were willing to defend what they saw as the best version of me—the parts they knew, the parts they liked best. Maybe it was painful to have them so angry now, but if they could only see—

"Dammit, someone put a lampshade over this woman," Lulu muttered, glancing my way.

It was faint this time, and not just my hands, but covering my body in a faint golden haze. If we hadn't been looking for it, we might never have seen it. It flared softly and dampened again like I was a lovelorn firefly.

Ma slapped her hands on the table. "Let's stop wasting time. Kenji, you need to go through those papers and find out why this—" Ma gestured at me, "this thing happens. Then we find out what it does. If it really helps anything—or if it hurts her."

"All it seems to do is make people fall asleep when they're around me so far," I said. "But we have to find out why it's happening now. Why do I keep dreaming of Yi-beh? Why is she trying to tell me something?"

"Maybe you can take a few days off work," Lulu suggested. "In case you start doing that again."

I shook my head. "I wouldn't want to leave Parisa in the lurch right now. It's been a tough few months. Not just for me. Hospitalizations are up. Everyone seems to be on edge, no one's getting any sleep. Even this accident seems to be a part of it. Parisa was telling me about her husband—" I stopped and frowned. "So much of this has been about sleep and dreams. And Yi-beh was saying something about how the dead can travel in dreams."

Ma looked then at something beyond my shoulder. "Maybe . . . she's a hungry ghost."

Something about the way she said it made me shiver. "What does that mean?" I thought of how those dreams made me feel, like I was being drained.

"I don't know much about it." Ma sounded unsure of herself. "My mother sent me to a Presbyterian school. She tried to take some of those beliefs away."

But Lulu pulled out her phone immediately and started to look it up. "Hungry ghosts are the spirits of those who haven't been buried properly," she read aloud. "At certain times, they can leave the temples to roam free and feed their appetites."

It seemed easier for Lulu sometimes. She could look things up about our background, things I didn't know how to search for when I was younger.

"What kinds of appetites?" Kenji asked.

"Food, entertainment, souls," Lulu read.

"They leave the temple to watch Netflix and chill?" I said, snickering nervously.

"Mom, please don't joke right now."

I swallowed. I was making cracks because I didn't like where any of this was leading. "Someone has to."

"Your Yi-beh disappeared during a summer like this one," Ma said quietly. "Strange weather, people acting oddly. No one could sleep."

"When did this happen?" I asked. "What month?"

"Sometime in mid-August."

Soon.

"Is she warning me?"

"Mom," said Lulu. "Stop. You're scaring me. Yi-beh's not warning you. We know nothing. The connection is tenuous. Just because one thing is happening with you doesn't link it to all the accidents going on in the real world. Correlation is not causation."

I clenched my hands, feeling a grim recognition of all the pieces that were starting to fall into place. "What's happening to me might not be a consequence, or the other way around. But what if *I* connect it? Maybe I can do something."

Although I really, really didn't want to think of what kind of heroic, life-shortening measure I might have to take to fight against—what? What was it that I had to battle? Some sleep-deprived drivers trying to keep it together? Ghosts who just wanted some chicken nuggets? I was just an ordinary woman with an extraordinary kid, a determined mother, a pretty nice boyfriend, and a strange luminescence. I wasn't looking to become a superhero or fight a villain.

My phone chirped with Parisa's tone.

"I have to take this," I told them, getting up.

I limped partway through to the living room. "Parisa, I was just telling my family about something you said."

"Leeann, it's Zana." Parisa's husband's voice broke. "Parisa's been in an accident."

◆ 15 ◆

THE NEXT FEW DAYS were a blur of redistributing Parisa's clients, adjusting the work schedule, and trying not to break down in tears. I wasn't allowed to see her. She was in intensive care. Not even my mother was able to bully her way past the nurses. But Zana sent me updates when he could, and Lulu and I spent time with her kids, who were both only a little younger than Lulu. We made sure there was always food in their house, Lulu ran the dishwasher, and I limpingly vacuumed a couple of times. But Parisa's extended family had it well in hand, and it wasn't like there was anything to clean—when the boys weren't at school or the hospital, they stayed silent and hidden in their rooms, emerging gaunt and exhausted, but still so polite when we called to them. The younger boy, Nasir, seemed even to have forgotten his crush on Lulu.

What we did wasn't enough—what I was doing was not ever going to be enough. They thought Parisa had fallen asleep at the wheel. Too many long hours and late nights had caught up with her.

If I hadn't been taken out yesterday evening, she wouldn't have had to come see me at the hospital. I'd stretched her day out longer. If only I noticed she was tired sooner, I could've sent her on her way.

Even now I wondered what else this *thing*, this glowing, useless thing was for. For all I knew, I could do something.

I pulled into our street. I was tired. I'd had too many late nights this week. But when I tried to rest, I thought of my friend at the hospital.

"Lay your hands on her," Ma had said on the phone earlier. "I'll distract the guards."

"They aren't guards. They're nurses. You're friends with some of them!" Ma snorted, although I wasn't sure whether it was because I'd said she had friends or because I'd insisted they weren't a security force. "Anyway, we don't even know if I can do anything."

"Something must happen," Ma said. "You have the power. Your Yi-beh knew."

I was beginning to doubt everything about Yi-beh's ghost, but I didn't let my mother know that. "Ma, she only gave me some papers. Plus, it doesn't make any sense. We're midwives. What does that have to do with summoning lightning and dream ghosts?"

"You deal with the beginning of life, Leeann, that spark. Of course you see the end of it, too."

"What the hell is that supposed to mean?"

But she'd already hung up.

I thought I'd wanted my mother to have faith in me—no, I always thought I wanted her to think I was extraordinary—but it turned out it made me feel like I was about to disappoint her even more than usual.

Yet, I couldn't just do nothing for Parisa.

I switched off the ignition and sat in the driveway. My eyes felt heavy and I couldn't think clearly, but of course I'd never be able to rest. *No one was sleeping.* The dead were visiting us in dreams. I turned the thought helplessly over in my mind, but it was like an orb, seamless, round, admitting nothing else. There had to be an opening. A reason.

I called Kenji to see if he'd made any progress on my great-aunt's notes.

"I'm sorry," he said distractedly. "I haven't really had a chance to look at anything. I've been packing, and my little niece has been testy lately. I was at Andrea's all day while she was in meetings, and Rosie fought her naps."

I didn't know what to say. This was important. But it all was important, wasn't it?

"Maybe I can have the papers back for now."

"No, I'll—" His voice faded for a minute. "Can we talk in person? Where are you?"

"I'm back home. Are you at your place or Andrea's?"

"I'm at mine now."

"I'll be there in 10 minutes."

I was too weary and heartsore for an argument or sex or anything more than taking the box of my Yi-beh's things. I could hire someone from the Japanese department at the university to translate them. But who was to say it wouldn't take even longer. I could . . .

Do something, a voice urged me. But I didn't know whose voice it was or what it was I ought to do. I was too tired to argue with it.

I found a parking spot on Main, and when I looked up Kenji was striding toward me. "You came outside," I said, dully.

"I didn't want you to walk up alone, and I knew you wouldn't call. I waited until I saw your car."

I got out and locked the door. The sun hadn't set yet. I stared at the sky for a few minutes wishing night would fall so that it could at least get a little cooler—not that it was cooling off much these days.

Kenji took my hand and led me toward his building and up the stairs. "Have you eaten? How is your friend?"

I shook my head and closed my eyes against the ache growing behind them. "Can I just have the papers?" I asked.

"Leeann, I can get them for you in a second if that's what you really want. But why don't you sit down? Let me at least get you a glass of water."

I shook my head, but I took my shoes off anyway. I folded myself onto the couch, almost too numb to register it was new, while Kenji moved around in the kitchen.

"She's my best friend," I said as Kenji flitted in and out of view. "She was one of the first people to believe in me. To see something in me, even though at that time I felt like such a disappointment to everyone else. You didn't even get to meet her."

I hadn't even told her about him. It wasn't something I could talk about over text, but I didn't know why I'd been taking so long to work up to it when it could have been something we might have giggled over together. She had the best laugh.

I buried my face in my hands.

"There's still a chance," Kenji said.

I wanted to believe that he knew something, anything. But the need was so sharp and desperate that instead I decided to be furious. "You don't know that. You don't know anything."

He brought out a sandwich on a plate with some chips, and a glass of ice water that I didn't realize I'd needed. I gulped it down greedily.

"I know you're worried," he said. "But you should eat something."

"I'm not hangry. I'm just regular angry. And heartsick and worried and guilty. I hate that this happened to Parisa. I hate doing nothing. The idea keeps growing in me, Kenji. If I could be alone with her for one moment and summon up the—whatever it is. The glow. But she's never going to be alone. She was a longtime member of the hospital staff. Her husband is the chief of neurology. People are going to be keeping an eye on her around the clock."

"You sound like you are already planning on doing something."

My voice came out hard. "And you want to try to talk me out of whatever it is."

He looked at me, quiet and gentle. It was probably how he gazed at his students, or at baby Rosie when she was screaming. "I'm not planning to talk you out of anything," he said. "But I am here to listen."

"And maybe to bail me out of jail. *Officer, I am guilty of glimmering gently. For luminescing. For unexplained phosphorescence.*" I took a savage bite out of the sandwich, and it shut me up for a while.

"Is that all you're planning to do? Slip in there, try to do your magic, leave?"

"I don't know enough to do anything fancier." At another time, I may have sounded snarky. But I only felt brittle. One tap and I'd be in a million sharp pieces.

"What if it doesn't work?" he asked me quietly.

"Like, if I'm caught?"

"No. If she doesn't get better."

"I might not be able to summon up the light at first, but if I have enough time, what harm could it do?" I said it bravely, but at the same time, I didn't know. I didn't know enough.

"Right, but what if she doesn't wake up healed the minute after you've done that?"

"It doesn't hurt anything."

"It hurts you."

"So far I haven't noticed a drain." *Was that true?* Maybe. The only thing that exhausted me was dreaming of Yibeh. "I'm not getting paler, less energetic. My ego is not on the line here."

"It's not your ego I'm worried about. It's your faith. In yourself. Other people have the luxury of learning through mistakes, but you aren't giving yourself that here."

I swallowed. The sandwich was too dry. I needed more water.

"Faith is supposed to be tested, isn't it?"

"But is this a fair test?" Kenji pushed. "I'm sorry I haven't had time to translate your great-aunt's papers. I'll try harder. But if we just knew more. My point is, if nothing happens with your friend, if she goes into a decline after you've gone and seen her and done what you think you need to do, I hope that you'll be easy on yourself. And that it doesn't mean you won't try to help people in future because you think it went wrong." His words came slowly and his voice was still gentle, but I didn't want to hear it.

I put up my hands. "I don't have a choice. This has to work."

He swiped his hand through his hair. It was the only sign of frustration he ever gave. "But it might do something different, or it might not work in a way you understand."

"All I understand is that I'm trying to do something, and you're second-guessing me."

If he didn't believe in me, then the only one who did was going to have to be me.

"I'm not—I'm not trying to undermine your confidence. I'm asking you to go into this with open eyes. I'm asking you how you'll feel if things don't turn out exactly the way you envision it the first time you attempt to help someone."

"Because I fail at everything."

He shook his head. "You know that's not true. You're a smart, professional woman with the respect of so many people in this community, and you do something important and awesome. And you have a kid who's going to make as much a mark on the world as you. I've told you I worry that I'm not together enough for you. But that's not the point." He ran his hands through his hair. He looked as tired as I felt. "I feel like I know you. And you want to do something—anything—rather than just sitting around. I understand that. But is simply doing *anything* really what you want to do? You may blame yourself if it doesn't work right away. You're used to taking responsibility for so much."

"What do you mean? I mean, if anything Lulu's the responsible one."

"But who has nurtured her? She didn't spring out of you fully formed. Your miracle glowing hands have been all over her life, just like they've been on all the children you've delivered. Just because you're used to occupying one space in your family doesn't mean it's who you really are."

I'd said as much to Ma and Lulu.

What could I really do? All I had was a vague family story about miraculous healing. A strange glow. I had nothing—no proof, no real expertise, no training or deep history or legacy that I could understand, no real deep-down certainty in myself, no special knowledge. I wasn't a neurologist like Zana, I was a midwife.

And yet . . .

"Do you think something will go wrong?" I asked.

He let out a long breath. "I don't doubt that you have something. But even people who have talent or knowledge hope for the best and prepare for the worst. It's like you told me earlier today, I don't know anything. I know less than you. Leeann, I care about you. I'm not trying to second-guess you because I don't have faith in you. I think you're remarkable. I think I'm in love with you."

He'd shut his eyes and mouth abruptly, as if he'd said too much at the wrong moment. I wanted to tell him that I felt the same, that I'd known for a while. But the words got stuck in my throat.

"You'll blame yourself if your friend doesn't get better," he continued in a normal tone, "and I don't think you deserve to take on that burden when you're trying your hardest with what little information you have."

He knew me so well. *He loved me.* So why didn't he understand?

"I'll never forgive myself if I don't try."

* * *

"The simplest plan is best," Lulu said.

She didn't like the magic. But she did enjoy solving problems—even if it meant bending the rules to get me in to see Parisa.

"You should wear your scrubs," she added. "Plus a mask. Try to look like you belong. Which you do. You've been affiliated with the hospital for years."

"I've never had to work in the ICU though."

"Act like you're familiar with it. I'll convince Zana and the boys to go get something to eat with me. You slip in and, I don't know, talk to her. Glow. Do your thing. Tell her I love her, and I wish I could be there, too."

"Lulu," I said softly.

She gritted her teeth. "For the record, I hate this."

"I know."

"I'm only agreeing to this because . . . because I also hate not doing anything."

I pressed my lips together. "I know, baby."

Any minute now she was going to cry. "Your stupid Wu woo better work."

"I'm going to try," I whispered.

In the end it was easy getting in. Parisa's husband Zana and the kids went along with Lulu without protest. Clad in my gear, I slipped into Parisa's room.

I stood looking at my friend for a moment.

Her face was yellow with bruises, her head still bandaged. She had an IV in her arm, and I knew that under the covers her body was broken, the bones and muscles and blood vessels trying to stitch themselves back together.

I wasn't going to cry. This wasn't the time. But my throat felt heavy.

I closed my eyes and tried to tune out the beeps and hums of the machines around us. I concentrated on the soft, ragged sound of my own breathing and listened for the resonance underneath it all.

A few inhales and there it was, right in place, as if I'd spotted the illusion and now couldn't unsee the strings. But as I reached out to grasp it, it vanished. I couldn't hear it or feel it anymore.

What the hell.

A thin line of sweat began at the back of my neck. That was fine. I could do this.

Breathe.

I relaxed my fingers around Parisa's hand. I let it come over me once more. When my mind was quiet again, this time, I didn't reach. I let the feeling overtake me, and I opened my eyes.

Parisa was looking at me.

Oh shit, I hadn't counted on her being awake. But she was there. Her eyes were as sharp as ever, taking in my hospital garb, my features behind my mask. The glow.

"I was wondering why I hadn't heard from you yet," she said, her voice a hoarse thin sound. I could hardly hear her above the swoosh of machines.

"Parisa." Tears tracked down my cheeks.

"Ugh," she said, looking at her hand in mine. "No wonder Zana won't let anyone see me. I look bad, don't I?"

I had to pull myself together. "You look like you fought a car with your face. Which you did."

"You should see the other guy."

I let out a gulping sob.

"Hey, hey. Stop that. I'm too tired to make you feel better, and your boyfriend is going to be sad I made you cry. Tell me what you're going to do with that glow stick in your hand."

I wiped my face in my elbow. I wanted to heal Parisa, not get snot on her. "I'm going to try to help you. But I don't know if it'll work."

If she could've shrugged she might have. But I could tell she was fading. "Worth a shot," she said, her face tightening with pain again. "You always had a talent."

I grasped her hand tightly as if it would make the connection between us stronger and watched as she fell asleep. I tried to direct the glow to her, but every time I tried too hard it faded. So I concentrated on just being there with her.

Who could tell if it was doing anything at all?

I don't know how long I stayed with her. The plan was I was supposed to get in, touch her with the glow, get out. But Zana found me. Because I'd fallen asleep.

How could I have let that happen while I was supposed to be alert and helping Parisa? I was supposed to evade detection.

I was lucky he didn't call security and have me ejected from the hospital. I'd never seen him furious before, but I could tell he was angry. He didn't say anything to me even as he escorted me out into the corridor.

"I have no explanation for you," I said.

His voice was clipped. "I know you're a medical professional. I know you didn't mean any harm. But you can't go in there."

"I won't again, I promise. I just wanted to talk to her."

He shook his head. "I can't believe I have to explain this to you, but the next few days are critical. If she doesn't wake up—"

"What do you mean if she doesn't wake up? I—"

"We've been monitoring her closely. She's been in a reduced state of awareness state this whole time."

I opened my mouth, then shut it. "But I spoke with her."

"It might have seemed like she heard you. She makes little movements and sounds sometimes. But Leeann, she's not—there's no telling if she's ever going to be the same." His voice broke. He felt as helpless as I did. More.

But I had talked to her! She'd made jokes! She'd spoken like she'd been aware and awake.

I reached out to hug him, but he stiffened, and I dropped my arms. A nurse walked by and looked at us curiously.

"I'm sorry, Zana. I really am. I won't do it again. But do the monitors pick up all changes in neurologic activity?"

He frowned. "Why? Did she open her eyes? Say anything to you?"

A few more people hurried by.

"We had a whole conversation," I whispered. "She was really there. It was her—her personality, the toughness, the way her eyes smile even when she's saying harsh things."

"You must have dreamed it. You were sound asleep when I came in." His face softened a little. "I dream of her, too. When I can sleep. And then I open my eyes."

He rubbed his face.

I'd been about to protest that it had been real, but Zana looked like he was on the verge of tears. It would have been cruel to insist. Almost as terrible as awakening from seeing and talking to someone you missed—to someone *I* missed—to believe they were alive and aware. Then for it not to be true.

"I'm sorry again," I mumbled as he escorted me out.

He took a deep breath. "No harm done," he said.

As he left me, I wondered if that was true.

⋆ ⋆ ⋆

"You fell asleep?"

"Lulu, I don't know what happened."

We were driving home after our half-successful attempt at intrigue.

"All you had to do was glow, touch, exit. That was the whole plan."

"Technically, the whole plan was you distract, I sneak in. Then glow, touch, exit. And that involves complications."

Truth be told, I was ashamed. It was supposed to be so simple. But somehow, I'd managed to mess it up. And no, being tired was not an excuse. I hadn't even been drowsy—not more than usual.

"The point is Zana probably won't mention it to anyone. I didn't get you in trouble, either, if that's what you're worried about."

"For crying out loud, I'm not worried that my own mom sang like a canary."

"Sang like a canary?"

"Snitched, ratted me out."

"When you were applying for American schools did you study for a criminal edition of the SATs or something? How do you know all this?"

Lulu snorted. It was probably the closest thing approaching a laugh I'd heard from her since the news of Parisa's accident.

That made me hesitate to tell her the next part. "The other thing was, I talked to Parisa. She talked to me, I mean."

"But the boys told me she wasn't waking up." Lulu shook her head, and I knew she was going to have trouble believing the rest. How could she? I doubted what happened myself. Parisa had seemed so real, so much like herself.

But even if she had woken, she couldn't have been so sharp, so lucid.

As I searched my memory for what Parisa had said to me, I realized she'd known about Kenji.

I'd hadn't mentioned him yet—I'd been waiting to tell her in person. All we'd had lately was a bunch of snatched text messages and that moment in the ER. But she had teased me about him from her ICU bed. How could she have known?

She couldn't have, unless the whole thing had happened in my head.

"Can't manage to pass the Bechdel test even during a hallucination," I muttered, turning to the window. "Never mind me."

Lulu said, "In a way I'm jealous you were able to sleep. I feel like I haven't been able to close my eyes for more than a few minutes at a time all summer. And especially now with what happened with Parisa."

My mind stirred. "Say that again?"

"I've been worried because of Parisa? Or you mean . . ." She stopped. "No one's been getting any sleep," she said slowly. "Almost all the accidents we've heard of, except for that lightning strike, were human error."

"More than one dry strike. And the dreams I've been having—those have been strange. Do you think there's a connection?"

Lulu let out a breath. "I don't know what to think anymore. I almost want to believe you."

"Don't hurt yourself."

Lulu pulled into our driveway and got out of the car. I followed more slowly. I could still feel the faint stir of electricity in the air and realized that was the other thing that had been making me uneasy all summer. I went to the trunk and pulled out an extra scoop of seed for the birds. They flapped down cawing for their friends before I even managed to close the bag.

Lulu leaned against the car and watched me. "I never worried you'd turn into a cat lady, you know. You like birds too much."

"Isn't that just substituting one kind of animal collecting for another?"

"No, I mean you're busy. You have too many ties and friendships around here. You have Parisa—well, and her family, and all your work friends, and the people you've helped over the years. People you know from high school. You're out there in the community. I never thought you'd end up lonely when I was gone. And now you have Kenji, too."

The last part was said reluctantly. But it was there.

When I didn't answer, she sighed. "And yes, you love these wild birds too much to get a houseful of cats."

The birds liked me because I fed them. At least I understood that relationship.

"What if Parisa doesn't get better?" I asked. "If she's in that state between sleep and death and I did something to her that made her appear in some dream of mine, maybe that's a sign I made it worse."

Kenji had been right. Guilt and worry over my own uncertain powers surged over me in a wave so strong I had to close my eyes.

"Or it could be a sign that you've been thinking about her and wishing you could talk to her. It could just be a dream about your desire to see her again and maybe it won't affect it one way or the other."

But I'd had dreams about people before, and they were never like this. I couldn't feel the scratchiness of the sheets under my hand. I couldn't smell that faint tang of disinfectant in the hair. The dream wouldn't have supplied me with the consistent beep of machines, the sheen of fluorescent lighting on Parisa's skin.

And in dreams if I concentrated too hard on a face, those faces always changed, became something or someone else.

"No," I said, certain. "It was real."

16

THE NEWS FROM ZANA remained the same. Parisa was stable, but she hadn't woken up.

At least Zana was still talking to me.

I went through the rest of the week like an automaton, shouldering most of Parisa's administrative work and taking on a few of her patients, trying not to break down every time I had to explain what had happened. Most of them already knew, but they wanted to talk about it anyway, or they wanted updates. Many times, I told myself to breathe through the pain, exactly the same way I'd been teaching them, especially when I had to keep saying there were was no news. My attempt at laying my hands on her had accomplished nothing. The stitches in my leg still throbbed sometimes, as if to remind me that these days would leave scars.

But Lulu and I were back at my mother's house that Friday. Except this time, when we pulled into the drive, we saw Kenji's car. And in the doorway with my mother, Kenji.

"I wanted to get to know him better," my mother explained with a wide-toothed grin.

It reminded me of the Tiger Aunt story she used to tell me when I was a kid. *What is that you're eating?* the little girl would ask the old Tiger Aunt, who claimed she'd been sent to watch the children.

I'm eating peanuts, the Tiger Aunt would lie as she crunched on the fingers of the girl's unfortunate sister. But the Tiger Aunt could never hide the swishing of her tail.

I took a quick look at Kenji's hands. All digits accounted for. Everything else seemed intact. Kenji smiled at us as if he hadn't arrived too early—been invited too early, I suspected—to have a one-on-one chat with my mother.

I hadn't seen him for a few days, since our . . . was it an argument? I didn't even know what it was. But he kissed me in front of Ma now and searched my face. Whatever he saw there had him squeezing me to his side.

I found it reassuring, damn me.

"How's your friend?" he asked.

"The same."

He nodded and kissed the top of my head for good measure.

My mother, on the other hand, looked sulky. "He made a cold soup," she said by way of explanation. "With uncooked peppers." Despite her healthy tendencies, my mother did not always trust raw vegetables. At the same time, I suspected Ma was a little relieved that she hadn't had to produce a meal for her ungrateful family.

"It's gazpacho."

"He used the blender," Ma added.

Lulu didn't look impressed. "Great."

"I think it sounds wonderful," I said.

To be honest, I didn't know if a garden-y soup was quite what I wanted, but I was petty enough to be happy that Kenji had thwarted my mother. Plus, everything was better when I discovered Kenji also had also been invited early enough to go out, buy some crusty bread, and to toast it under the broiler before we'd arrived.

"He made the house too hot," my mother complained to Lulu.

"So, turn on the air conditioning," I muttered.

Apparently, she'd set the table in the dining room while Kenji was busy. We all sat solemnly around it. Not that it was any less easy than our usual Friday routine. But I could tell that Lulu was already comparing this new normal against what she was comfortable with, and she didn't love it. One person changed the dynamic entirely. It wasn't that Ma was better behaved or that I felt much more supported—and observed.

"So what's the deal with the translation?" Lulu said as soon as Kenji took a mouthful of bread. Her eyes were challenging.

He glanced at me. "I made some progress," he said carefully. "I have a bunch of notes. Most of it was about your great-aunt's cases. But I think she wrote about you, Leeann. The years match up. She was taking care of a young girl and watching her grow."

It didn't make sense. I was too young to remember her, but it was like someone had reached into my chest and squeezed my heart tight. My only memories of Yi-beh, if they could be called memories, were in my dreams.

I stared at my plate.

"Near the end she started writing more. She was worried she was becoming—" He paused. "Unstable. And she didn't have anyone she could really talk to about it. Her family were too busy and too far away. Most of her close friends had died by then, and there was a new district nurse, so she wasn't doing as many deliveries. Also, people thought she was strange, and she knew it."

Lulu did not look at me. Ma frowned.

I stared at the bright soup in my bowl.

Lulu was the only one eating. She spooned food steadily into her mouth, because she was a sensible girl who knew she needed her nutrients to outrun us older weirdos. She avoided my eyes.

"Go get the papers out, Kenji. I want to see them," Ma said.

"Kenji's eating," I said. "And you can't even read them."

"It's fine," Kenji said, getting up. "But I don't want to get soup on your family history."

Ma fixed him with a glare. "You won't get soup on them because if you do, I'll yell at you."

To be fair, this would probably work.

What was I feeling? There was guilt that I didn't remember Yi-beh, mixed with anger that the whole family had forgotten her. How could we have done that, let her soul wander without a proper rest?

Kenji went out to his car and in a few minutes came back with the box and folder. He pulled out a few pages. "This is the main thing that stands out near the end of her life," Kenji said, scanning the paper quickly. "She says she had prophetic dreams and no one in her village was sleeping enough. Her writing seems to match up with that. All the half-finished thoughts, the way her handwriting became erratic, and the entries stop being dated. Then she starts talking about making a big sacrifice."

A sense of foreboding sat in my breastbone. "Is there any wine?" I asked, getting up.

"Aren't you still on painkillers for your leg?" Kenji asked.

"No."

"There's vodka under the sink," Ma said.

I was surprised it had taken me this long to find out about Ma's stash. I located the bottle, unscrewed the top, and tipped some into my soup. Then I passed it to my mother who did the same.

"You two aren't going to be able to pay attention if you're drinking," Lulu snapped.

I tried to keep my voice light, but fear kept thudded dully in my chest. "I *have* been paying attention. Something about a big sacrifice that the people with magic have to make to save a village that isn't sleeping. That's why I broke out the alcohol."

I took a generous spoonful of gazpacho and grimaced. It wasn't delicious but maybe it would do the job.

Ma said, "Before you go around getting ideas about doing something big, whatever your great-aunt did, it didn't work. The village was wiped out anyway. She disappeared. We assumed she'd died. No one ever found a body. She left you."

A pause.

"I know it's not right. Nearly forty years later, I'm still angry at her for leaving you."

And me, were her unspoken words. But they rang out in the pause that followed her surprising words.

But I didn't want to show her I'd heard the grief in her voice. It seemed too emotional, and she'd taught me not to acknowledge her weaknesses at least. "Drink up, Ma."

Surprisingly, she obeyed.

I sat there as Kenji and Lulu and Ma argued around me as I ate my soup steadily and thought about the way Ma's words sounded. *She left you.*

Yi-beh hadn't left me behind promising to come back for me the way my mother had. She'd disappeared.

Except now Yi-beh was haunting me when I was asleep.

"The ghosts come in dreams," I said slowly. Like Yi-beh. She was a ghost. "But if we were all practically sleep-walking half asleep, half in dreams they'd be around us all the time. The ghosts come in dreams, but people *are* seeing them during waking hours."

I thought of the flash of surprise that came over the expectant father's face before he'd collapsed, the student who'd accosted me outside the restaurant. They'd both perceived things they shouldn't have been able to see if they were fully awake.

"That's part of the problem. They're coming to our world."

Ma blinked. "We're seeing them," she repeated.

"Who is it?" I asked Ma sharply.

Her face shuttered. "I've sensed your father before," she said quietly. "Sometimes I think he's there, a flash in the corner of my eye. But now sometimes . . . he appears."

My skin felt cold. The way she talked made it sound like he was not a welcome presence.

We all stayed quiet for a moment.

Lulu was the one who finally broke the silence. "So what are you saying? If everyone stopped sleeping—"

"Which is what's happening now, isn't it? No one has been able to get a decent rest. That's what I keep hearing this summer. People in the area are irritable, acting wild, sometimes having accidents because everyone is exhausted."

I tried to concentrate, but my mind was reeling over the fact that my father haunted my mother. I took a breath. "The lines between the ghost world and ours are blurred if no one can sleep. They'll be among us, and," I added reluctantly, "they'll want to stay."

Ma dropped her spoon on the table. She was almost never clumsy, but her eyes turned to me, startled. "You think they can get stronger?" My mother was scared.

My fingers twitched with the urge to touch her, to pat her hand. But I couldn't move because I knew I was right about this. This was what Yi-beh had been trying to warn me about.

They come in dreams.

"So, they want us to be in a half-asleep state," Kenji was saying slowly. "All of this heat, and these weird incidents are symptoms of the conditions they're creating so they can come to our world."

I shivered and tried to think clearly. "That's why what I keep feeling around us isn't just heat. It's . . ." I didn't know the words for it. "It's almost like the weather has a personality. Maybe it's some kind of psychic energy trying to press us all down. Lightning bursts, winds around the clocktower. And exhaustion. Like they're eating at us already."

I breathed more quickly, thinking of the heavy feeling of loss whenever Yi-beh came to me, how drained I felt, how hollow. How I always felt I never knew enough about her after. How that always left me yearning. Yearning for something I would never know enough, and that she could not give me.

I could almost feel the edge of her hunger. She wanted to warn me, but she also wanted my energy. There were too many unknowns; I couldn't trust her.

"What do they want?" Ma murmured as if following my thoughts.

"They want to swallow the living world. And because we Wus have this . . . this ability to channel energy they want, they're using us. Yi-beh would know this." I wanted to get up and pace, but my leg still hurt. My heart hurt.

I felt the slow realization of betrayal seep into my bones as I spoke. I'd thought she was coming to find me because she missed me, because she wanted me to know about her and our family. But this made more sense. All those sad secret longings I had of wanting to belong somewhere where people knew me, she'd exploited them.

She wanted my energy.

"Listen, I don't know if any of this makes sense. But what we do know is that accidents are up—we've all had more this summer than before. More patients at our clinic are showing signs of postpartum depression, the neurology team is logging a lot of people complaining about insomnia, we're having this strange hot summer and it won't rain or offer us any relief. We're exhausted. And when we're not sleeping, we're all vulnerable. My best friend, who's been a midwife for years and is used to strange hours, was so tired she fell asleep at the wheel. We can't let this continue."

Lulu stirred but she didn't contradict me. I knew she wanted to.

"The connections are tenuous, I know that, Lulu. And maybe this is the irrationality of my own lack of sleep talking, but something's happening. Can't you feel it? You can't tell me you haven't felt it pressing around us all summer. And we're the only ones who can do something about it because we can control this energy that they want. But also, in a way, we're the cause of it *because* we have this power." The more I spoke, the more I felt it made sense. Until it didn't. I felt a little dizzy and the heat seemed to stir once again as if I'd poked it. Of course, the warmth from the vodka was probably helping.

Lulu gave a short, sharp nod.

That was the thing that made me want to cry. I didn't want her to agree with me that she'd been feeling this way, too. I wanted to be wrong. All at once, I tried to push my soup away. It slopped over the side of the bowl. "I'm sorry, Kenji," I said a little blearily. "You worked so hard on this meal and I'm spilling it all over."

"It's fine. It's all a lot . . . for everyone."

"It's too weird. I don't want to think I'm supposed to save the world from being swallowed by ghosts." I laughed uncomfortably. "That would be ridiculous. I'm just a middle-aged woman who's tipsy on three spoonfuls of spiked gazpacho."

"You could, though," Kenji said quietly.

I clenched my fist. I'd wanted to be special. Now here I was. "How do you know that? You tried to warn me, and Parisa's still in a coma."

"I wasn't warning you so much as telling you not to blame yourself if nothing happened."

Lulu put her spoon down. "With all due respect, we should cover our bases. We can work on this magic thing. Keep working on it," she said with a guilty flush. "But if it really is an 'outbreak' of insomnia and other neurological issues, we have to tell someone, too. A public health official. Infectious disease doctors or an epidemiologist. Or someone who specializes in environmental health."

"Like who?" I asked.

"Zana, for one. He's the chief of neurology. Whatever is happening right now, this is having an effect on our nerves and brains. You said yourself he'd been seeing an uptick in weird cases."

I shook my head. "We can't talk to Zana about this. Not now that I had been caught sneaking into Parisa's room. And besides, we don't have any real evidence. Unless your water testing turned something up."

"No, there was nothing." Lulu's shoulders sagged.

I nodded. "You're right, Lulu—I'll figure something out to say to public health officials, but I don't know that they'll hear me out if I have nothing to go on except that people are not sleeping during a hot summer. The same thing happened to my great-aunt. I don't have any more scientific evidence than my gut feelings and anecdotes of what we've seen."

"Mom," Lulu said more desperately. "I know what it seems like to you, but you aren't alone, and you don't have to do something drastic."

My baby girl, she really was starting to get scared. I wanted to joke to make her feel better. "Okay, maybe we'll just save Reineville and the surrounding tricity area then."

"I don't think the clinic requires you to cover this."

I squinted at her. She was trying to tease me back, but for some reason it made me sad and even more frightened.

"I'm know I'm not a hero, Lulu. I'm not a witch. I'm a midwife, and I might be a little magical, but my life isn't from some fairy tale. I've been a very ordinary woman for most of my life. Most people don't even notice me."

"I noticed you," Kenji said. "There are many ways to be extraordinary."

My heart squeezed painfully again. The people I loved were here in this room, and I was such a chickenshit in front of them. I didn't want my life to end in a typhoon, not that we'd be getting them in Ontario, Canada. But I didn't see that I had much choice other than to try something again. "You've said it yourself. I have this effect. One of the things that I do, aside from the weird glowing, is I make people sleep or relax into it." I thought again of the man who'd tried to put his hands on me after my date with Kenji, the parents who'd fainted or dozed off in my presence. The names of people they thought they'd seen before they slept on their lips. I swallowed. "Or it could just be my boring personality."

"No way," Kenji said.

"I wouldn't call you restful," Lulu interjected helpfully.

"You don't have to discount my powers by insulting me."

"To be fair, both choices you offered are insults."

I held my head. "I'm supposed to save the world—sorry, tritown area and I can't even follow an argument. We have to make a plan."

"What kind of plan could we possibly concoct?" Lulu said. "You can't go around touching everyone in town and causing them to pass out. You can't let them know about your whole phosphorescence thing, and even if they did find out and were cool with it, it would still take too much time. We have to think of this more like a numbers problem than a magical problem. We have to find a way to distribute whatever it is you have over a wider range."

I threw up my hands. "We could do something with the reservoir. You keep saying there's something in the water."

"I didn't mean I thought we should go out and deliberately add something to it. We'd never be able to anyway. It's not like sneaking into the ICU. We would be in serious trouble for attempting to tamper with the reservoir. And even if we did, what do you think we'd be able to do? Take an enormous bag of chamomile and dunk it in the reservoir? Maybe empty a honey bear into it, too? Sleepytime tea? That's the big plan?"

We were all breathing too quickly, trying to keep it light while talking about the end of our world. I held out my hands. "No, we're going to work together, like you said, Lulu. After the accident, we made tea together, and we managed to channel something that time. We were all glowing. We all have it, not just me."

"I've been trying on my own and so has A-mà. We can't reproduce the results. That makes it a failed experiment."

"Let's try it again now that we're together." I meant to jump up, but I was a little unsteady on my feet. Kenji stood and caught me, and maybe I sagged into him a little. It was nice. Why couldn't I just let myself be caught instead of having to do things?

But Lulu, sleepless but energetic Lulu, was still picking at the theory. "Why? Even if we can get it to work, the three of us can't go around just randomly groping people so that they fall asleep. And even if we make them do that, what's to say they'll be able to sleep the next day or the next."

"It's not groping exactly," I muttered.

But she had a point. There were too many people and too few of us. If we could get more people to conduct the same energy, then maybe it would be possible.

I delivered babies one at a time. Twins and triplets went to hospital. I had one parent, one child. That was the scale I was used to dealing with.

Ma finally spoke. "Your great-aunt, she tried to do this herself. She had to because no one would believe her. She shouldn't have had to do this alone. But you, Leeann—this is different. We don't have much information, but that doesn't mean we can't stop some of it. This world already has enough ghosts." She reached out and touched my hand.

It was so rare, this contact, that I almost withdrew. "Are you saying you believe me, Ma?" I swallowed. "All the ghosts and glowing and strange science and . . . my ability to do this?"

She nodded. "Yes, that's what I'm saying."

I gripped my mother's hand. I knew what we had to do. "Lulu, sit down. Kenji, take cover."

I didn't give them any warning except for the flock of birds that rushed up, temporarily darkening the kitchen window. Then there it was, the flash of white in the sky, except this time, holding my mother and daughter's hands, I could sustain it. I had so much control.

It was exhilarating.

Ma jerked in my hold and Lulu screamed. Out of the corner of my eye, I saw Kenji, outlined in white, looking as if he was going to spring on us to protect us from that awful, seductive light.

I found it difficult to let go, but I eased my hands and the light winked out.

My mother slumped and Lulu drew in a shaky breath.

"So," I said. "That's what we can't let them have."

⋆ ⋆ ⋆

I was still not Zana's favorite person, but I'd promised Lulu I'd try to talk to someone about the sleep problem.

"She's the same," Zana told me when I approached him in the cafeteria.

He was alone surrounded by crushed coffee cups scattered around him like buoys warning of rocky shoals.

"Thanks," I said carefully. I sat down across from him uninvited. "I've been reading your updates."

He placed another coffee cup between us. Directly in front of me.

Message received.

"Don't ask how am I *really* doing," he said.

"I won't."

"My wife is in a coma and has likely sustained brain damage, and even though I'm a neurologist, I can't do a thing about it. That's how I'm doing."

"I'm sorry."

He scrubbed his face with one hand. "I know you didn't try to harm her when you went to see her, but sometimes it's hard not to convince myself that you falling asleep next to her didn't cause her condition to worsen. I know it doesn't make sense."

I stayed silent.

"If she doesn't show some sign of waking soon, then I don't know," Zana said.

I clutched my hands together and squeezed. My glow hadn't helped Parisa.

Zana said, "Did she ever tell you how we met? We were young. Our families were friends. I always knew she was the one for me. But I wasn't patient enough, and she didn't want to marry me the first time I asked. My mother was scandalized. What kind of woman turned down a good offer? And what kind of ungrateful girl wouldn't want to marry her Zana? Her son was going to be a doctor! But Parisa was in the middle of her training—so was I. Maybe I was annoyed at the time, too, that she didn't want to commit when it was convenient for me. But part of me always understood that I should be with the kind of person who knew her opinions and life and work were just as important as mine. So, I was patient. The next time I asked, I waited until she was on her vacation, and she'd rested well, and that her glass was full of juice and there was food on the table in front of her. She was relaxed. And then I begged her humbly."

I had to laugh. "You learned."

"It took me a while, but I did." He looked at the coffee cup in his hands and sighed. "Now when I can manage to sleep I dream of my mother. Not my wife. That's probably a good thing. I doubt those two would get along enough to be in the same dream together."

I took in a breath. "So, you are sleeping a little bit."

"Snatches here and there. And when I sleep, I dream."

"Does your mother say anything to you in the dreams?"

Zana rolled his eyes. "She always has something urgent to say to me. It's funny, though, because she always used to smell like lemons. I could swear I still smell them when I blink awake."

He looked pensive, and stubborn. Parisa had described that look on her husband's face often enough, but I'd never seen it until now. I could see I probably wouldn't get more information out of him about those dreams.

I changed the subject. "Before Parisa's accident we were running numbers, and we realized we had an unusually large number of patients reporting depression, sleeplessness, irritability, and other disorders."

He nodded. "Parisa mentioned it."

"She also said your department was having a busier-than-usual summer. I pulled some of the numbers from our practice."

"Why are you telling me this?" Zana asked tiredly.

"It's just . . . I think there's something to the fact that so few people are sleeping well. It's why Parisa lost control of her car, isn't it? If there's something in the water or some environmental cause for this . . ."

Or something else that was making Zana dream constantly of his mother who'd died at least four years ago.

Zana just stared at me. Finally, he said, "I know you feel like you need to find answers. That Parisa's accident had to have some meaning. I was that way, too. But these things happen."

I shook my head. "You make it sound like you've given up on her."

"I'm being realistic," Zana said.

I wasn't—at least, I was trying to argue something I couldn't believe. I should've gotten Lulu to make her own case. She would have busted out phrases like *public health crisis* and *contaminated groundwater.* But Zana wouldn't have listened to her either. She was a kid in his eyes, after all.

Zana was still talking, still locked in his own thoughts. "Look, I know what survival rates after this are like. Even if she pulls out of this, there's a good chance she won't be the Parisa we used to know. No, not just a chance. This is a trauma. Physically, but also emotionally. If she survives, she may never heal completely. Even if they regain their motor control, patients report being more angry, more fearful and aggressive. They become impatient and lose impulse control. Or these patients become more prone to depression, anxiety. She'd be a ghost of her former self."

"She isn't a ghost yet. And she's not a patient, she's your wife."

But Zana wasn't hearing me. I'd been wrong, the coffee cups scattered around him weren't warning buoys. They were a graveyard.

I wanted to zap him.

I kept calm and reminded myself I was here to simply tell Zana about Lulu's backup plan. Zana was our best chance of getting an authority to see that something was wrong—or to confirm that what we were seeing was real.

But Zana had retreated behind his expertise. I thought about how Kenji had told me that I would blame myself for failure because I didn't know enough—but sometimes knowing a lot more still wasn't enough.

"Maybe just consider there's something else going on here," I said, standing up.

But Zana had stopped listening to me long ago, and I could hardly blame him.

So I did the only thing I could do. I went home and practiced my magic with my mother and daughter.

♦ 17 ♦

"EVERYONE IN TOWN IS here," Kenji said in my ear as we pushed our way through the fairgrounds.

His shoulder was proving very useful. It was a hot, crowded night, and although I didn't usually feel short, the fair sometimes made me realize that I was small. Almost insignificant. How did I think I could save anyone?

"It draws a lot of the summer-cottage people," I half whispered and half shouted up into Kenji's ear. "But most of the locals work it or attend at some point."

I started to pull him toward the area that held the craft booths. At least it would be a little quieter there, although a guy hawking reproduction medieval wear was blasting Whitesnake out of a pair of deceptively tiny speakers.

"I remember coming as a teen with my childhood best friend," I told Kenji. "My mother was working, and I was supposed to be spending the night at Jen's. But we went out to the fair at night, and I remember how bright it was, how noisy and disorienting, with the blaring of music from every different ride, the local bands screaming their songs onstage, urging everyone to sing along."

"It sounds like you didn't like your taste of freedom."

"I hated it. We were going to meet up with some boys, maybe drink beer. I was terrified. But I knew I was supposed to love my teenage rebellion. I tried to throw myself into it. And the first thing I did was lose Jen in the crowd. We didn't have cell phones back then. I spent most of the evening being swept through groups of people, searching for her."

I'd kept trying to rebel after that. The last time, I ended up with Lulu.

I paused. "Jen has twins now. They're 12, and they live in Winnipeg. It won't be long before they start pulling shit like that on her. She and I are Facebook friends."

My babbling was loud, but not enough to drown out the deep bass of the music from a distant bandstand; the beat made my heart thump nervously. If I could barely hear myself, how was I supposed to do my work?

I still didn't like crowds. But here I was about to plunge into the middle of a huge surging living thing.

I didn't feel festive. I kept thinking of Parisa in her hospital room, her body still, even as under her skin, cells and bone clamored and fought to pull her back together. I could almost hear them pumping blood into those vital spaces, cobbling broken bones, always building, building.

Another series of deep thumps from the fair.

I closed my eyes and took a deep breath. Kenji put his arm around me.

My mission was to stop and talk and briefly touch everyone I could, everyone I knew. From the other corners of the fair, Ma and Lulu were doing the same.

We'd practiced together more intensely than ever, trying to put that feeling, that glow into our connection.

Sometimes it worked, lightning up our space with brilliance; most of the time it stayed wan. Lulu wrote down all the variations of everything we tried. Holding hands, not holding hands. Closing eyes. Allowing Kenji into the room. Trying an iteration of whatever we'd done together with tea, coffee, kombucha—anything and everything.

We ended up meeting every night before the fair started. Sometimes Kenji would arrive with takeout, which caused Ma to make noises about being healthier. But she always ended up eating what was in front of her. Kenji listened with tolerant amusement, which was probably the best way to deal with my mother.

Then he would retreat into the background. Once, after a frustrating session in which no one had managed to relax enough to produce more than a tingle, I found him in the upstairs bathroom cleaning the filter of the tap so that it would flow freely, and I almost pulled him down onto floor and had my way with him. But restraint, discretion, and all those grown-up things I was supposed to understand prevailed, and we went to his place for an hour or so and did other types of adult things, and despite the other failures of the night, I managed to sleep. In fact, other than one brief midnight trek to check on what turned out to be Braxton Hicks contractions, I had slept more-or-less well that week, exhausted, seemingly dreamless bouts that did little to make me less worried about what the future held.

On a few dark nights, we stood outside, daring lightning to come and strike us, but aside from a few flares, we saw nothing like my previous displays of power. Sometimes, a flock of birds would cock their heads and observe us as we stood utterly still in the backyard, so still that sweat trickled down my forehead and back. By the time our session ended I needed to drink an entire pitcher of water.

I tried to teach Ma and Lulu to reach into themselves, to still their minds long enough to hear and feel that resonance. But they weren't the quiet types. Lulu was impatient and unbelieving. Her fingers twitched every time I said something about connecting with the hum of life. Ma, by contrast, was too greedy. I could feel her practically rattling with the desire to grab all of the threads for herself. But the more she tried to grasp at them, the more they eluded her.

Still, we managed consistently to reach some sort of reluctant glow, a sometimes anemic thing coming from our joined hands, sometimes much more.

I guess this was one way we were all getting closer, although it wasn't quite the quality time I'd envisioned spending with Lulu before she left, it was ours, a ritual we'd made out of an old gift, but in a new way. After a good session, Ma would even tell us a story about her life, and that brought us closer, too.

Lulu still held out hope that a public health authority would respond to the strongly worded and heavily footnoted letters and emails she'd sent to them.

"I think they've decided I'm a crank," Lulu said.

"You so aren't," I told her loyally. "Would a crank use AMA format citations in her letters?"

"It's not a big deal. There's a generator—you just have to plug in the information."

My darling nerdy girl. I could only hope that she'd find like-minded people in university who would listen to and understand her.

But tonight, before we dispersed in the fair crowd, we'd gathered at my house one last time, heads bowed together. "This is like how backup dancers psych themselves up before a show," I whispered into our silence.

Ma glared. Lulu looked at me blankly.

We had a lot of work to do—probably should have started talking more, sharing more years ago. But the anniversary of Yi-beh's disappearance approached too quickly. We had no choice but to launch our plan on this sultry evening.

Ma muttered before she drove off that the weather felt a little too much like Taiwan. I looked at the gray sky. It was still unrelievedly hot. I hoped nervously we weren't walking into a typhoon. But worse, for me at least, tonight we had to . . . socialize.

Again, it wasn't much of a scheme. All I could do was make contact with everyone I could. Ma and Lulu were also going to have to do this. The rule of the evening was that everyone I saw who I knew, I had to talk to. I had to try to touch a shoulder or a hand, to focus on them but tune in to my resonance, to exchange and interact, to hope something would stick.

Our first test came when I saw one of the EMTs, Daywin, at the next booth. "My girlfriend's holiday shop," he explained. "She makes all the jewelry herself."

I nudged Kenji. But it wasn't until I said, "And this is my . . . boyfriend," that I realized that I'd rarely spoken the word aloud before.

I paused to look at a simple but beautiful silver necklace while trying to process what I'd revealed to Daywin, to Kenji, to myself in order to start the conversation.

This was why I didn't like to socialize.

"Why don't you try that on," Kenji suggested.

"Oh, no I—"

But Kenji understood better than me that it was a good opportunity to talk. And as I fingered the pendant, a small smooth bird much like the ones I often fed, Kenji said, "Say, Daywin, I don't understand the clasp. Would you . . . ?"

Right there, Kenji had given me my first real opportunity. I tried to send some energy into Daywin's fingers, and I could swear I saw a light travel from me into him. Damn, that had gone a little better than anticipated.

Daywin and Kenji examined the necklace critically for a moment, then Kenji reached for his wallet.

"Oh," I said once again to try to stop Kenji. I was clearly not doing my best on the word front.

"Can't I buy some jewelry for my girlfriend?" Kenji asked easily.

But Daywin said, "Oh no. Please. It's on the house. Actually, Leeann, I was thinking, we haven't told anyone, but my girlfriend and I are trying for a baby, and you know more about this than anyone else. We'd both love it if you'd meet with us."

I gave him my card. Another brief contact of our fingers, and I murmured a wish for him to get some sleep. Maybe it was enough.

The next person was one of the admins at Kenji's new school. I smiled and grasped her hand lightly when I was introduced, then fingered my new necklace as Kenji and she talked.

She was flirting with him—unconsciously, probably. Touching her hair, smiling a lot. But her eyes, when they met mine, were rueful. "We were all hoping Kenji was single," she said.

"I have no idea how to respond to that," I said honestly. "But I guess I'm lucky."

Kenji laughed softly in my ear and pressed a kiss to my temple.

I silently wished her better sleep and good dreams (though not of Kenji), and we went to next person.

It did not, unfortunately, get easier.

Over the next two hours, we chatted with one of the nurses at a birthing center, shouted over the stereos at Lulu's old gym teacher, danced a little with my favorite cashier from the grocery store, high-fived two neighbors I didn't know very well. The best, of course, was when I ran into my former clients—a couple of whom had their now-much-bigger children with them.

At least I had Kenji with me. I ended up having to introduce everyone I saw to Kenji as my boyfriend, but somehow, after that first hurdle, it became so easy to sink into it. *Boyfriend. Boyfriend. Boyfriend.* The word slipped off my tongue. He seemed to be having no trouble adapting to the identity. He was happy to be take part in all of these small interactions, these tiny crisscrossing lines of webbing binding us together. As if he'd been waiting for me to do it all along.

It was an odd, tense day, but I realized something about him: He was always going to let me shine.

Even as I talked to people and touched them and tried to be present and tried not to let the thumping bass of the music get to me, at the back of my mind, I worried about Lulu and Ma.

Lulu also had a friend with her. I thought I spotted them a couple of times somewhere through the crowd. They both dutifully stopped for everyone and probably answered the same questions about graduation and school that everyone asked. Ma, on the other hand, had looked at me blankly when I suggested she bring someone.

"Don't you have a friend or colleague you could ask to take the edge off?" I'd said. "You know, a wingman?"

But even as I asked, I knew. Ma wasn't chummy. She treated her patients respectfully, but of course, they were nothing like friends. She kept her colleagues at a distance, almost never attending the holiday parties or after-work gatherings. She'd chosen isolation, and I'd never questioned it.

Lulu was right. When she left, if I stopped going to see Ma, she'd be alone.

So, it was a surprise when I crossed paths with her early that night to see her with Dr. Ricardo Marín, a silver-haired gynecologic surgeon I'd occasionally consulted with myself.

But what gave me pause was that he had his hand on the small of her back. And she was smiling and laughing.

Ma wasn't aware that I was watching her. She wasn't looking at anything. She was tucking her hair behind her ear, a little uncomfortable, a little itchy based on the way she couldn't seem to be still. But I could tell that even though her gaze wasn't on him, her energy was. As it should be. Because that's what we were doing, wasn't it? Moving energy around.

His attention certainly was on her. Dr. Marín *was* divorced. Right?

Kenji and I were near the bandstand by now, but I kept craning my neck to keep sight of my mother. Dr. Marín's hand hadn't moved.

"She's fine," Kenji said in my ear.

"I think he's been married at least two times. Maybe more."

Kenji raised a brow. "You believe all the gossip?"

I tugged his head down so I could explain everything. "As long as I'm not the subject of it, I like to keep my ear to the ground. Besides, it's Ma."

"Your mother can definitely take care of herself."

He wasn't getting it. "But she's never had to deal with an interested party, and that party is definitely interested."

Kenji looked like he was trying not to laugh. "I'm pretty sure at some point she has."

"Oh. *Oh.*"

Fuck. How was I supposed to distribute calming energy with *that* thought in my head?

Kenji had led me to the area near the concert stage, which was empty for the moment, thank goodness. I didn't think I could take more noise. But Kenji whispered in my ear that we had another person incoming. Sarah McCaffrey. She looked bright-eyed and a little too giddy. Her cheeks were red. I gazed at her uneasily as she swayed.

"It's you!" Sarah said, plowing through the center of a group of teens in order to reach me. She got close—very close—smelling like she'd had more than a few beers. She grabbed both my hands. "You were, like, always so cool. And you're still the same."

Not this again. "Thanks," I said cautiously.

It was good she felt this way, wasn't it? I just felt uncomfortable with the praise because I wasn't sure what I'd done to deserve it. Maybe Sarah had always wanted to be my friend, and I'd never noticed.

I wasn't sure how I felt about that.

But I couldn't deal with Sarah right now. I still had about two or three thousand more people to talk to.

Sarah wasn't letting me go. "I told myself after the last time I saw you that I'd go and live it up like you are!"

"I wouldn't say I'm doing that exactly—"

"I'd date around and quit my job—"

I tried to keep my face expressionless, but I did not need this right now. "I hope you didn't."

"I didn't. Because I always do the right thing." She was clearly disgusted with herself.

I said, "Oh hey now, that's not so bad. And you have friends." I wasn't sure that was true, and I'd certainly tried to avoid her earlier in the summer.

My uncertainty must have come through. She looked at me frustrated. "Easy for you to say." She narrowed her eyes at Kenji. "I'm taking her," she announced.

Sarah grabbed my arm and started towing me toward the stage. I glanced back at Kenji, who was following, but he'd gotten stuck behind a group of chattering seniors paused in front of a food stall. He waved me on smiling, unaware I didn't really need a heart-to-heart with Sarah.

Should I shake her off? I could get away from her, but I noticed the slight glowing from my palms. My skin was almost adhering to her sweaty hands. Was this a sign that I was on the right track? But if my fingers were that lit up, why wasn't Sarah asleep right now, instead of . . .

Energized.

We were almost at the bandstand when I started pulling back. "What are you doing?"

"We should sing a song!" Sarah shouted enthusiastically.

This was definitely not part of the plan. I started to back away. "This isn't open-mic karaoke. We're going to get in trouble."

But Sarah kept her grip on me firm. "I can't believe Leeann Wu is afraid of getting in trouble."

"What's that supposed to mean?" I asked more exasperated than insulted.

"This is the *fair*."

"Yeah, not exactly known as a hotbed for punk. Giant crops? Yes. Dirtbags? Nope."

And I had people to save. I was feeling desperate. But short of stomping on her toe, I didn't see how I was going to escape.

Sarah was starting to sound stranger and stranger. "Remember that year Sandra Lysenko got on stage and started berating the judges for not awarding her apple pie first place?" Sarah asked, as she dragged me onto the stage.

I groaned. "I heard it was cherry. They probably have some corporation running this fair now, and you know how the suits love schedules."

"Fuck the suits!"

"You wear suits!" I yelled.

She gestured at her off-the-shoulder tee and denim cutoffs and looked up at me triumphantly.

She didn't seem like herself.

I tried for a conciliatory tone but inside I was getting frantic. I had to be around more people, talk to more people, not just one sad ex-classmate. "Most of the time, you do. My point is you aren't acting like yourself, Sarah." Had I zapped her with too much juice? Why couldn't she just fall asleep? "There may be something wrong with you. Let's get down before we get in trouble."

In answer, Sarah kicked an amplifier, which promptly screeched.

The sound cut right through the entire fair and everyone looked up.

Oh gods, if stopping and talking to everyone had been exhausting and humiliating, this was worse. I took a deep breath to calm myself, and my hands flared to life again.

"Oh, you've got a lighter!" Drunk Sarah grabbed my hand and held it up high. "Hey everyone!" she yelled.

More feedback sounded from the amps, but everyone was looking up, looking at my hand glowing softly in the evening light of summer. *Fuck.* I curled it in on itself, but it didn't make the light disappear. I needed to turn it off. Why the hell didn't it have a switch or some sort of power button?

But a few people in the crowd were now holding up their phones with the lights on. People I knew. People I'd grown up with. "Yeah!" said Sarah in a voice overlaid with a desperate hunger.

I glanced at her again. Was this something more? Was she being influenced by a ghost? Before I could formulate a thought, she yelled, "Tonight, we're going to sing!"

Oh no, *we* weren't doing anything of the sort.

Sarah McCaffrey, my clean-cut high school classmate who wore pantsuits in the heat of summer, launched into an a cappella rendition of Whitney Houston's "The Greatest Love of All," taking my arm along with her as she swayed to the rhythm.

Sarah, or whoever she was, it turned out, had a good voice.

My hand vibrated. I could feel a sudden connection to something, as if it had been waiting out there for me to just put my hand out, the resonance thick in the air, heavy and hot. The fairgrounds seemed to still except for this music coming out of the speakers, out of the microphone. The waves were made visible as people one by one started to sway their phones in the air to the sound of Sarah's haunting voice. A flock of birds came out and swooped through the air, almost like they were drawing secret signs.

Sarah's own face was flushed red, her eyes bright, her neighbors, the people who knew her as one thing, watching her transform herself into another.

I held up my other hand so I could sway too, willing myself to radiate peace and sleep to the crowd. I had no idea if it was working, but the connection was strong, and I felt a rush through me. Whatever this was, it was stronger than any of the pulls I'd felt before, and it seemed to buzz all around us, through the growing collection of people attracted to Sarah's voice.

But as Sarah moved into the last repeat of the chorus, a jagged flash of lightning tore silently across the sky.

⋆ ⋆ ⋆

All was quiet for one moment.

Then someone in the crowd screamed as several bolts fissured the atmosphere, almost seeming to trap us under a net of light. The tang of electricity singed the air.

The evening had been turning pink and orange just moments before as the sun began to set, but now when the brightness died down it was dark and eerily silent, and everyone seemed to be waiting, waiting for that crack of thunder that never came.

The birds had scattered as the first streak appeared. But now they came back cawing and circling in the air as one—a murmuration. Their wings were dark against new streaks of white light that threatened overhead.

My hands were still raised, but Sarah had dropped her arm. "This is like that other time, in the parking lot," she whispered, staring at me. She was wild-eyed, but seemingly herself again. The deep boom when thunder finally hit made her drop the mike, triggering another huge sound.

She squealed and scrambled off the stage.

That was when the crowd began move toward the exits.

I should run, too.

The lightning streaked down bold and fast, filling the heated air with the stench of fire. I was on a stage, exposed. Tarps snapped angrily as howling gusts of wind threatened to tear down the structure at any minute.

But I didn't move, didn't even lower my arms.

Because I felt a connection with the lightning. That was the most frightening, exhilarating thing.

It was mine.

As it flashed above me, as the wind howled and the microphone stands and equipment clattered across the stage and tent flaps struggled to escape their tethers, I felt its fascinating pull guiding my hand higher still, stretching out my fingers. The light felt sharper under my skin. I could taste the burning on my tongue, I could almost hear it—a higher, keening note, unlike the gentle thrum of before, as if all the energy were arrowing toward me.

The only people still trying to get to the stage were Kenji, Ma, and Lulu, fighting their way toward me in a crowd determined to sweep them to the exits. Kenji may have been shouting something, but he was too far away for me to hear it. Ma's face was resolute.

Lulu was closest. She looked scared.

They seemed so far away.

"Mom!" Lulu called from her distance. "Mom, please come down from there. It isn't safe!"

A twang, a different note. I wanted to tell her I would be all right. I'd never felt stronger.

The birds drew their patterns in the air.

I could get swept up in this, pulled high into the sky where the humming in my veins told me I'd live forever.

The crowd may have been making sounds, but I couldn't hear them. I could hardly hear anything except the wind and the rush of connection to that vast well of power filling my bloodstream and crackling under my skin.

Lulu finally managed to break free of the fleeing sea of people, but she couldn't seem to reach the stage. It was as if something were preventing her making her way across the now empty space. Kenji and my mother were struggling, too, but there was too much energy blocking them—too much of *my* energy.

I could hear my daughter, like a murmur in the distance. She was pleading. "Mom, please come down and save yourself. You don't have to do this. You don't have to make this sacrifice."

That's right, I thought dispassionately, I hadn't really wanted to make a sacrifice, had I? But this was nothing like giving up. It was like being filled with all the gifts I thought I didn't have. It was extraordinary. I wasn't just some sad mom whose purpose was over because her kid was grown. I could almost, almost see why Yi-beh had done this, had given herself over to the electricity.

I'd go out in a blaze of glory having saved the town and maybe the whole tricity area that I covered.

I paused, remembering my former life. What was it I did? Who was I?

Lulu's frantic stream of words penetrated. "Think of all the people you help all the time. Your ordinary life is already more than enough. You don't have to be magical when you're already extraordinary. You have to be *here*. You can't disappear on me—on all of us."

But her words seemed to fade in the rush of my power.

"Mom, don't leave me! This was not part of the plan."

That was such a Lulu thing to say. Lulu, my daughter.

A sign ripped from its moorings and smashed into a pole near the stage. One of Lulu's hands reached out to touch the closest thing. My foot.

When she was a baby, I would curl her small toes in my palm to prove to myself she was real and here and with me. And now she was doing the same to mine.

I gazed down. Of course I wouldn't go. She was the one who'd move away soon. Find her own path. She was her own person. But I would always come when she needed me. I'd promised to be here for her.

The pole teetered. The stage was going to crash on me.

It was going to crash on Lulu.

No.

I had to stop the wind. I tried to draw my arms down, and it was so hard, much harder to do that than to keep them up where the sky wanted me.

Ma reached Lulu and with her other arm tried to grab onto me, grounding me when I threatened to be swept away.

It was what I needed. I mustered all my strength, pulled my arms to my sides, and clapped once. My hands flared as skin met skin, and then there was the sound. The deeper, warmer resonance I knew.

Another boom of thunder flowed out from it and saturated the air and debris from behind us began falling as clouds opened in an enormous rain that had been gathering since early summer.

The sky had teeth.

There went the birds streaking and cawing through the sky one last time, one last shard of nightmare, and another clap of thunder before the rain, finally released came pouring down from the sky.

My hands were no longer bright.

"Mom!" Lulu screamed and she tried to scramble onto the stage as if the barrier keeping her from me had suddenly fallen. She was lurching into danger.

I didn't even have to think. I ran forward with my hands outstretched to push her, the last light bursting from my hands away as a huge piece of scaffolding teetered. And I fell. The last thing I heard was the crash of the stage as it collapsed under the spot where I'd been standing.

♦ 18 ♦

WHEN MY EYES OPENED, it was to the sound of gentle rain and Kenji's deep breathing beside me in my own bed.

I didn't know how I'd ended up back home. With the rain pouring down and the stage collapsing, all I could do was make sure Lulu was safe before I blacked out.

At least I hadn't woken up in the hospital again.

I didn't feel quite steady, but I managed to pad to Lulu's room, where I saw Ma and Lulu asleep on her bed. I resisted the urge to check them for injuries, trusting that if they'd made it there and seemed to be sleeping well, that was enough. I padded to the bathroom and cleaned myself up before heading back to bed. And Kenji.

I had only one other memory from last night, and that was my dream of Yi-beh.

We sat on my back porch, my small child hand in her dry, papery one as we stared out at the rain. Part of me ached, but not because I'd lose her again, but because I had so many people with me who cared about me, who supported me even when they couldn't always quite believe me. Because I knew now that in the end, she had been alone, twisting in that uneasy current of power.

We sat and did nothing for a long time. But when I'd grown up enough in the dream, when I remembered everything again, I turned to her and asked, "Why did you do it?"

"I was greedy. I wanted more than this half life." She gestured around us to my yard, the birds huddled in the trees, the rain. But when I tried to focus on one thing, it was like it blurred out of my vision.

"So, it was your hunger? All of this happened because you wanted to return. You tried to use me to come back."

She looked at me for a moment, narrow-eyed. "When you were a child, you were supposed to listen to everything I told you to do."

I didn't let go of her hand. But I said, "I got older."

I kept growing into myself in the dream, too. Yi-beh smiled so softly, but I could feel the seething, restless power underneath. A part of me wanted to reach out and grasp it for myself, even when I knew the danger. But she said mildly, "I didn't do it on purpose and I didn't do it alone, Mei mei. All I did was wish, like many other spirits before me have done, like all the ones who followed me to you these months. But when you are a spirit, sometimes wanting strongly is enough to change the course of the mortal world. So many of us have regrets. I regret abusing my power then trying save everyone alone—and my regret and desire, and those of everyone around me made the air heavy. And that created its own danger."

"So, you wished to come back."

"To you. To your mother. I wanted your mother to think about me and remember me."

I hadn't remembered Yi-beh. And that probably hurt. "But Ma does. I think she misses you, more than anyone."

"But she never talked about me before all this." The ghost sighed, and she squeezed my hand. "She had to bury all of that—me—in her mind. But once I reawakened in you and in her, once you started to talk about the past, I began to want. Then soon I wanted it too much."

"That was why the air was so heavy the whole time. Why we couldn't sleep. Spirits like you wanting something."

Yi-beh nodded. "Spirits wanting to change their past, wanting something new, and sensing a power in people like you—in people who can receive life in their hands."

"There are more like me?"

"Of course there are. You all have gifts," she said. She added portentously, "But it is also a curse."

I managed not to roll my eyes. Yes, I'd definitely grown. "Yeah, I figured. You know, after the lightning almost drew me up with it."

"You're like your mother. You like to talk back to your elders."

Her scolding couldn't hurt me. I gave her a lopsided smile. "Call it another Wu power."

She frowned, but I could see the twist of laughter in her lips, a small indicator of how she'd been when she'd been alive, of what had made me love her. Was there a possibility . . . ? I tried to isolate the spark to see what I could do with it, but Yi-beh shook her head as if knowing what I thought. "You can't bring me back to life with those kinds of tricks."

I dropped it, ashamed, and her face softened. "To be able to heal someone is wonderful, but sometimes I enjoyed using my gift too much." She squeezed my hand. "In the end, you didn't forget who you were."

But I found out there was more history, more power to me than I imagined.

We stayed there longer, looking at the shifting sky. I wasn't facing her as a child anymore. I was an adult now. I should have been angry with her, but I could understand the desire to come back to all of this, even if loving people was sometimes as much a responsibility as it was a pleasure.

"I miss your mother," Yi-beh said. "I never got to say goodbye to her. I never got to say how much it meant to me that she let me take care of one so young. You will have to tell her."

"Why can't you tell her yourself?"

"Her dreams are crowded with too many others."

"Who?"

"It's her story to share."

I sighed. "I'll be waiting another forty years for that."

Yi-beh smiled sadly. "I hope not."

Her face flared, then started to fade. I tried to reach for her, knowing I probably would never see her again so clearly, already forgetting exactly what she looked like as the layers of sleep began to dissolve.

But this time as I swam out of that dream, I wasn't left with the same sadness. Her face might not be fixed in my mind, but the essence of her was in my memories.

Now, pressed against Kenji, I tried to keep still and fall asleep again, partly to hold on a little longer to that sense of peace. Everyone else in the house certainly needed and deserved their rest, too. But I couldn't stay still. My mind was energized. I wanted to get up and start living my life again.

Kenji breathed deeply beside me. Was this what it would be like, I wondered, skimming my hand down alongside Kenji's, gently so I wouldn't wake him, trying to take as much care of him as he'd taken of me—of all of us last night?

But he turned over suddenly and shimmied down so that we were nose-to-nose. "I've never been surprised you were extraordinary," he whispered. "If I was surprised, it was only at the direction it all took."

Part of me had been anxious that things would change after last night. But in essence, it was the same: He was always going to let me shine.

"Do you always wake up sweet-talking like that?" I asked.

"We'll have to find out." A pause. "You know, this is the first time we've ever slept together."

I opened my mouth to contradict him, but he clarified, "Spent the whole night unconscious next to each other. In a real bed."

It was true. "'First time' implies there will be others."

He stroked his fingers between us, over my belly, underneath the t-shirt. "I hope so."

My breath hitched. "We'll have to be quiet."

He watched me with heavy-lidded eyes as he pulled me toward him and slid one hand smoothly down into my sleep shorts. His fingers were cool at first, then hot.

The bed creaked as my hips began to move. He kissed me slowly, first my nose, then my eyelids. His teeth closed gently around my jaw.

"How do I taste?" I whispered.

He chuckled. "The same as always. Delicious and real. But let me check down here."

He pulled the shorts down, trailing his fingers down my thigh as he went, pausing to nudge his nose between my legs.

I raised myself on two pillows and pulled my shirt tight so I could watch the progress of his dark head. I looked at his hair falling over his eye. He was looking at me, all the hidden parts of me, following my desire with his tongue and lips and fingers. A wet click, a muffled groan as he slicked himself along me.

I opened my legs more fully, enjoying the strain of the stretch and tilted my greedy hips, making myself a wider canvas for his strokes. My breath came in harsh pants, or were they his? But my body thrust up higher for him, my ankles pulling and digging into his sides as if to bring him closer to me, until the throb of my body, of his, overwhelmed me.

I stared at the ceiling. "Yeah. That was . . ." I croaked.

He hauled himself up and rubbed his face on my shoulder. I could feel the beginning prickles of his stubble. "The day I met you, I told you that you performed miracles every day, and you do."

I huffed out a laugh. "Is this your way of getting me to tell you that you perform miracles, too. Do you want more praise for your efforts just now?"

He kissed long and leisurely and smiled. "You can praise me when I'm done," and pulled off my shirt.

Much later we stumbled down the stairs together. Kenji's clothes were still a little damp from lying in a heap on the floor all night. But he didn't seem to mind.

Lulu was downstairs sitting at the table checking her phone and eating while my mother was making . . . pancakes?

"They're buckwheat," Lulu said.

"Where did we get buckwheat?"

Ma said, "I gave you a sack for Christmas."

Oh, right. "A heartfelt gift."

"Heart *healthy*," Ma snapped.

I should've considered myself lucky. The year before it had been an industrial-sized tub of fish oil capsules.

She set down a plate front of Kenji, and I felt the world becoming right again in a small way. Although my mom making pancakes in my kitchen and Kenji spending the night after I'd been a conduit for lightning and thunder could not really be called normal.

But it was peaceful. The rain still fell lightly. The window was cracked open so that we could all smell that dampness, that freshness, rising up from the outside. Lulu was humming while she ate.

Ma glanced at my messy hair. I tried not to look guilty.

"So do we know what happened last night?" I asked.

What I meant was, *Do you think it did anything?*

But we'd never truly know what we managed to do, if there was anything at all. That was the thing about trying to stave off disasters: not much changing was a success, but it was hard to tell what then had truly been altered.

"Well, I slept well," Kenji said. "Apparently so did my niece. Andrea texted to say she was out from 8 till 7 this morning—and so was Andrea. When she woke up, she wasn't sure whether to be worried or proud."

"Welcome to the ambivalence of parenthood, Andrea," I said, raising my coffee cup.

"I heard on the news the stage was totaled," Lulu said. "But strangely, the rest of the fair is fine—if wet. So performances are canceled, but they're still judging the pies and desserts today."

Ma spoke up. "I think we know that it accomplished something. So much power." Her eyes gleamed. "We need to figure out a way you can do that again, Leeann. Maybe if we keep practicing."

"Ma, we all almost died last night. That stage I was on? And that you weren't far away from? It's gone. If you all hadn't been there, if I'd been alone, I would have given myself over to the wind and lightning."

"But you didn't," Ma insisted. "You have a gift, and we have to learn how to use it."

"No, Ma. The fireworks look impressive, but it's not as important as how I live the rest of my life. That's how I've made a difference. All that power isn't mine to own and use anyway, at least that's what I believe. What I felt last night didn't come from me. It's from somewhere else, and if I let it, it could take me over. I'm just a conduit."

I turned to Lulu. "Something you said to me—you said my ordinary life was more than enough. I didn't have to summon thunderclaps and glow strangely and do all these magical things in order to help people, to be happy, to . . . to lead a worthwhile life. I have done good for people. I don't always do my best, I make mistakes, but I am trying, and I'm here for you, and for my clients. I have to learn to use my own gifts from my own sources the best way I can. I was always enough. This whole time, I was always enough."

Ma didn't argue. Turned out, there wasn't time. My phone sounded, and it was Monique Masson in labor. And Lulu had to get to work. Ma's messages went off, too. Kenji cleaned up the kitchen and watched us while we scrambled to get out into the world.

Later that day, we'd find out that Parisa had woken in the morning. That she'd had a coherent conversation with her husband and her children—well, as coherent as it could be, considering how surprised and overjoyed and relieved they were. The news met me as I came out of a delivery at the birthing center, and I sat down right in the middle of everything and cried in relief and gratitude. Her physical recovery would end up taking a long couple of years, and she never did come back to work full time. But when I introduced her to Kenji, she said she'd known about him all along, and sometimes, she'd take my hand and squeeze it, and I understood she remembered our conversation. I had my friend back, my friends had their wife and mother back, and that was more than enough.

The fair became known as the place Sarah McCaffrey had her breakthrough and decided to sing professionally—or at least become Reineville's queen of weddings and karaoke. The fact that lightning had destroyed the stage after she'd stepped off of it became part of that legend—in our town at least.

Hardly anyone remembered I'd been there with her at all. Ma was usually outraged over that detail, but she kept her grumbles to herself—or less discreetly between us. "They could at least be grateful."

But it was for the best that no one suspected any abilities I or my family might have. Also, I wasn't about to have it twisted around so that it seemed like we'd solved our problems in the most Taiwanese way—through karaoke. I'd let Sarah have that.

Lulu would pack for school later that week, her boxes clearly labeled and the entire move too smooth and quick for my comfort. But I went to visit her on a couple of weekends that fall. She came up a few times with her friends, filling the house with late nights watching movies and the smell of baking and laundry.

After almost a year, Kenji moved in with me. He ended up cooking for the weekly dinners I had with my mother, which suited all of us better.

And some months after that, I traveled with my mother to Taiwan. I sweated a lot, despite the fact that it was barely April, and my younger cousins gave me rides on bright scooters through Taichung's streets. My aunt plied me with food, introducing me to wax apples, and varieties of guava, and the joy of eating sticky rice at the night market. We ran for the train to take us into the countryside, my mother panting along while I hauled her luggage and mine up steps, warning me that Taiwanese trains only had minutes between transfers and were never late. It turned out this was true, and we made our connection without a second to spare. When we arrived in the place where my great-aunt's village once stood, we swept clean the tombstone that had been put up for Yi-beh on land that my mother still owned and left our offerings to her.

Late at night, in our shared rooms, sometimes my mother would tell me a little bit more about my father. As Lulu had suspected, he hadn't treated my mother very well. But that was really more her story to tell. We returned home exhausted, but buoyant, and able to put some of our issues behind us.

The glow never really returned to my hands, although sometimes I could feel its echo in me. Instead of freezing, I learned to trust the feeling, and in doing so, trust myself. But although I never saw it again, sometimes on those weekends when Lulu came down, and the table was full with family and friends who had stopped by to laugh and talk and argue, I'd look around and feel it emanating from all of us. I could hardly say I missed the power when it was still there.

ACKNOWLEDGEMENTS

THANK YOU FOR READING *The Glowing Life of Leeann Wu*. This book was a messy labor of love, and I hope that it spoke to you.

I owe much to my parents, whose stories make up so much of who I am, and especially to my mother, who was a nurse-midwife in Taiwan. To the midwives out there, thank you for what you do. You ARE magical. All errors in the depiction of contemporary and historical midwifery and Taiwanese spiritual and cultural traditions are very much my own.

Thanks to my agent, Sarah E. Younger, who has been a shining beacon of serenity and wisdom.

Much gratitude to the team at Alcove: Julia Abbott, Thaisheemarie Fantauzzi Pérez, and Monica Manzo, copyeditor Debbie Stone, and many others have worked so hard to bring these books into the world. Natalie Olsen of Kisscut Design created the striking cover with art direction from Rebecca Nelson. A special shout out goes to my brilliant and insightful editor Jess Verdi, who edited my first books and who I've been so glad to work with again.

Jenny Holiday, Emma Barry, and Tara Gelsomino read early versions of this, and I very much appreciate their input. Wendy Muruli of Tessera Editorial gave me useful notes on how to make this story stronger.

Olivia Dade, Kate Clayborn, Jackie Lau, Farah Heron, and Jasmine Guillory all listened to me at various points while I tried to figure out what to do with this strange book. Thanks also to Toronto Romance Writers and especially to my TRW write-in buddies.

I know I mentioned Emma Barry before, but she made me believe in this novel when I was ready to give it all up. I am grateful for everything she's done.

Finally, for my husband and daughter, who've endured with me through all the less-than-magical moments, I love you.

DISCUSSION QUESTIONS

The Glowing Life of Leeann Wu

1. In stories, many characters in stories gain their powers in childhood or when they're on the cusp of adulthood. What difference do you think Leeann's age makes in her approach to her powers, how she feels about them, and what she does with them?
2. Both Leeann's mother and her daughter push her to be what they think she should be. What do you think of Leeann as a character? Are any of the other characters' self-assessments accurate?
3. The Wus are caught between being scientifically minded and not being able to explain what is happening to them. Do you believe in magic or things that have nothing do with science? Have you had spiritual and/or supernatural experiences?
4. Leeann is scared to take action once she realizes she could die trying to help her town. What would your reaction be if faced with having to save your community at great risk to yourself?
5. Many of the characters and side characters complain about insomnia and sleep problems. What do you think

of how sleeplessness affects the townspeople? How do you think this affliction could affect people long term?

6. Leeann worries Kenji is too young to love her and Kenji worries Leeann is too powerful and accomplished to love him. What do you think of their relationship and how do you see it progressing down the road?
7. What did you think of the friendship between Parisa and Leeann? What do you think of the notion that Parisa brings up of histories that are passed down among women?
8. At one point, Leeann's mother says, "I have never understood how to talk to you. . . . I don't know how to tell you about any of these things, because there is something more than language that separates us." Do you speak a different language from your parents or other family members? Does that complicate the preservation of your family history?
9. How do Leeann and her mother's understanding of each other change as they learn more about Leeann's abilities?
10. When Leeann and her family start practicing their magic together, Leeann says, "It wasn't quite the quality time I'd envisioned spending with Lulu before she left, [but] it was something of ours, a ritual we'd made out of an old gift, but in a new way." Have you heard of the term "third culture kid," that is, people who were raised in a country or culture other than that of their parents? Does your family have traditions that take elements from your culture of origin and those of the one you live in to create a third, blended tradition?